Another World

Praise for Philip Stott's Novel

I remain very impressed by this novel. As far as I know, nothing like it has ever appeared in print. I would be surprised if it should be anything less but very well received by the Christian community at large. *Another World* provides a window into a past world that looks and sounds eerily familiar; a world only separated from us by a little time and a lot of water. No one who dares to compare that world with ours can escape its fearful implications. Philip Stott has written a novel that may be called, as he himself says, Biblical science fiction. It is certainly Biblical, and it is scientifically tenable. That leaves precious little fiction to hide behind. May all who read this account of the first world's terrifying ruin by flood be driven to seek refuge from the judgment that is yet to come by fire.

—Rev. Barry Beukema
Pastor of the United Reformed Church of Thunder Bay
Ontario, Canada

Scientist, educator, and author Philip Stott takes us on a harrowing journey back to the future. The time: a few thousand years ago. The place: a world we can barely imagine—and may not want to. Here there is much to amaze, but there is also much to appall. Here, all but a few have forgotten God; here, none but a few realize that God's judgment is coming—terrifyingly—from above and beneath. To enter that world is to risk seeing our own. But enter it you should—the better to prepare yourself for another world that is soon to come.

—Dean Davis
Director, Come Let us Reason
Author of *In Search of the Beginning: A Seeker's Journey to the Origin of the Universe, Life, and Man*

Another World

A NOVEL

Philip Stott

Noble Novels

VENTURA, CALIFORNIA
2010

Another World

published by  a division of

Copyright © 2010 by Philip Stott

ISBN: 978-0-9796736-9-6

Library of Congress Control Number 2010922966

Theology and Manuscript Editor, Ronald Kirk

Original Cover Art and Interior Illustrations,
Henning ven der Westhuizen

Designer and Managing Editor, Desta Garrett

Copy Editor and Proofreader, Kimberley Winters Woods

Another World is a work of science fiction. Apart from the well-known actual people, events, and locales that figure in the narrative, all names, characters, places, and incidents are the products of the author's imagination or are used fictitiously. Any resemblance to current events or locales, or to living persons, is entirely coincidental.

Printed in the United States of America

NORDSKOG PUBLISHING, INC.
2716 Sailor Ave., Ventura, California 93001 USA
1-805-642-2070 • 1-805-276-5129
www.NordskogPublishing.com

Member

Christian Small Publishers Association

For Margaret,
who has brought me all
the worldly assets worth having —
wonderful children,
a delightful daughter-in-law, and
lovely grandchildren.

Another World

Some of the Science
Behind the Story

THE floating forests were inspired by the work of Dr. Joachim Sheven. His research shows that a great deal of the world's coal probably comes from forests that once covered much of the ocean.

Huge meteorites striking the earth were first proposed by Dr. George Dodwell after many years of research into the changing tilt of the earth's axis. His work points to an enormously catastrophic impact only a few thousand years ago.

Use of the Earth's formerly powerful magnetic field for transportation was put forward by Professor James Hanson.

The theory of hydro-plate tectonics comes from Dr. Walter Brown.

Ideas concerning dinosaurs come from a number of researchers who have not always come to exactly the same conclusions. They may or may not be accurate.

The contributions of a number of scientists are outlined more fully in the APPENDIX — POSTSCRIPT beginning on page 243.

Some information and illustrations regarding dinosaurs and mag-sleds is also given in the APPENDIX, pages 251–263.

See also a short biography of the author beginning on page 265, and the Publisher's Word beginning on page 267.

1 The Planet

"In the beginning God created the heavens and the earth. And the earth was without form, and void; and darkness was upon the face of the deep. And the Spirit of God moved upon the face of the waters…"

"You're not serious!"

"Surely that must classify as hate speech!"

"I always knew you were a liar."

"Come on, Shell, he can't have said that!"

"I'm telling you. That's exactly how he started the lecture. His very words!" insisted Shelah as he looked through a steadily thickening alcoholic haze at his friends seated around the battered, beer-stained oak table.

A waiter arrived with five large mugs, set them down, collected the empties, and held out his hand for the money. The five young men grinned sheepishly. By the yellow light of smoky oil-lamps hanging from the low, oak-beamed ceiling, it was easy to see that these were freshmen, still wet behind the ears. New arrivals revelling in the novelty of being away from home for the first time. Their table was far from the door and even farther from the bar—not the most popular spot in the large, noisy room, but even here there were only a few empty places. They had to bellow to be heard above the surrounding chatter.

After the waiter left, Asahai looked at Shelah with a long, deliberate, half-inebriated stare. "Shell, you scandal-monger, you ought to pay for two rounds after a story like that."

A murmur of approval ran around the little group, which had already downed four rounds and begun to sound very merry.

"Great idea. You can have mine, Shell."

"No. It was my idea. He can have mine."

"Why not both?"

The youngsters laughed. They didn't notice a group of seven men swagger into the bar through the swinging doors. Everyone else did notice and looked uneasy. The general hubbub of conversation began to fade. Rendo, the leader of the new arrivals, had a self-satisfied smirk on his face as he savoured the hush. His smirk sagged to a scowl when laughter bubbled up from a table on the far side of the room. Rendo swung round toward the sound and peered through the smoke. His thin lips narrowed to a hard line.

"I suppose it could be true," Hoshea's loud voice slurred. He had obviously drunk more than he could handle. "Professor Zalomo just might have said something like that. His daughter's married to one of Old Doom and Gloom's sons."

"Come off it!"

"It's tall story night!"

They all laughed again.

"No tall story. It's true!"

"Oh yeah, and where'd you get that from?"

"My dad went to school with Doomy's eldest. He's called Japh. He used to come and visit us now and then."

"Didn't mind associating with a sled-man then?"

"Well, actually, he did the sled-men's course at Super Swift with my dad. I was just a little kid then. Didn't finish and get a licence though; went off instead with Old Gloom to Tarshish or some such God-forsaken spot."

"Pity they didn't stay there."

"If they had, they'd 've been strung up long ago. You know what goes on in Tarshish!"

They chuckled again, not noticing the general hush in the room. Nor that the newly arrived group was heading in their direction.

"Your dad wasn't scared to be seen with him?"

"And the neighbours didn't burn your house down?"

"They'd want to fumigate the neighbourhood after a visit by anyone connected with Old Gloom!"

Another ripple of laughter went round the table.

Several of the other patrons looked uneasily from the new arrivals to the noisy bunch and back again. One or two looked as if they were trying to catch the attention of the youngsters. But the cheerful group were oblivious to it all.

"Well, that was a few years ago. Doomy used to be quite popular once. A bit before my time, but my dad told me about it."

"They say he used to try and scare people by telling them they'd end up burning on a bonfire."

"So why did he change his story to say everybody will get drowned?"

"Well you see, all that water puts the fire out!"

All five burst into howls of laughter. Their faces were wet with tears, their sides were sore and a lot of beer had been spilt by the time order returned to the group. They had been too distracted to notice the spivs sitting down at the table next to theirs.

The Planet was almost exclusively patronised by students of Salem University. The new arrivals were obviously not students. A little too old, for one thing. Too flashily dressed, for another. And a bit too surly... and they all had knives in their belts. But Rendo, as a one-time drop-out astronomy student, considered himself part of the scene and he liked to invite his buddies to The Planet now and then. Rendo demanded fear and respect from the students. He was not one little bit pleased that the five freshmen at the next table had failed to notice him arrive. Neither was he at all pleased with their talk.

Asahai beckoned a waiter and ordered another round. His

friends drained their mugs and banged them down on the table. They were still smiling from ear to ear and giggling sporadically when their beer arrived. Another waiter, with a worried expression on his face, hurried with a tray of drinks for Rendo and his gang at the next table.

"Is it the unmarried one that your dad knows?"

"Yep," said Hoshea, after a long draught.

"I suppose he'll stay that way," said Loshan. "Not much chance of finding a girl who'd be prepared to even talk to him."

"Why not invite him to marry your sister, Loshy?"

The group guffawed loudly.

"No good—he's sure to be looking for a virgin!"

The group sprawled helplessly across the table spilling beer, gasping for breath, holding their sides.

"They're an endangered species!"

"All but extinct!"

"Stamp out virginity!"

"Definitely no prospects for him in Salem!"

As the half-drunk students spluttered and choked with laughter, Rendo, at the next table, glanced toward them. His eyes darted from one to the other. He had remarkable eyes; both brown, but very different. The left was hazel with little flecks of green; the right was dark, almost black. He turned his gaze back toward his sidekicks. They sat staring at their mugs. Not saying a word. Maybe they were thinking the same thoughts he was. Why was everybody always talking about that miserable wretch of a preacher and his three lousy sons? These stupid little creeps hadn't even noticed him. He and his buddies got up to some nasty cool stuff. Why wasn't somebody talking about that?

"Hey, Loshy, you know old Jeremiah's daughter? The ugly one who's so cross-eyed you can't tell if she's looking at the professor or the clock on the wall? I'm sure she's got a king-size crush on you. We could take her to meet him. You could stand next to him and she'd say 'yes' not realising it was him doing the asking."

The drunken quintet thumped the table and held their aching sides, tears streaming down their cheeks.

Rendo's hard lips pursed into a scowl and two shades of hatred smouldered behind his angry glare. How dare those worthless scum joke about a girl just because her eyes are a bit different!

He leant forward and murmured something to his gang. They stood up to go.

Rendo made a show of tripping over Hoshea's foot as he left the table.

"What'd you do that for?" Rendo demanded angrily.

"Oh, sorry," said Hoshea, withdrawing his foot from the aisle.

"Trying to land me flat on my face in all that beer you jerks 've spilled on the floor?"

The students at the next table got up and hurried for the door as unobtrusively as possible.

"Hey, he told you he was sorry. It was an accident," managed Shelah through his alcoholic haze.

Tables throughout the room were emptying rapidly.

"Yeah, it was just an accident. Leave him alone."

Rendo's gang waded in with boots flying and fists flailing.

2 Interrogation

"Come in."

The door opened and two male nurses entered, supporting a heavily bandaged figure.

"Bring him here," said the middle-aged police-inspector seated at the far side of the bare, spotless, white table. He pointed to an empty chair opposite him.

A tall young doctor in a creased and rather grubby white coat rose from his seat to the left of the inspector, pulled out the empty chair and helped the limping youth to sit down.

While the new arrival tried to get comfortable in his seat, a policewoman on the other side of the inspector moved a clean sheet to the front of her clipboard and wrote a few words at the top of the page.

"How are you feeling?" asked the inspector.

"Terrible," mumbled the young man through his bandages.

"I'm sorry about that, but we have to ask you some questions."

"Couldn't it wait till tomorrow? I'm feeling rotten."

"Unfortunately your friend Shelah may not live till tomorrow. We need your help right now."

"What about Loshan and the others?"

"They're in intensive care. They're expected to recover, but they won't be answering any questions for a few days. Go ahead, constable."

"Name?"

"Hoshea."

"Age?"

"Nineteen."

"Occupation?"

"Student."

"Father's name?"

"Taban."

"Father's occupation?"

"Sled-man."

"Place of birth?"

"Salem."

"Place of residence?"

"Salem."

The policewoman scribbled on her pad. The inspector leant forward with his elbows on the table and looked into Hoshea's bloodshot eyes, scarcely visible through a slit between thick bandages. "Tell me all you can remember about last night's incident."

"Don't remember much. Must've been drunk. My head's hurting. Can't think straight."

"Have you anything for a hangover?" The Inspector looked at the doctor.

"We've already given him an alcofen injection. It wouldn't be advisable to give him another."

"So, young man, you'll just have to try your best. Remember, your friend is likely to die, and it's you we're relying on to catch the culprits. Do you understand?"

"Yes sir."

"What did the attackers look like?"

"Don't know. Hardly noticed them. They were at the next table. Very quiet. Didn't look their way much."

"Why did they attack you?"

"One of them tripped over my foot. I was sprawled out a bit…I was a bit drunk…didn't think I'd be in the way but he came very close and caught my ankle."

"What did he look like?"

"Oh…uh…thick, black hair…spiff black outfit with gold trim…knife in his belt…something funny about his eyes…can't think what it was, though."

The inspector and the policewoman glanced at one another. The inspector's expression hardened. "Age?"

"Don't know. Thirty maybe. Everything was a bit blurred.

I'd had a lot of beer. I wasn't seeing too straight."

"And the one who went for Shelah. What did he look like?"

"Don't know. They all looked about the same to me. Nattily dressed. Mostly dark colours. They all had knives."

"Was one of the preachers sons among them?"

"Why, no! No. I'm sure of it. Didn't look anything like the preacher's sons. Not at all."

"But you just told me you were drunk and couldn't see very well. How can you be sure one of the preacher's sons wasn't among them?"

"Well…they wouldn't go to a place like that, would they? They're older than those guys, anyway. The preacher's sons are around my dad's age, about a hundred. If one of them had come into The Planet there'd 've been a riot. They'd 've chucked him right out. But why should you think it might have been one of them?"

"Your friend Shelah has been delirious since he was brought in. He keeps saying 'I shouldn't have bad-mouthed the preacher's son.' Isn't that so doctor?"

"Yes. He's said that at least twenty times."

"Now why would he say something like that if it wasn't the preacher's son who hit him?"

"We were joking about Japh, the unmarried one,…about him not standing a chance of finding a wife."

"And that angered the fellows at the next table and they came to beat you up."

"They didn't say anything about that. They said something about me trying to make them fall into some spilled beer."

"Hmm…uh….now…let me be straight with you, Hoshea. I'm looking for your help. There are a lot of people who are very upset by that wretched preacher's threats of death and destruction. Your friend was also upset by him. So upset he's as good as dead.

If we don't stop that troublemaker, who knows how many more innocent people are going to get hurt or killed? We need some evidence to put him away. It's obvious your friend has been very badly affected by his nonsense. I'm sure you could help us to find something to nail him with. You know what a problem the fellow is. You know what a service to the community it would be to have him hanged—or at least locked away. Now surely you can come up with something."

"But what makes you say Old Doom and Gloom got to him?"

"He keeps saying 'I'm going to die; but I won't drown; I'll burn.' Isn't that so, Doctor?"

The doctor nodded. "I've heard him mumble those very words a dozen times or more. 'I'm going to die; but I won't drown, I'll burn'."

"Now, who would put such an idea into his head except that wretched preacher or one of his sons? I'm telling you, Hoshea, there's a lot of folk suffering psychological trauma like that. It's spreading throughout the community like a cancer. And it's all because of them. Now, didn't that Japh fellow terrify him with such talk last night?"

"Well, actually, we were joking about the burning and drowning stories before we got onto Japh not being able to find a wife. I don't think Shelah's ever actually seen Old Doom and Gloom. He's heard about him—hasn't everybody? But I'm as good as certain he's never actually set eyes on him. Or any of his sons, for that matter. Shelah lives in Zohan and he's only just come up to the university. It's his first year and the term's just started."

The inspector sank back into his chair with a deflated and disappointed look on his face.

3 Mercy Mission

It was very unusual to see a group of only three mag-sleds speeding along the sledway. Ever larger bands of robbers had led to ever larger convoys. Only the foolhardy would think of going in a convoy of fewer than a dozen. But this one consisted of an ambulance, a police escort, and an army personnel carrier—not a very attractive target for robbers. The sleds raced along the cleared way between the tall, beautiful trees of the lush coastal forest, soaking up the warmth of the midday sun.

"D'you think he'll last till Zohan?"

"Not a chance. He's going fast. Isn't even rambling and mumbling anymore. Hasn't said a word for at least an hour."

"Waste of time if you ask me. I didn't think we'd make it when we left Salem yesterday. I was even more sure of it when we left Noph this morning. But the way the authorities got into top gear after that telemessage from his dad, it's obvious he must be a real big-wig. No good arguing with people like that. Lose your job before you can blink twice."

"You're right there—and with everybody in such a rush to get moving, I missed my breakfast. I'm starving."

"You're not the only one, mate."

The sleds began to slow down for a bend in the way. The sled-man, who had been on ambulances for many years, was considerate of his patients and prided himself on the smoothness of his driving. He slowed down to just a few miles per hour for the bend.

A narrow stretch of ocean, squeezed between a long, low promontory and a great expanse of floating forest, came into view on the left. The gentle sea breeze wafted a delicious smell toward the sled and, as it reached the end of the curve, a stall

Another World

Name: Date:

came into sight next to the sledway thirty yards ahead. Dishes, spoons, cups, and jugs were neatly arranged on the makeshift counter. Behind the stall was a large cooking pot set over a heap of glowing coals. A lean, wiry, athletic-looking man lifted the lid to stir the contents.

"Hey, let's stop for a bite to eat."

"Great idea. Oi! Vanesh! Let's stop and get something to eat. We're starving—we didn't have any breakfast this morning."

Vanesh pretended to be reluctant to stop. It was against the regulations. But that delicious smell made his mouth water. And if there were any repercussions he could say the medics insisted. He pulled over to the side of the way, hovered beside the stall for a few seconds, and slowly reduced lift to let the sled settle gently onto the ground. The hum of the sled died as he switched off the power.

The corporal in charge of the army detail set his men on guard and headed for the ambulance. He arrived at the same time as the sergeant from the police escort.

"What's up?"

"Patient's in a bad way. Needs a complete rest with no acceleration for a while, otherwise he won't make it to Zohan."

"Hmm, sounds a bit fishy to me. Just happened to take a turn for the worse next to a food stall, eh? Still, that smells really good, doesn't it?"

"I'll treat you to some. Hey! You with the soup ladle! What's your name?"

"Malech, Sir."

"Well, Malech, we'll have some of that food you're cooking. What is it?"

"Fish stew. My own special recipe. You won't taste better anywhere, though I do say it myself."

The medics, all three sled-men and some of the police and soldiers were soon enjoying the most delicious stew they could ever remember eating.

"How's the patient?" asked one of the police escort.

"Not so good. We'll be lucky if we can get him to his family in time. By the way, before we left the hospital yesterday, I talked to one of the male nurses. He told me that Doom and Gloom's son Japh hired a gang to do him in. Have you heard anything about that?"

"No, I haven't," said the tall, dark-skinned, craggy-featured sergeant, after a few seconds of chewing a mouthful he was obviously enjoying too much to hurry. "But I can tell you exactly what's going to happen. That story will spread till everyone in Salem—and lots of other places, too—will be up in arms and demanding a lynching. Then we'll be sent to investigate and it'll turn out to be a load of codswallop. It happens so often I can tell right away when I hear a story like that. It's just wishful thinking."

The disapproving glances from the medics and the soldiers were not lost on the police sergeant and he hastened to add, "Look, I'd be as glad as anyone else to get those scumbags put behind bars. I'd be very happy if someone would come up with something against them that would stick. But people come out with things that even the judges can't put their names to, like the last one. You know the story that was doing the rounds a month or two ago—about them murdering a whore because they're all fired up against prostitution. You can't imagine how many policemen were sure we'd got them at last. Then it came out that Gloom and all three of his sons were in Uz when the woman was killed. And plenty of witnesses saw them there, too, making trouble, stirring people up just like they always do with their stupid stories about everybody getting drowned. They'd taken a break from chopping down trees and they'd been in Uz for a week. Didn't get back to Salem till two days after the murder."

A glum silence descended on the group while they finished off the last of their stew.

"What's in the jugs, Malech?"

"Grape juice in this one, orange in the other two. Fresh and delicious. I squeezed them just a few minutes ago."

"Give me orange."

"I'll have grape."

"Me too."

"Orange for me."

The jugs were soon as empty as the stew-pot.

The customers handed over their money and returned to their sleds.

"How's our patient doing?"

"Looks a bit better. The stop must've done him some good. Might even last long enough for his parents to see him before he snuffs it."

"You could be right. He does look a bit better, and it's less than an hour till Zohan."

"Hey, look what's crossing the way over there."

"Wow! You don't see stegos as big as that very often."

"Good job they get out of the way when the sleds get going."

"Yeah, wouldn't like to run into one of those!"

The sled-men flicked their power switches and the sleds began to hum. One after another they eased forward the lift levers. The sleds rose until they hovered two feet above the ground.

A hundred yards away, the stegos bellowed and lifted their heads a few feet, rippled the great angular plates running down the length of their backs menacingly, raised their spiked tails and hurried into the trees by the side of the way. The sled-men adjusted their thrust controls; the sleds accelerated smoothly and, in a few minutes, disappeared into the distance.

4 Bronto

Malech emerged cautiously. He heard the usual clamour of the forest—birds calling, pteros screeching, insects shrieking, small creatures scurrying and disappearing into crevices between the roots. There was a pile of fresh dung to the right. No sign of the animal that had left it—probably a lambo judging from what could be seen at this distance. Better keep a look out, he thought to himself. Don't want to disturb one of those!

He stood motionless for a full minute, eyes scanning as much of the landscape as could be seen from the mouth of the tunnel. The pool a few yards ahead open to the sky, blue as always. Birds and pteros wheeling and flapping, appearing and disappearing behind the foliage. Everywhere else the trees of the floating forest almost completely hid the sky. Looked safe enough. The area before him coming into view little by little, inch by inch. Another full minute of scanning and listening.

The trunks of the floating forest trees were thick enough to hide lurking creatures. A multitude of criss-crossing trails between the trees were well cleared—all the low branches had been broken off by the passage of very large animals, and the undergrowth had been flattened by their heavy feet. But in other places the ferns and bush were dense, often joined to the branches above by hanging creepers; perfect cover for some very dangerous animals. No good taking chances. Didn't survive here for four years by taking chances.

Satisfied that there was no immediate danger, he stood up

and lugged his bag toward the pool, eyes darting from the mat of roots to the surrounding trees to the pool ahead, ears alert for unfamiliar sounds. Every few paces stopping to glance left, right, backward. An antelope twenty or thirty yards to the left, almost hidden by the trees, was looking at him. As always…never see them before they've seen you. Not likely to be any predators in that direction.

A twenty-foot-span ptero had been circling overhead since Malech emerged from the hole in the roots between two trees. It half folded its wings and streaked toward the water. Just as it seemed it must splash into the pool, it opened its long, narrow wings to full stretch and skimmed above the surface, stabbed downward with its massive beak, and brought up a fish. A big fish. The ptero had to struggle to gain height, wings flapping laboriously, rising painfully slowly. The surface of the pool erupted and a mass of jaws and teeth on a snake-like neck burst through the spray. Long curved teeth crunched into one of the ptero's leathery wings. After a few moments of screeching, flapping, and splashing, the ripples faded away. Then there was only the usual sound of insects, birds, and pteros.

Malech's heart was pounding. First time he'd seen that kind of plesio here—not that he'd seen many in his whole life. This was a fairly young one, probably no more than thirty feet long, but scary—very scary. Better be even more careful near the pool in future.

Up to that moment it had been a reasonably normal and very successful day for Malech. He had been in his usual place near the bend in the mag-sledway. His steaming pot of fish stew was just fully cooked and giving off the most tempting aroma when the ambulance sled with its escorts had pulled up to his stall. Convoys were not allowed to stop between recharge stations and this was the first time that mag-sled people had been his customers. They had finished off everything he had to sell.

Malech had asked double his normal price for the stew. Sled-men, medics, and police-men earned good salaries. Still, what he charged was quite a bit less than they would pay in Zohan.

His usual customers were pedestrians trudging to or from the city. They were usually poor, often fugitives, but never very hungry since plenty of fruit grew by the way. But his stew smelled so appetizing that he generally found enough travellers wanting a change, and prepared to pay his modest price.

Malech always added a good pinch of salt to his stew. Not only did it enhance the delicious flavour, but it made his custom-ers thirsty. He had asked three times his normal price for the grape and orange juice and they had been only too willing to pay.

And now he squatted near the pool to wash his cooking pot and dishes. He was allowing his thoughts to wander. Dangerous. He gazed at the water and the crockery he was washing. His mind's eye started replaying the spectacular end of the ptero.

He was not paying attention to the forest.

Malech's thoughts drifted to his successful morning's busi-ness; then to his little pile of cash. Not so little anymore. Malala would have a bit of a nest-egg if anything should happen to him. Of course, there would be no reason for her to stay here if he were gone. But then, would there be anywhere better for her to go? He really must get her some new clothes. Everything was worn out except a few drab things that didn't do her justice.

A few yards to his right, a large, brown rat emerged from a hole in the roots and looked around, its nose twitching as it sniffed the air. Its head swivelled toward a scraping noise coming from the trees twenty yards to his left. It darted back down the hole. Malech was too deep in thought to notice.

Maybe he could get Malala another book of plays. She missed her plays. He could tell that even though she never said anything. He'd pretended he didn't know her ambitions and dreams of being an actress in the old days. He'd just steered her away from them as gently as he could. Not that he wanted to rule her life like a tyrant, but he'd always tried his best to keep her away from anything that might end up hurting her. What a joke; he'd landed her here, in a floating forest, of all places. Ah, well. Maybe he could get some other books, too—another Enoch perhaps. That would mean a search in the secondhand shops. Bookstores didn't sell such works anymore; nothing but witchcraft, sex, and violence these days. Enoch's books had been out of print for years.

A sound of tearing leaves high in the branches close by broke into his day-dreaming.

Suddenly wide awake, tense, and shaken, Malech glanced around.

A bronto stood less than ten yards away.

A young one, of course. The thousand-year-old giants were too big for the floating forests—they stayed on the mainland. But even this was awe-inspiring. The neck and tail disappeared from view into the foliage. The intricately patterned green and yellow legs and massive body filled the space between the trees in front of him. Amazing that such a monster could even move through the forest, never mind come so close without making enough noise to rouse him! He backed away. His foot caught the pile of crockery and cutlery. It toppled over with a crash.

Malech raced for the tunnel.

Boughs above him were snapping like matchwood. The huge tail crashed through a splintering mass of twigs and branches. Then the ground shook as a ton-and-a-half of muscle and bone crashed down. Malech's smashed cooking pot flew twenty yards before splashing into the pool. Shattered remains of dishes, cups, and spoons showered down behind it. Malech scrambled into the hole.

He turned to see the bronto bringing its head down for a closer look. Such a small head for such a huge body! But big enough to tear him to pieces with its jagged teeth if he wasn't careful. It sniffed and followed its nose to the entrance of the tunnel. Malech backed further inside holding his breath. The head swayed two or three times across the entrance, eyed him for a few seconds, snorted, withdrew, and moved off to graze a little farther away.

5 Convoy

"Hey, Caro. What were you jawing about with that freeloader at the station—and who is he anyway?"

Caro turned his eyes from the forest bordering the sledway and looked across to Esdras, who sat strapped into the seat between himself and Ulm, the sled-man. He pushed back his helmet far enough to scratch an itch on his forehead. "Funny guy, a bit quiet, friendly though, name's Japh. He don't drive for no company. It were his own sled."

"Wow, he must be loaded—that sled's new! So what were you doing talking to a plutocrat? Trying to wheedle your way into a better job?"

"No, man, we was just chatting. He were telling me some interesting things."

"Like where to pick up the best tarts in Noph?" Esdras chuckled as he glanced across at Caro. As expected, Caro did not look amused.

Esdras' grin widened and he looked again toward the forest

speeding past the racing sled. He was warm under his heavy uniform in spite of the strong breeze from ahead; a bead of sweat trickled from his arm-pit. Both he and Caro wore the uniform of Top Guards Inc. And very smart the uniforms were, too, made of tiny rings of Tubal-Cainite linked together. Worked into the dull, mat silver of the ordinary T-C-ite were three narrow bands—black, yellow, and purple—running like a sash over the left shoulder and down to the waist on the right. The black was rust-proofed by a sulphur treatment, the purple by a phosphorus treatment, and the yellow was brass. Their helmets, of beaten T-C-ite, also had the company's distinctive narrow black, yellow, and purple stripes. Esdras glanced at Caro. He was definitely not happy. Esdras was a good-natured fellow and wanted to humour him. He put on an air of being interested. "So what was he telling you, then?"

"He were telling me about Professor Zalomo. You know, that astronomer what invented those hi-tech telescopes and stuff."

"You getting into star-gazing then, Caro? I bet your misses will be pleased about that. A whole lot cheaper than floozies! Ha ha ha ho ho ho!"

Caro scowled. He never appreciated Esdras's jokes. That made it all the funnier for Esdras and he laughed even louder.

"You'd do a whole lot better watching out for a raid instead of laughing your head off. I don't fancy having to fight bandits all by myself while you're rolling around on the floor, splitting a gut."

"Oh, come off it, Caro, just a little joke, and anyway, only a mad gang would take this outfit on. Twenty-six sleds, most with two guards—except that freeloader, of course."

"Don't be so sure about that. There's some big gangs around —and some nasty tricks they gets up to these days. One of my cousins caught it last week in that raid other side of Cainan. That

one where they felled a tree on the lead sled. All but five of the
sleds smashed into it. Must've cut through the trunk so only the
last little bit needed chopping out when the convoy came. You'd
do a whole lot better watching out for trees swaying more than
usual instead of laughing like a drain."

The smile left Esdras' face as he thought over what Caro had
said. It was true the gangs were getting up to some very nasty
tricks these days. His eyes went back to the trees beside the way;
three-hundred feet tall, some of them. Wouldn't be much left of
a sled if one of those came down on top of it! He wondered if it
would be possible to spot a tree swaying in time to warn Ulm.
His eyes scanned the trees ahead for a few minutes. Then his
attention started to wander. He fidgeted in his seat. His uniform
was getting too tight around the waist. He'd have to watch it.
He'd changed uniforms for a bigger size earlier in the year and
his belly was already feeling the strain. They didn't make uniforms
much larger than the one he was wearing. All the guards were
big, burly fellows—security companies didn't accept average-sized
men. But the uniforms were very expensive. Anything made of
T-C-ite was expensive. If he got any fatter than the standards,
they would not make a new size especially for him, they'd fire
him. He looked across at Caro, gazing at the sledway leading
straight as an arrow toward a bend a few miles ahead—almost
invisible in the distance.

"So what did Freeloader tell you about Prof Zalomo? And
how does he know him, anyway?"

"The Prof's his brother's father-in-law. And he were saying
we'll be out of a job in a couple of hundred years or so."

"Oh, come off it, Caro! You don't believe stories like that do
you? Zalomo's one of those old-fashioned religious types. Does
he think he's going to preach the bandits into becoming good

guys so nobody needs us anymore? Fat chance! Or is he going to set up one of his telescopes to keep an eye on them? Come on, Caro, get real. In two- or three-hundred years' time, when you're still having to get up two hours before dawn to make your convoy on time, just remember I told you so."

"It weren't nothing to do with the robbers. The Prof says that in just a few hundred years, the magnetic field won't be strong enough for sleds to work no more."

"What! You don't fall for such utter bull do you? What do astronomers know about magnetic fields? He should stick to his star-watching... and his preaching, if he must."

"Well, Japh said it were him what invented the mag-sled drive, so maybe he knows just a little bit more about it than you do."

"Invented the mag drive! Give me a break, Caro. You must be a real sucker if you believe that freeloader's tall tales. He must think you're as green as the grass."

"Well the recharge is coming up just after the next bend. I'll take you to meet him and you can talk to him and call his bluff."

"Maybe I will. And you know what? After the recharge, the route goes pretty close to West for a long way. Bet that free-loading amateur'll slow us up big time."

"Well, I've been taking a look behind us every now and then. He seems to be doing fine."

"Big deal! Even I could keep a sled on track on this part of the trip. Not far from dead South we're heading. Straight down the line of the magnetic field. Child's play."

"There was a few bends and he didn't do too badly," said Caro.

"Well, we'll see after the recharge."

❖ ❖ ❖

The recharge station, at the fork where the way to Noph branched off to the right, was growing rapidly. When Caro had first done this route almost fifty years earlier, it was just a plain and simple recharge shed with its power house and cottages for the station attendant and the technician.

Expansion had started some twenty years ago, after the rise of organized robber gangs had forced sleds to travel in convoys. A shop had been the first unofficial addition. A bar had followed soon after. All sled-men and guards were prohibited from drinking while on duty. The bar was licensed only to sell liquor to passengers. Now there was a restaurant, a brothel, a sled workshop, a tea room, a gambling den, a raunchy magazine shop, a general dealer, and a few dozen houses. To recharge twenty-six sleds took two hours, and plenty of business was done besides recharging before the convoy was ready to form up again.

Caro scowled at Esdras as the sleds started to assemble. "You ain't supposed to tank yourself up on duty. How much good d'you think you're going to be when the bandits attack if you're sozzled?"

"Oh, come off it, Caro. I only had four."

"And that's four more than you're supposed to have."

"I wonder if your missus would think you're 'supposed' to spend so much time with that redhead at Sophie's."

"That ain't nothing to do with you. It don't make me no less ready to fight bandits."

"It will if she gives you RAK!"

Caro had no time to spit out a cutting reply about Esdras' fast-growing beer-paunch before Esdras went on, "Hey! Look, Caro, that freeloader's just in front of us. Better tell Ulm to watch it. He might not know he's got an amateur ahead of him. Just our luck to have him in front when we're going so near to West."

"I don't suppose you talked to him like you said you would— too much like a waste of valuable drinking time."

"Well I couldn't, could I? He went straight for the tea room. The others would never let me hear the end of it if I'd followed him in there, now, would they? And anyway, you said you'd take me to meet him. Streaked off to Sophie's too quick for that, didn't you? Afraid somebody else'd get to that redhead first!"

Caro looked around and noticed that the two passenger sleds had formed up just behind them. He scanned the faces of the passengers. As he had expected, there were no pretty girls. Not like the good old days; too many had been captured by bandits. They fetched enormous prices in the big cities. Now the only passengers were worried-looking businessmen and even more worried-looking grannies going to visit their children in Noph.

He also noticed that three slasher sleds had joined at the rear. They had come with the previous convoy, but one of them had needed some repairs at the sled workshop. That would explain why the way from Salem had been so clear. There would be more bushy growth and taller weeds on the way ahead, so progress might be a little slower. Pity they didn't put the slashers at the front instead of the back. But, come to think of it, it wouldn't be so good travelling through a spray of finely chopped vegetation. And, with the three of them side-by-side across the whole way, it would be difficult for the sleds behind them to spot a convoy coming in the opposite direction—or an ambush, either. The slashers would be paying attention to their work and might not be looking out. Maybe it was just as well they were at the back.

The convoy master gave the signal and the sled-men nudged their control levers. Current surged through the lift circuits and the sleds rose above the way, humming gently, turning slightly from side to side as the sled-men went through the standard post-recharge checks. Caro had a worried expression on his face. He looked around to see which would be the lead sled for this leg of the journey. He spotted it moving slowly toward the barrier beyond the recharge shed. It was a big one, well over thirty feet long, ten feet wide—the maximum allowed—and, at the highest part of the cargo bay, it must have been more than nine feet tall. It was painted in the bright red, green, and white swirls and flashes of Super Swift, Salem's famous sled factory. It was loaded with parts for the workshops of Noph. Caro breathed a sigh of relief. Zenano, the driver, had, like himself, spent the break at Sophie's, not at the bar. He would be stone-cold sober. The barrier swung open, the convoy pulled away and accelerated toward the intersection where the route to Noph turned toward the West.

"Hey! Just look at that!"

"What?" said Esdras with a start. He was obviously feeling a bit drowsy. His eyes had been half closed, head hanging forward. He followed Caro's gaze to the freeloader's sled in front of them.

"Did you ever see anything like it?" asked Caro.

"Well, I've seen wheels before, but not on a mag-sled. Wheels went out years ago. Too much friction."

"Inefficient, everybody said. But it looks like he's got a good idea there—look, he's pulling them up again."

"I get it! He just lets them down till he's got the right control settings and then pulls them up," observed Esdras. "That'll make it dead easy to drive a sled."

"Look out, sled-men! Your big fat pay settlements are going to be in trouble when this gets around and sleds come standard with retractable wheels! And it don't take years of practice to get a full licence."

"Well, maybe you'd better introduce me to him when we get to Noph. I want to find out a bit more about it."

"You wanting to become a sled-man then, Esdras?"

"Pays a whole lot better than being a guard, doesn't it?"

"I wonder if it's his own invention. Or maybe he got it from Prof Zalomo. The papers say he's always inventing things."

"Bet he won't be inventing things much longer. They're getting rid of all the religious types at the universities. Narrow-minded bigots who use the G-word for anything but cursing are a bad influence on the younger generation. I guess it's only because Salem's an old-fashioned town they haven't got rid of him already."

"But he's the cleverest chap in the world according to the papers," said Caro. "Don't see how they'll get rid of him."

"Just wait and see. It won't be long."

"Not long to Noph either. Roll on!"

"Eh, Caro. What did you say Freeloader's name was?"

"Japh."

"Remember to introduce me to him before you hightail it for Dora's. Right?"

"Right!

6 Ambush

"Well, it's your choice. Looks as if about twelve sleds will leave at first light tomorrow; thirteen if you go, too."

"Is that enough to be safe?" said Japh.

The overweight, slack-jowled, baggy-eyed transport official studied his clipboard, making a show of being busy with some figures, and said nothing.

Japh had not offered anything to grease his palm. Little chance of further advice—or any kind of help—without it. Still, rather take a chance than go against his principles. Twelve sleds. Fifteen was considered the safe minimum these days. The convoy he'd missed had only ten.

If it hadn't been for those two guards, who had slipped over from the sled behind him the moment the convoy came to a stop, he would not have been here. He would have found out that the convoy he wanted to join from Noph to Zohan had just left and he would have sped after it. But Esdras and Caro had been interested in his retractable wheels. What a pleasure to talk to people who didn't treat him like dirt! When had that last happened? Hard to remember. He had chatted with them for more than half an hour, thinking there was plenty of time before the next convoy would form up.

On entering the office to make enquiries, he learned that the Zohan convoy had left a few minutes before his arrived.

Only ten sleds. If he could catch up it would make eleven. Not so far from the mark, but he carried no guards. He didn't count as far as sled-crews were concerned. Even though he was armed, without guards everyone looked down upon him as a "freeloader." That wasn't really fair. A sled without guards had to pay a bigger convoy fee.

Japh glanced around the little office as if looking for inspiration. The walls were decorated with aging, dog-eared official notices vying for attention with large, glossy, expensive-looking calendars advertising sled transport companies, sled repair shops, and sled dealers—all sporting images of scantily clad women in provocative poses. He looked out the window. The outskirts of Noph were bathed in the bright sunlight of mid-afternoon. There was plenty of daylight left. His recent memories of Noph were not pleasant and he didn't want to spend the night unless he had to. Was it really worth waiting until tomorrow for two more sleds in the convoy? Pity that all twenty-six in the group he'd come with from Salem were swapping cargoes and going straight back again. Next week there would be a lot of traffic from Noph to

Zohan, but he certainly wasn't going to spend the weekend here.

With his light, empty sled, he might be able to catch up within an hour or so. He'd been pleased with the way it performed on the journey thus far. But he must decide quickly—that convoy was getting farther away all the time.

"Well, thanks for your help, sir. I think I'll have a go at catching up to the one I missed."

The flabby lump shifted his ungainly bulk in the swivel chair and kept his attention on his clipboard. Not a word. Not a gesture. Not a sign that he had even heard.

❖ ❖ ❖

Without other sleds all around him, it was easy to speed along the sledway with his mind on autopilot. He had to keep watch for animals crossing the way in front of him, but that was easier than keeping track of sleds behind, in front, and to the side of him. His thoughts wandered. It had been a long time since he had held a friendly chat with anyone outside the family. He had really enjoyed talking with Caro and Esdras—it had made him feel almost normal. He was used to being scoffed at, insulted, and threatened.

And for what?

What if his dad was way off with his predictions?

What if he had got it all wrong?

After all, if he was a prophet, why couldn't he prove it so that everyone would take him seriously? He would only need to predict the outcome at the stadium every week for a month and the whole world would come flocking to hear him preach. They would be hanging on every word he said instead of doing all they could to hang him—and his sons.

Japh loved his father and had always tried to be loyal to him, but things were getting just too tough and he thought again about what would happen if he decided to pull out and just go his own way. How close they had come to being lynched the last time they were in Noph!

Maybe his dad was right.

But didn't they all deserve what was coming to them anyway? Why should his family spend so much effort trying to tell people what they didn't want to hear and didn't deserve to hear, anyway?

A few times in the last year, Japh had come close to giving up. It was only the encouragement of Sarai's father, Professor Zolamo, that had kept him going. What a great guy! What a lucky chap his brother was to have found not only a terrific wife but the best father-in-law anyone could ever hope for.

The sight of a herd of mammoths on the sledway only a few hundred yards ahead wrenched him back to reality. He slammed the thrust control into reverse and slowed to give the monsters time to stamp off into the forest, trumpeting angrily.

❖ ❖ ❖

Cush was getting nervous. The last convoy of the day should be coming around the bend any minute. That fat pig from the transport office had said there would be only ten sleds. He got a cut, so he wouldn't deliberately give them bum information. But maybe there'd been some latecomers—it happened sometimes. But what if there were a lot of latecomers? The convoys were getting bigger and more heavily armed all the time. And the Elrod gang was now dangerously small—seven men lost in the show last week near Cainan. And those two greenhorns had died of their wounds after a drunken knife-fight last night. They were good fighters, too.

What if bounty hunters had offered that flabby lump of blubber a bigger cut? Can't trust anybody these days. Just our luck to get done by a sell-out transport official.

Cush looked at the rest of the gang hurriedly piling on branches. They were tense and jittery. There were only seventeen of them. And what if the sled didn't perform as it should? They'd been too rushed crimping their mat of mesh onto the sledway. Shouldn't rush a job like that. What a chore it had been! The sledway's mesh was so firmly embedded into tangled roots it had taken much longer than expected to expose enough to crimp onto. There would probably be no time to do a test run. Such a big sled. Would there be enough control if the crimping wasn't right?

The goat, tethered in the middle of the way, started to tug on its rope. Cush caught the movement from the corner of his eye. See that, Boss? Gotta get ready, Boss.

"Get ready!" barked Elrod from behind a clump of bushes thirty yards away.

The men left the last few branches on the ground and scurried to the undergrowth by the side of the way. Cush and Toom jumped onto their sleds.

The goat became more agitated. Joash ran to the tether, pulled out the peg, and hung on as the animal struggled to get as far from the way as it could. Joash knocked in the peg a few yards beyond the edge of the cleared way. The goat was still not happy and kept straining at the rope.

Cush wiped the sweat from his palms and eased the lift control forward. The sled lifted as easily and hovered as steadily as if it were already on the way. So far so good. Maybe Joash knows something about crimping mesh after all.

Sweat oozed from the back of Cush's head and trickled down his neck. He steadied his fingers on the thrust levers. The sled was an exceptionally long one, captured in last week's heist. Now it looked like a ten-foot-high pile of branches, almost invisible among the trees next to the way.

Now the last of the sleds was well clear of the bend and the convoy was at full acceleration. All ten were in full view. Cush's fingers stiffened. Time to go, Boss! Time to go!

"Go!" roared Elrod.

Cush eased out of the dense little clump of elder and across the sledway. Toom slipped in behind him with a normal size sled—not much more than half as long as Cush's, but long enough to leave the way blocked from one side to the other.

Cush grabbed his weapon, jumped down, and dashed for the undergrowth.

The nearest sleds were only a few yards away. Cush could see the panic throughout the convoy. Every sled-man had his thrust controller on maximum reverse, easing back on the lift, trying to get as much braking from the ground as possible without going into a spin—struggling to keep control, light sleds trying to dodge the more sluggish and heavily laden ones likely to ram them from behind. Guards readying their weapons while leaning back to maintain their balance against the deceleration, free hands moving to the quick-release buckles of their harnesses. Fear written all over their faces. Eyes scanning the bush to see where the attackers would spring from.

Two sleds had already hit each other before the first smashed into the barrier.

Cush winced. Pity to make good sleds bash themselves up like that. And the cargoes. Anything fragile ruined for certain. Bottles of booze? Smashed for sure. What a crime! But with so many armed guards you've got to adapt. Got to put them out of action long enough to put them out of action for good.

The first sled to strike the barrier was a very big unit, heavily laden, hard to slow down. It rammed into the front of Toom's sled, punching it sideways, leaving a gap in the barrier. But it slewed—side-swiped the back of Cush's big-rig and rolled over. Three other sleds hit the barrier, the other six managed to stop before reaching it, but two of those had collided.

Elrod's gang surged forward.

In less than four minutes, it was all over.

Cush counted thirty-eight of them. Ten sled-men, sixteen guards, and twelve passengers. Easy pickings there, sure to be some fat wallets and handbags.

But three of the gang were dead, too. And Zeek was on the ground clutching his belly, trying to hold in his ripped intestines with blood-soaked fingers, the stink of torn guts stronger than the smell of blood. He's trying to pretend it's not too bad. Face twisted with fear. He knows what's comin', poor blighter. Toom's in a bad way, too. Toom sat on a box which had spilled from an upended sled. He bent forward clutching his bleeding chest, coughing blood, and making a strangled, burbling noise. Not much chance for him, either. His best buddy. But we can't leave no one to blab to the bounty hunters. They'll be here in a few hours. Even if we could get them to a hospital the police would be there in no time, wringin' information out of them—more vicious than the bounty hunters. Don't really care if their suspects blab before they croak—less work for them if they don't. Bounty hunters have a whole lot more incentive. Sure hope Elrod doesn't tell me to do it. Wouldn't be so hard with Zeek, but Toom—we've come a long way together. But you do what Elrod says. Right away. That's just the way it is. And just like him to tell me to do it, Cush thought. He always gets a wounded man's best buddy to finish him off—less chance of bad blood in the gang afterwards.

But Cush needn't have worried about that. Without a word Elrod himself finished off the two wounded men. One blow for each. The boss never used more than one blow.

"Get cleaned up!" roared Elrod. No sign of concern about killing two men who had shared his life for the past three years.

They headed for a spring close to where Cush's long sled had been hidden. They put down their weapons and washed the blood from their hands. You never know what's in the cargo. No good spoiling stuff. Like two months ago, other side of Salem. A crate of beautiful white lace spoiled by blood stains. And if there's food, it tastes better without blood on it. They'd clean their weapons later—too eager to get to the sleds to do it now. Always a thrill to find out what's in the cargo bays. And some things classify as finders keepers—like guards' or sled-men's personal belongings. Nobody wants to be last at the pickings.

The gangsters headed for the wreckage. Cush splashed water over his head, wiped away as much of the sweat from the back of his neck as he could, and hurried after them.

"Ay-ay-ay-ay-aiiii!"

Cush turned from the sled he was about to board and raced toward the cry. So did everybody else. Joash had opened a case in the cargo bay of one of the sleds which stopped without crashing. He lifted out a bottle to read the label. Elrod prised open a case and pulled out a bottle immediately recognizable by its shape—Royal Amber!—the finest 20-year-old whisky. Within seconds, every one of them had ripped the top off a bottle and was swigging contentedly.

Twenty minutes later, Cush was opening a crate in one of the cargo holds, a smile on his face, a half-full bottle on the floor beside the crate. This was the only part of life worth living. He wanted it to last a long time. What luck! Enough booze for five or six nights. It's nights that get you—somehow you can't stop thinking about the people you did in at the show. Need a lot of booze at night. But now he took another big swig and enjoyed the burning sensation warming his throat and stomach as he forced back the lid of the crate. It looked as if there might be a good chance of finding toiletries in this one. The packing was the kind that pharmacies liked. He was hoping for a supply of deodorant. The sweat from his head soon took on that peculiar rancid smell, which embarrassed him. And his head sweated whenever he was tense and on edge. It happened with every raid.

Before he could get a good look at the contents of his crate, he heard an urgent yell. Jumping up he saw Big Hoon racing toward one of the fallen guards. The giant bent to wrench a weapon from the dead man's grip.

A sled was threading its way through the wreckage. Impossible! No more convoys due till tomorrow. Must be seeing things. Must be the booze. But everybody else was getting into action. The sled veered slightly and accelerated to smash into Big Hoon as he straightened up with the weapon in his hand. He went down like a sack of potatoes, both legs broken. The sled reached the barrier and manoeuvred its way through the gap.

"Come on!" yelled Elrod.

They raced to the pool, grabbed their weapons, and made for the Flying Viper. Cush slipped behind the controls and pushed the lift lever while the last men jumped onboard. The Viper was Cush's pride and joy. Sleek, streamlined, and powerful, it was one of the fastest, most expensive sleds on the market. It was a bit sluggish and touchy till he got it over the mesh of the way, but then it surged forward, pushing Cush back in his seat, streaking toward the rapidly disappearing smudge in the distance.

Cush's grin spread from ear to ear. Piece of cake, these dumb clucks in their lumbering cargo tubs. With a racing machine like this, it's like taking candy off a kid. He ran his fingers lovingly over the controls waiting for the boss's orders.

"We'll catch him just before the bend," roared Elrod. "Don't slow down till he's only ten yards away. Hakim and Joash! Get ready to jump! We don't want that sled crashing. It's a new one and we'll get plenty for it."

Twenty seconds later, Cush's grin began to fade. Must be a real amateur driving that tub. Doesn't that nutcase know he's got to slow down for the bend? Oh, Rats! We're going to lose that sled. We'll have to make do with the cargo if it's not too badly smashed. Time to slow down, Boss... Come on, Boss, time to slow down... Boss, we gotta slow down! You drunk or something, Boss? Rot your guts, Boss! We gotta slow down!

Cush, like the rest of the gang, was more afraid of Elrod than sled crashes. He kept the thrust on full. Sweat poured from the back of his head and streamed down his neck.

❖ ❖ ❖

Elrod was drunk. It had suddenly hit him right after he gave the last order.

While the others had been ravaging the cargo bays, he had been hiding in one of the wrecked sleds, pouring Royal Amber down his throat, trying to blot out the ache in his heart.

Zeek had been his only son. His only child. He had meant even more to Elrod than he had been prepared to admit. He had intended to tell Zeek he was his son in a few years' time—maybe when he retired. He would hand the leadership of the gang to him and give him advice from the sidelines. He thought of Zeek's mother. He'd never been able to get her out of his system. He'd left town in a hurry as soon as he found out she was pregnant. But he couldn't stop thinking about her and decided to go back and marry her. Trouble was she'd married a sled guard while he was away. A big, burly bear of a man. Intelligent too. Not the type to pick a fight with. Elrod could never remember the fellow's name, but thought of him as *Gorilla*.

Elrod joined a gang, hoping to kill Gorilla in a raid. He desperately wanted to marry the widow. But he never came across that particular guard in an ambush and, a few years later, Gorilla was promoted and got to be an administrator in the security company. Even worse, when he followed her to the shops one day and cornered her in a quiet café, she'd told him she didn't love him anymore.

Elrod had returned to Noph every now and then and kept a discreet watch on the boy. Three years ago he'd met him in a bar, half drunk, and persuaded him to join the gang.

Now he was dead.

After he had splattered his son's brains out all over the sledway, it was all he could do to stop himself from burying his head in his hands and weeping in front of his men. He hated himself for striking that blow, but he'd had to do it. Couldn't let him suffer for hours—no chance he could live with his guts torn and spilling out, not even if they could have got him to a doctor. Couldn't let anyone else finish him off, either.

But he'd had to put on a show of indifference. In a gang like this, the first sign of weakness would mean a knife in the back before the day was out.

He pulled himself out of his alcoholic paralysis. Through the blur, he saw the bend in the way approaching at a frightening speed. That crazy fool ahead was going to crash. Then he saw an astounding sight: Wheels descending from the sled in front. He was suddenly shaken out of his stupor.

"Slow down!"

"Rot your guts!" growled Cush bitterly as he slammed the main thrust controller into reverse. "Now you tell me."

❖ ❖ ❖

As soon as the wheels were down, Japh reduced the lift to settle more of the sled's weight onto them. He pushed the turn control hard and hung on as he tossed sideways. The sled slewed toward the inside of the curve, heeling over with the inside wheels clear off the ground and the outside wheels squealing. Japh reduced control, overcorrected, and swung toward the outside. As he struggled to keep the sled in the cleared way, he had no time to look back to see how close the thugs were approaching.

❖ ❖ ❖

As soon as he slammed the thrust to maximum reverse, Cush reduced lift as much as he dared in order to gain some braking by scraping the bottom of the sled along the way. Then, just before stabbing the turn control, he had to increase lift again. At this speed, he'd be sure to get into a spin if the sled touched the ground when it was travelling even slightly away from a dead-straight line. With the consummate genius of a born sled wizard whose skills had been honed to a fine edge by years of practice, he judged to a fraction of a second the moment to hit the turn controls and the exact pressure to give them. The sled sheered into the curve almost clearing the growth by the side of the way. It barely grazed a young maidenhair sapling. A small enough touch to be hardly noticeable, but, at the speed he was travelling, it was enough to swing the sled a tiny bit away from the line he had to aim for. The edge of the sled went just beyond the mesh at the apex of the curve. The Viper swung away from alignment with the magnetic field—too far for Cush to correct in time. It careered across the way, and smashed into a huge oak.

— ❖ —

7 Lambo

Malech crouched motionless at the end of the tunnel as he always did when he reached the shore. His eyes scanned what little could be seen of the narrow beach to his right and the lush, dense foliage beyond. A lion dabbed a paw lightly into the sea and flicked a fish onto the shell-covered beach. Nearby, his mate sucked the flesh from the bones of another. Three huge crocodiles waddled past and slipped noiselessly into the water. A few seconds later, Malech slid forward out of the tunnel, dodged through a few yards of dense vegetation and straightened up, taking a firm grip on his heavy staff as he looked around him. In a few steps, he reached a wide track beaten hard by the daily traffic of immense creatures on their way to drink at the beach between the promontory and the edge of the floating forest—the beach where the lions had now finished their meal and were slaking their thirst at the water's edge.

A hundred yards further inland, the track made its nearest approach to the mag-sledway. He stopped to look it over as far as he could see. To his right, the way disappeared into the trees around the bend where his empty stall stood forlorn and unattended. To the left, the way ran straight as an arrow into the distance before it merged into the hazy green of the forest at the next bend, seven miles away. A few hundred yards from where he stood, the sledway from Uz joined the main way in a wide intersection with sweeping curves to both left and right. There must have been slasher sleds with a late convoy yesterday. The way was now clear. Yesterday it had been quite overgrown. It would make his journey easier, but there would be plenty of scavengers eating up the dead frogs. Strange that frogs didn't get out of the way when sleds approached. It seemed that only frogs and people could not sense whatever it was that radiated from the sledway's mesh.

Malech hated to go to Zohan. But there were no other towns within striking distance for a pedestrian. Besides, even if he could have got to another town, there was little chance that things would be much better. He scolded himself again for his carelessness the previous day and moved to the right-hand side of the way. The cleared way ahead led straight into the distance. Huge trees on either side hemmed him in and, overhead, birds and pteros circled beneath the unbroken blue of the sky.

After four and a half hours of steady running, he reached the tollgate on the outskirts of Zohan. As a pedestrian he paid no toll, but he offered a nod and a greeting to the toll man, who raised his eyes from his *Kinky-Teens Torture Dungeon* magazine just long enough for one contemptuous glance.

It took him almost half an hour to reach a large store which sold not only cooking utensils, crockery, and cutlery, but also hardware and salt.

More than a year had passed since Malech was at this shop. It took him aback to see the changes that had happened in that time. The shop-front had been repainted in rainbow colours, but the area in front was littered with wrappers, peels, and assorted rubbish. A smell of rotting fruit hung about the street. The houses on either side were totally neglected and looked shabby and drab, making the shop seem even gaudier in its loud colour scheme. Idlers and street urchins sat on the curb, or slouched on the sidewalk or in the street near the door. They turned to look him over as he crossed the way toward them.

Malech moved his right hand as unobtrusively as possible to his pocket and held it there, pressing the wrist against his purse. He always took small-denomination coins with him on his infrequent visits to civilization. He left the valuable ones at home. This had the advantage that his savings were not an inconveniently large heap, but it meant that his bulging purse always looked as if it held more than it really did. Four of the youths to the left of the shop huddled together and mumbled something under their breath. Malech brought the staff in his left hand in front of his body and took a two-handed grip, without moving his right hand away from his pocket. The hairs on the back of his neck tingled as he passed three shabby young men whose eyes had been following him as he progressed down the sidewalk. He stayed as far away from them as possible. He could hardly stop himself from glancing back at them over his shoulder as he reached the door and hurried inside.

Pictures advertising the goods that the shop sold had always been a feature of this business. They were plastered on the walls and counters. But now, every one featured a scantily dressed or totally undressed woman. He looked at a poster for a pipe-joiner. A naked woman held the tool so that it just hid her private parts. "What have women got to do with pipe-joiners?" he muttered as he approached the crockery section. He did his business and hurried out as quickly as possible.

His pack was heavy and his purse light when he left the store and headed back the way he had come.

The stares that followed him were even more worrying now that his pack was bulging. He thought of a new robe for Malala, but it was late and there were even more of the idlers on the street outside the shop than when he had gone in. A convoy was moving along the way not far from the shop and he hurried to join it. None of the sled-men objected to his walking next to the convoy. Nor did they do anything to make him feel welcome. None of the sled-men suggested he put his pack on a sled. He thought to himself how different things had been just forty or fifty years earlier.

At the gate, the sled-men paid the toll. All had full batteries so there was no need to stop at the recharge counter. They got back onto their sleds and turned up the current. The convoy took the route dead North and was soon speeding into the distance. Malech set off down the less-used route curving gently to the East. On his own now, he looked frequently over his shoulder, expecting at any moment to have to run for the heavy vegetation flanking the route. He was confident that he could escape pursuit by any of those he had seen. He knew they would be no match among the trees for a man who spent his life in the floating forest.

But no one was following him, and he settled down to a lengthy spell of running, his long, powerful strides steadily eating up the miles. He had to stop once to wait for herds of antelope, buffalo, giraffe, and horses to cross the way. His shoulders were hurting where the straps of his heavy pack pressed into them as he passed the turn-off to Uz and approached the curve where he would slip off to the game track and disappear like a phantom. But what a nuisance! There, up ahead, a man stood next to a mag-sled, looking out to sea. The fellow was dressed in forest green; he had a broad belt with a weapon hanging from it on his left side. He was bare-headed and his hair and beard were short and neatly trimmed. The nearest point Malech could conveniently join the game track was close to where he was standing. He slowed to a walk and approached cautiously, taking a two-handed grip on his staff, scanning the surrounding vegetation for lurking thugs as he drew nearer. A lone sled-man these days was rare. Very suspicious.

The stranger smiled and called, "Hello there!"

Malech noticed that his face was open and friendly; his

features were sharp and his nose showed none of the bulbous pin-cushioning of the hard-drinking libertine. His whole bearing was one of fitness and well-being.

"Something out there caught your eye?" asked Malech.

"It's been years since I last saw the sea—must be nearly sixty. As soon as I got a glimpse, I knew I just had to stop and have a good look. Strikes me there's much more floating forest than I remembered."

"Yes, there's more than there used to be. Some would say there's too much of it. It's a bit strange to see a sled-man alone these days. How come you're not in a convoy?"

"I tried to join one, but robbers got to it before I did. I managed to give them the slip. Now I don't have much choice but to travel alone."

"You're a lucky man. Robbers don't leave survivors these days. By the way, I'm Malech."

"And I'm Japh. I'm from a town called Salem, it's a few hundred miles inland." He offered his right hand.

Malech transferred his staff to his left and took the offered hand in a firm grip. He noticed the stranger's hand was strong, rough, and calloused. Not the sort of hand he would have expected of a sled-man; it was on the end of an arm that was muscular and sunburned. The stranger was definitely built more like a guard than a sled-man.

"Glad to meet you, Japh. You don't look like most of the sled-men I've come across."

"Well, I spend most of my time felling trees. I usually only drive a sled to transport the timber—through the forest; not on a sledway."

"Your sled doesn't look as if it's done much work in a forest."

"Oh no. This is a new one. The ones we use in the forest are much bigger—and slower. My dad or one of my brothers drives one, I drive the other, and we move the tree trunks suspended between the two sleds. The trees we fell are over two hundred feet tall, so they really take some moving."

"And they must really take some felling too! But tell me Japh, what brings you to this part of the world? It must be pretty important to make you risk a solo journey."

"I've come to get some woodworking equipment in Zohan."

"Don't they have woodworking gear in Salem? I've heard of the place but never been there. It must surely be big enough to have equipment shops?"

"Well, it is a fairly big place—bigger than anything within two hundred miles. We've got the third-biggest sled factory in the world. You've heard of Super-Swift?"

Malech nodded.

"We do have shops that sell woodworking gear, but not the very heavy stuff. My dad's building something really big. We thought the shipyards of Zohan would probably use the type of thing we need, so I'm going to look for a firm that supplies the ship-builders."

Malech was keen to keep talking. He liked this young man. He had an open and friendly air about him. Malech was eager to hear something about what was happening in the rest of the world and Japh was the first person he had met for four years that he felt like spending time with. He liked to talk to Malala, of course, but since she never went much more than a hundred yards from their home she was no source of news of the outside world. His customers were usually secretive, suspicious, scared, silent, and very rarely friendly.

"It's getting quite late. Tell me, Japh, where are you planning to spend the night?"

"I'll look for an inn when I get to Zohan."

Malech's thoughts were racing. Would it be safe to invite a stranger to his hideout? Would this young fellow be prepared to spend a night in what was little better than a cave? Would Malala be safe with a strong young man like this around? Would he be alive in the morning if he took this fellow home with him? But then, he seemed such a decent chap; he would love to spend the evening hearing of far away places and having some conversation a bit more stimulating than Malala's narration of the day's chores and a reading from one of their few books.

"It's pretty dangerous in Zohan, you know. By the time you get there it'll be almost dark, and the place is full of thugs who'd think nothing of killing you for your sled, not to mention the money you must be carrying for the woodworking gear. The whole of Zohan seems hell-bent on provoking divine judgement these days."

"You know, Malech, you remind me of my dad. He talks like that. I'm actually feeling a bit uneasy about going into Zohan. I've heard a lot of stories about the place."

"Funny you should say I remind you of your dad. What does he do?"

"Oh…er…he's a preacher."

Malech noticed that Japh seemed a bit uneasy saying that. He had dropped his eyes to the sledway and seemed almost ashamed of what he had just said.

"A preacher. That's unusual in this day and age! How does Salem take to his preaching?"

"Well, to be honest with you, these days not many come to hear him. Nowadays it's usually just my mom, my brothers, their wives, and myself."

Malech's blank expression concealed his speeding thoughts. He remembered hearing of an outspoken preacher from Salem a few years ago—before he came to the floating forest. That one had three sons as far as he could remember. But this couldn't be one of them. Probably a different preacher; must be a few in Salem. He looked the young man squarely in the eyes.

"Japh, how would you like to spend the night at my place? It's not much. It's small and primitive, but it's safer than Zohan. I know a good place just over there where we could hide your sled. It would be fine for the night."

"Well, that's very kind of you, but I wouldn't like to put you to any trouble. I'll be fine in Zohan." He extended his hand. "It's been good talking to you, but I'd better be on my way. Hope we meet again sometime."

"Japh, I know Zohan pretty well. It's a sea-port. That makes a big difference. It will be no joke getting there just at the time when the worst kind of thugs hit the streets, and it might take quite a while to find a room. You really would be most welcome at my place and it would be no trouble."

"Your family will be wanting a quiet evening with you and I wouldn't like to put them to any inconvenience."

"No inconvenience at all, come on, let's get your sled hidden for the night. We'd better hurry. We have to use a game trail and there'll be some pretty big brontos using it to go for a drink at the sea soon. Let's go."

A few minutes later, they were hurrying down the trail. Malech stopped, looked around, dodged between a mango tree and an avocado, took a few steps and dropped to his knees, pushing aside thick undergrowth to reveal the mouth of the tunnel.

Soon the gentle slap of water beneath them signalled that the tunnel was in the root system of the floating forest. Although it was fairly dark, enough light seeped through to enable each to make out the figure of the other. After a slight bend, the tunnel widened, and light ahead meant they were near the end. Malech stopped. A few moments later he pressed himself against the side of the tunnel and beckoned Japh to squeeze forward next to him.

Malech was sure that Japh would never have seen a sight like it. He waited a few seconds for him to take in the scene. The air-passage-filled root system entwined to form a thick raft through which the water could only rarely be seen. The stocky trunks, looking oddly slender in proportion to the enormous mat of roots, carried sturdy branches whose luxuriant foliage blocked out the sky, except over the pool just ahead. The pool, about a hundred feet in diameter, clear and blue, was surrounded by a rim of intertwined and knotted roots. Over the pool, birds and pteros circled. Many more announced their presence by incessant calls from the dense foliage.

Malech pointed to what looked like two large, smooth stones lying not far from the water. "Lambo eggs," he whispered. He then indicated to the left—a tyrano approached. His head was almost ten feet above the forest floor. His thick tail pressed against the roots for balance. His enormous jaws were open, showing long, sharp teeth. Puny little forelimbs hung in front of his chest. Powerful back legs strode carefully over the uneven mat of roots. His body moved with practiced ease between the tree trunks lining the well-beaten track, where all the lower branches had long since been broken off by large animals. The tyrano's shiny scales were iridescent green from the neck down, merging into a brilliant blue at the hips, and becoming a rich purple by the end of his tail. No doubt about this one being a male. He had found no carrion that day in the forest and his eyes lit up as they took in the eggs. A few strides and he reached the first. One bite and it collapsed in a shattered cascade of broken shell. The tyrano slurped loudly as he sucked up the contents with obvious relish.

An outraged howl rang through the forest and a lambo bounded into view on their right. It was nearly as big as the tyrano, had powerful back legs, a strong tail, and small fore-limbs, but there the similarity ended. Its head was dominated by its bulbous bony nose sticking out like the bill of a platypus, and by the hatchet-like crest on the top of its head. In a fury to protect her eggs, the lambo rushed forward, bellowing fiercely. The tyrano stood his ground and opened his jaws ready for a mighty snap. It never came. The lambo stopped, thrust forward her bony snout and fired two reeking jets of boiling acid at the tyrano's face. Sparks shot crackling from her nostrils behind the scalding streams. Acrid fumes roiled around the tyrano's head, and with a roar of pain he staggered back, his eyes blind and burning. He tripped over a root and toppled sideways into the pool. For several seconds he thrashed around wildly. His puny forearms clutched at roots, but did not have the strength to pull his huge bulk out of the pool. His strong back legs kicked power-fully but found nothing to push against. His struggles served only to attract the attention of a krono, which swam swiftly toward the commotion, caught the thrashing tail in its ten-footlong jaws, and pulled the tyrano under the floating mat of roots with a few deft strokes of its four powerful flippers. Calm returned to the scene. The sound of the forest settled back to the chirping of insects and the calling of birds and pteros.

"Those eggs weren't here this morning," whispered Malech. "The lambo's all fired up now, and it won't be safe to go any further till she's moved off a bit. Sorry, Japh, we might have to just sit tight for a few hours."

But the lambo had apparently decided this was not a safe place. With deft prods of her bony snout assisting her little forearms, she rolled the remaining egg over the uneven terrain out of sight.

Malech slid into the open, looked round, and helped Japh to his feet. Thirty yards farther on, he opened a crude but strong door beyond which a natural passage of intertwined trunks and branches led to another crude, strong door. He gave a few quick taps with his staff.

8 Floating Forest Hideout

"Lali, we've got a visitor," said Malech as the door was unbolted from the inside.

The door opened to reveal a young woman, poised and alert, with long hair and bright, intelligent eyes. She wore a faded brown robe.

"Japh, this is my daughter, Malala."

Japh politely held out his hand to shake hers and made a slight bow. "Delighted to meet you, Malala." As he straightened up he noticed her eyes and stood motionless for a second or two looking into them.

Malala looked down modestly and murmured, "Oh, please, do come in."

Japh helped Malech to take off his pack and put it on the floor. Malech moved his shoulders round in circles to ease the tired muscles for a few seconds and said "Well, Japh, this is my little hideaway. I don't suppose you've ever been in a place like it. Make yourself at home. I'll be back in a few minutes." He reached for a net hanging from a hook on the wall, went through the door and closed it after him.

Japh stood looking at the closed door for a few seconds before turning round to find himself completely alone.

He was in a courtyard about forty feet by twenty. At the far end, in the corner on the same side as the door, was a stone slab.

Blackened, it obviously served as a fire-place. In the centre was the thick stump of a floating forest tree. It had been cut off at waist height and made smooth and level for use as a table. The roots making up the floor of the courtyard had been levelled by chipping away the high spots and filling in the low parts. Three or four trees had been cut off at floor level. The walls of the courtyard were live trees whose branches had been trimmed so that they did not protrude into the courtyard. The spaces between the trees were closed by stout branches and tree trunks woven tightly together.

To the left of the door was a curtain of reeds hanging from a creeper stretched from one side of the courtyard to the other. He wondered if Malala had gone behind the curtain. He began to feel a little uncomfortable. Why was everything so quiet? He listened for the sound of movement behind the screen but heard nothing. He moved quietly toward it, looked round to make sure he really was alone, and gently pulled open a slit through which he could see a sleeping enclosure about half the width of the courtyard. He stepped quietly toward the other side of the courtyard and listened again for the sound of movement behind the screen. Hearing nothing, he pulled the reeds apart and saw another sleeping enclosure, this one obviously a woman's.

Japh was suddenly alert, the hairs on the back of his neck prickling, a hot flush burning his ears. What had he been think-ing to trust a complete stranger? One who, within a few minutes of meeting him, had steered the conversation to find out he was the son of the preacher of Salem…carrying a lot of money. And then, persuaded him to leave his expensive new sled completely unguarded! What a fool he'd been! What a sucker! He'd followed a complete stranger into the floating forest—just about the most dangerous place in the world. And now he was alone in a prison yard, the easy victim of a smooth-talking confidence trickster. How dumb can a man get?

And what had happened to Malech? Had he gone off to collect a band of fellow forest-dwelling thugs? What had happened to Malala? How had she disappeared so quickly?

Japh's hand moved to the handle of the weapon on his belt. With pulse racing, his eyes scanned his prison. The walls were not too high to scale, but what was on the other side? Japh moved toward the door, stopped, hesitated, and turned to the reed screen. He pulled the reeds apart and went in. There was nothing that caught his attention, just a pallet on the floor and a shelf with a few clothes and other oddments. He crossed quickly to the back of the enclosure. He looked around again, let go his grip on his weapon and climbed high enough to see over the wall.

He found himself looking over a tangle of undergrowth to another wall fifteen feet away. The undisturbed state of the undergrowth showed that the outer wall certainly kept out large animals, but he soon noticed the rustling of small creatures hidden by the dense vegetation. He watched for a minute or two trying to make out what caused the sound. He saw that some of the undergrowth carried long, curved, sharp thorns. He would have to be careful if he tried escaping through them. A large rodent of a kind he had never seen before emerged from the foliage, moving along a low branch. It was more than two feet long, its fur was grey, and its pointed nose twitched repeatedly. Its front teeth stuck out like pale yellow chisels. It stopped and stared at Japh, nose no longer twitching, whiskers motionless. Japh stared back for five or six seconds. Then he was startled by a flash of movement behind a branch to the right. The wide-open jaws of a large green snake streaked toward the rodent and fastened themselves around its neck.

Japh dropped to the ground shaken. He wouldn't like to have to cross that space to the outer wall. Definitely only a last resort. He returned to the reed screen and peeped through. Satisfied that the courtyard was empty, he slipped through the screen and faced the door again. Maybe he should bolt through it and go straight back the way he had come. He hadn't noticed a latch on the outside; it was probably not locked. Maybe he could get to the tunnel before Malech arrived with his band of thugs. But they might be waiting in ambush expecting him to do exactly that. Rather examine the rest of the courtyard and look for an alternative. He backed to the wall farthest from the door and started moving toward the far end.

He passed four thick slices of floating forest root. They looked as if they could be used as stools or movable tables. He brushed against one. It was very light. It was full of air-pockets. Might come in useful as a shield, or even as something to throw if necessary. He passed the other furniture, two sets of shelves made of homemade planks. One, against the opposite wall behind the tree-stump table, carried two bowls of fruit, some crockery and cutlery, and a cooking pot. The other, against the wall he was moving along, held a small collection of well-worn books.

As he approached the end of the courtyard, he scanned the stone hearth on the far side. It had been cleaned since its last use; there was no sign of ash. Three stacks of dry wood were neatly arranged against the wall, small twigs for kindling on the left, thicker branches on the right. Suddenly he noticed that the wall stopped before reaching the end of the courtyard. There was effectively a doorway directly opposite the hearth stone. He was almost on it before he saw it. His heart thumped loudly. Was this an easy way of escape? Or a trap? He edged toward the opening and eased his head forward till he could just peep round the doorpost.

He peered into another courtyard, larger but not as carefully made. Vegetables were growing in great profusion. He stretched his neck forward to take in more of the courtyard. He saw Malala next to a tomato plant harvesting the ripe fruit.

Had he been wrong after all? Surely if they were about to kill him for his money this woman wouldn't be calmly picking vegetables! He noticed how lithe and supple she was as she turned from the tomato bush and bent to pull some carrots. He withdrew his head; afraid she might look up and see him spying on her. He went back toward the middle of the room, confused. He came to the bookshelf. Books can tell a great deal about the people who own them. He looked around again to make sure no one was watching him. Then he turned to the books.

His eyes were drawn to two volumes he recognised instantly —*Fountain of Joy* and *The Highest Goal*. For a moment he was dumbstruck. His dad had all of Enoch's books, of course. You'd expect that since Enoch was his grandfather. But in this day and age you didn't expect to find them on a stranger's bookshelf. Maybe he'd been wrong about Malech. Surely a thug wouldn't have books like that? He looked at the rest of the little library. Two books of poetry, two of plays, one on geography, and one on vegetable growing.

He was about to open one of the poetry books when the door creaked. Japh stiffened and turned toward the sound, ready to drop the book and grab his weapon.

Malech entered with two fish in his net. He immediately noticed that Japh was tense and on edge. "Hi, Japh, don't feel guilty about looking through our books. I told you to make yourself at home. Not a great selection, but better than nothing. We know them all by heart."

Standing with his mouth open but not quite able to manage

a suitable reply, Malala saved Japh from embarrassment as she came in from the garden. In a homemade basket, she carried onions, potatoes, okra, tomatoes, carrots, floating forest tree leaves, and herbs. Malech took a chopping board from the shelf against the wall, put it on the table, and set the fish down on it. Malala brought her vegetables to the table, took a knife from the shelf, and began preparing the food. Malech invited Japh to come and look over the place.

Japh felt himself relax. Maybe Malech was not a con-trickster after all. If these people planned to rob him, it didn't look as if they were about to stab him in the back. Drug him maybe? He'd better watch carefully when the food was served. He followed Malech through the doorway.

The garden was well laid out and well-stocked with vegetables growing in a thick layer of compost covered with mulch. "Plenty of dung all over the forest floor," explained Malech, "and all the leaves we could ever want for mulch—best vegetables you'll taste anywhere. We water them from here." He took Japh to one corner, where a bucket stood next to a hole through the roots to the water below. He then led Japh to the opposite corner, which was screened off by a reed curtain, and discreetly pointed out another hole through the roots.

"How long have you lived here?" asked Japh.

"Four years," said Malech as they re-entered the first courtyard.

"It seems a strange place for people like you and your daughter to be living. What made you come here?"

"It's a sad story," said Malech, squatting down next to the stone slab and picking out some of the thinnest twigs. He packed them round a little bundle of finely shredded dry grass. "I used to be a preacher…in Zohan."

Japh shot a glance toward Malech. A preacher? He might be

sympathetic to his dad—and to him. But then, he might be just playing him for a sucker, knowing that his father was a preacher. Still, Enoch's books on his shelf fits better with a preacher than a con man. Better just keep a close watch.

Next to the slab were a small bar of iron and a flint that Japh had not noticed before. Malech picked them up. With a well-practiced flick of the wrist, he struck the iron against the flint, sending sparks into the dry tinder. At the second attempt, the kindling caught and he nursed a flame until the twigs were well alight. As he packed slightly larger twigs around them, he seemed to be in two minds as to whether he should say anymore. Then he continued, quietly and with much hesitation.

"We used to hold services in the main square every rest-day. My wife, our four sons, and three daughters used to help. They gave out tracts and talked to the people. Sometimes they would do plays; usually they got some of their friends to help. Lali was very good at plays—really made them come to life."

By now the fire was crackling and Malech arranged the cooking pot over it and filled it a quarter full with water. He remained squatting on his haunches, gazing into the flames, apparently waiting to see if any further adjustments were needed to the fire.

"Over the last forty years, things started to go downhill badly in Zohan. Mind you, I heard it was no better in other places. A kind of moral rot set in and everything went bad very quickly. I was preaching one rest-day and, as always, I ended by inviting the sinners to turn from their ways."

He added two thicker pieces of wood to the blaze.

"I invited the thieves, the drunkards, and the adulterers—I didn't expect many to come forward. None did. Then I invited the homosexuals, and a riot broke out. There was a gang there and they stormed at us, shouting abuse."

Malech's voice came up hard against a lump in his throat. He added some more wood, stood up, looked at Japh, and gestured toward the table.

Malala approached the fire with her board covered with coarsely chopped pieces ready for the pot. Japh and Malech made way for her and moved to the table. Each drew up a stool. They sat down facing each other. Japh said nothing.

"In a few seconds I was unconscious. I found out later that Lali was giving tracts to a group of whores who'd come to the door of their escort agency to listen. When she saw the mob attacking us, she ran to the police station, which was just around the corner. By the time the police arrived, we were all unconscious on the ground with the thugs kicking us. They ran as soon as they saw the police."

There was a long pause. It was obviously painful for Malech to recall the incident. His elbows leaned heavily on the table and his shoulders slumped forward as he continued.

"One of my daughters and all four sons were dead when the ambulance arrived. My wife died on the way to hospital...my other daughter died next day. I came out of a coma a week later."

Japh watched Malech gazing at his hands, clasped in front of him on the table. Many seconds passed before he went on. Japh felt guilty. How had he ever doubted this man? How had he ever imagined he was a thug? And he had thought it was only his family that faced opposition from the crowds. He was obviously wrong about that, too.

"Lali heard rumours that they planned to kill me when I got out of the hospital, so we slipped out in disguise and left town right away, taking only what we could carry. At first we lived very roughly. We came to the floating forest because we thought it would be safe from people—we'd rather take our chances with the animals."

In the stillness Japh could hear Malech swallow hard. The day was almost gone, but in the dim light of the dusk he could see the glisten of moisture in the corners of Malech's eyes. The sound of Malala moving the lid of the cooking pot seemed strangely loud against the background noises of the forest.

"I'm really sorry, Malech," said Japh softly. "I know a bit of what you've had to go through—my family's had to face a lot of hatred—but couldn't you find some other place a bit safer than the floating forest? Some village, maybe, where nobody knows you?"

"When we left Zohan, we went to a little village not far from Uz. Everybody wanted to know where we were from and why we were there. Within two days we heard there was a gang headed our way, so we ran away to the floating forest. We made ourselves at home here very quickly. We found the pool where you saw the lambo eggs. It's a wonderful place to fish. We found the tunnel. I don't know what sort of animal made it, but I light a smoky fire in it every week, and nothing uses it anymore. All animals are scared of the smell of smoke. It's much easier and safer to get to the mainland that way. Seemed like a good place to stay, so we made this hideout. It took time and we needed a few tools, but we made it comfortable."

Malala, who had been standing listening to the last few sentences, moved behind Malech's stool and gently put her hand on his shoulder. He reached up and laid his hand on hers. She smiled down at him and said softly, "Are you ready for supper, father?"

9 Moonlight

The fish stew had been enjoyed, the dishes cleared away, and Japh had been speaking for a long time. His audience urged him on, eager to hear news of the outside world, and enthralled by the story about his father's project. They plied him with questions and wanted to know every detail he could tell them.

The moon had risen while they ate, and now it was nearly overhead. They sat around the stump table with no need of a lamp. Japh grew a little tired of speaking, but not at all tired of noticing how the glow of the moon shone from Malala's long hair and lit up her smiling eyes. Nor did he grow tired of listening to the hint of laughter in her voice as she occasionally made comments, and asked searching questions about the project.

"It's full moon tonight," said Malech. "The eclipse started a while ago. I think we'd better call it a night and get the bedding sorted out while there's still plenty of light."

Japh looked up. He had not noticed the shadow creeping over the face of the moon.

Malala also looked up. She seemed surprised and disappointed to see how much of the moon was already covered.

Malech got to his feet and moved to the right-hand side of the reed curtain, Malala went to the left side. Japh felt a little guilty that he had spent time snooping and already knew that each had a sleeping area behind the curtain. How could he have thought these lovely people were crooks out to rob him?

Malech came back through the curtain with a bedroll in his hands. He offered it to Japh. "This has never been used. We made it when we made our own—just in case we had a visitor. You're the first."

Japh took it and looked around for a smooth place to lay it out.

"There shouldn't be a problem with the floor. Every now and then we have to level it out a bit as the roots grow, but it's only a couple of weeks since we re-did it. We took extra care over the area around the table, so that's probably your best bet."

"Fine. In that case I'll sleep next to the table."

"It's been a real pleasure talking to you this evening, Japh. I could have gone on listening for hours, but I know you've got business to see to in the morning, so you'd better get some sleep."

❖ ❖ ❖

Japh slept badly.

He found himself in the forest next to a pool, surrounded by lambo eggs.

He was certain a tyrano was not far away, but had no idea which way to run to get away from it.

Out in the forest he saw the gleam of fire from a lambo's nostrils. He was about to turn and dash off in the opposite direction when he realized it wasn't a lambo at all. It was moonlight glinting on long, silky hair.

He caught his breath and set off toward it.

He could almost see the ghost of a radiant smile. He was sure he could hear a faint echo of merry laughter. But that lovely hair was drifting away between the trees. He ran to try and catch up but suddenly the view ahead disappeared behind something black and menacing.

He made out the shape of a huge snake hanging from a tree just in front of him. Its jaws were open. Drops of luminescent venom dripped from its fangs lighting up rows of long, sharp, curved thorns among the undergrowth. He grabbed the snake by the throat and wrestled it out of his way, struggled past, and dashed along the path. In a clearing ahead he could see the moonbeams dancing. He tripped over a root, struggled to his feet, stumbled and saw the reflection getting further away. His legs were getting entangled in the undergrowth. Strands of creepers appeared from nowhere and wrapped themselves around him. He fought to tear himself free. That ghost of a smile was fast fading into the distance.

Bound by the creepers and the undergrowth, he could only watch helplessly as the last hint of moonlit hair disappeared into the darkness. A sense of dismay and loss washed over him as he struggled to get free.

Then he was lying on the bedroll sweating, writhing, kicking, and groaning. Malala was kneeling beside him, a look of alarm on her face. She was saying "Japh, Japh, what's wrong? Are you all right? Are you all right?" in a very worried voice.

Suddenly wide awake, Japh realised he had been dreaming. But Malala really was kneeling beside him. He propped himself up on one elbow and looked at her.

"Oh, I'm so sorry, Malala. I must have been making a dreadful racket in my sleep," he said, feeling very foolish.

Malala's look of alarm changed to a smile. After a few seconds of awkward silence she said, "That's fine. May I bring you something? Something to drink? I'm sorry you didn't sleep well. I hope it wasn't the stew…"

"Oh, no…no, the stew was absolutely delicious. I've never tasted anything so good in all my life…but what about your dad? Did I wake him up too?"

"I wasn't asleep. Dad is. We'd better talk quietly. He needs to rest; he had a long run today."

"Can I take you up on that offer of a drink?"

"Come to the table."

Japh got up, moved to one of the stools and sat down. Malala brought a jug of juice and two cups from the shelf and sat down opposite him.

"Was it a full-blooded nightmare?"

"Oh…I was in the forest…I got caught up in the undergrowth …you know that sort of dream?"

"You want to run, but you're up to your knees in treacle."

"Exactly!" said Japh breaking into a chuckle.

Malala quietly echoed his laughter and then silence descended. It seemed as if neither knew quite what to say. They listened for a while to the sounds of the night—insects chirping, frogs croaking, leaves rustling.

"Malala…" Japh began.

"Lal," she interrupted softly.

Japh hesitated, put down his cup and started again. "Lal… I've done an awful lot of talking tonight, but you haven't said much at all. How about telling me a bit about yourself?"

"Oh, there really isn't much to tell. I just stay at home and tend the garden, go out gathering wild fruit now and then, read the same books day after day…and dream about how things might have been."

"And how might things have been?"

"Oh…I often think about my mom and my brothers and sisters. Maybe…if it hadn't happened…I always wanted to be an actress. Trouble was things were deteriorating so badly when I was old enough to join an acting troupe, I knew there was just no chance. Standards were falling even faster among actors than with most people. It seemed as if the arts were competing with each other to embrace corruption. I knew it would break Daddy's heart if I got mixed up with such people. But then, things just happened so quickly. The family was killed, and Dad and I fled here. Funny how your whole life can change in an instant…"

"Yes. It can…can't it?" said Japh thoughtfully.

The hoot of an owl sounded above the background chirping of insects and the faint rustle of unseen creatures.

"But it's time you got some sleep," said Malala. "It will be morning soon, and you've a lot to do tomorrow—or should I say today. I hope you have better dreams this time."

She stood up slowly, smiled at him for a moment, said "good night" in a subdued voice, then turned and started toward the reed curtain.

As Japh watched her walk away a distant cry wailed across the forest.

"Aaagh…aaaagh."

"What's that?" whispered Japh.

Lal turned, straining to hear. "I don't know," she said. "I think it came from over there toward the middle of the forest. It sounded as if someone might be in trouble."

"Are there other people living in the forest?"

"I'm sure there must be, but I've never come across anyone."

"I'd better go and see if I can help."

"That wouldn't do any good at all. It's hard enough to find your way in the forest during the day. At night you'd get lost and be eaten by a leopard or a velo, or some such thing."

They stood listening for a few moments. The sound of a distant splash reached them. They looked at each other with puzzled concern.

10 Jethro

"Aaaagh……aaaagh."

Benaiah staggered back clutching his belly.

Jethro stood in front of him, a stream of his own blood running from his throbbing nose, drops of Benaiah's blood dripping from the knife in his hand.

Benaiah stared at Jethro for a few seconds with a stunned expression on his face. Then his legs crumpled beneath him and, with a groan, he collapsed onto the gnarled roots of the floating forest floor.

"Is he dead?" said a small, scared voice from the undergrowth.

"I don't know," said Jethro, stooping to wipe blood from his knife. "But he soon will be."

He grasped the ankles of the fallen man and dragged him to the edge of the pool. He straightened up and looked for the best place to stand, hardly noticing the beauty of the peaceful scene. The full moon was just above the trees on the far side of the pool, its reflection in the still water a perfect silver disc. Then he bent over, grasped the groaning figure, and heaved him into the water. The spreading ripples hardly reached the reflection of the moon before the surface burst into a mass of foaming spray and greedy jaws tore into the bleeding body.

Jethro stood transfixed. In a few seconds the commotion was over, the ripples already beginning to fade. He stood staring at the lovely scene. The enormity of what he had just done started to sink in. He had murdered someone in cold blood. Why should that trouble him? After all, he'd killed three other men with this same knife and that had not troubled him at all. His thoughts drifted back to his other victims.

He and Zilha had been married for less than two months. They had already been the targets of four armed robberies. They found themselves with no worldly possessions and an abundance of bitterness and hatred.

In the fourth robbery, they lost everything in their home, including their clothes and furniture, most of which were not yet paid for. The robbery had been done by a notorious gang led by Xeeka, an obnoxious, supercilious thug well known to have the police in his pocket. Not surprisingly, Jethro and Zilha had no success in getting any redress through the authorities, even though they had clear evidence of the culprits' identities. They decided to take their own revenge. The plan was to watch at the gang's drinking and gambling haunts and, as opportunity presented itself, Zilha would lure one into a dark alley, where Jethro would be waiting to cut his throat.

The plan had succeeded twice. But the third time, Xeeka rolled out of the Teeny Teens Pleasure Palace just as they slunk out of the alley. Without thinking, they had scurried away and his suspicions were aroused. He called three of the gang to take a look. They found the body. Jethro and Zilha fled in terror.

They had not been particularly sorry to leave Uz, with its crooks, drunks, perverts, prostitutes, corrupt police, and even more corrupt politicians—even though it was their hometown. They had made for the floating forests of the coast. Fortunately, the coast was only a hundred and fifty miles away. There was no problem with food; there was plenty of fruit growing by the side of the way. Still, the problem of avoiding Xeeka's gangsters had been compounded by the need to avoid the bands of robbers lying in wait for unwary travellers and lone sled-men.

When they were within a mile of the coast, they had come to an ambush. If they had been on a sled, they would have fallen into it, but Zilha spotted a glint of sunlight on metal through the undergrowth and they made a detour through the trees.

A few minutes later, Xeeka's gang had sped into the trap. Having set many ambushes themselves, they were up to the niceties of the game. The gang rolled expertly off the sled and into the undergrowth next to the way before straightening up with their weapons at the ready.

The robbers sized up the situation instantly. This was no commercial sled; there was no cargo to steal. There was plenty to lose in a fight with a gang as well-armed as themselves.

"Well, what have we got here?" sneered Xeeka, with the confidence that went with the fact that they were only twelve to his seventeen. "Looks like a bunch of cheap bandits wanting to steal our sled."

"Sorry gen'lmen, we didn't see you was a class outfit. Thought you was a bunch o' common scrubbers. We don't want no trouble wi' you guys. Now what d'you say to a case o' prime brandy wot we got from a little outfit as came along yesterday. You know, just to show there ain't no 'ard feelin's."

"Three cases. And make sure it doesn't happen again." Xeeka's voice was like ice.

The robbers stiffened and glanced from one to the other. But Xeeka stood his ground with a flint-hard scowl on his face. He seemed to be weighing the possibilities. To give up three cases might be more than they would stomach—maybe they would fight. That would be nothing short of a pleasure to a thug like Xeeka in other circumstances, but his quarry was getting away and the coast was not far off.

"But just to show there's no hard feelings, we'll only take two."

The members of the gang glanced from one to the other and then relaxed. Their boss nodded assent. He motioned to two of his thugs to fetch the loot.

"We're looking for a man, about six-five, green duds, and a woman about five-eleven, blue and beige. Should've been along here just a few minutes ago."

"Sorry, mate, we ain't seen nobody for the best part of a' hour. Mind you, we was 'avin a bit of dinner just before you come along. I suppose they could've 'idden somewhere when we wasn't lookin'."

Jethro and Zilha had heard the commotion of the attack and recognised Xeeka's voice in the opening challenge. Listening intently as they crept through the bushes, and spying on the gangs whenever the undergrowth thinned, they had reached the way. Then, while the gangsters sorted out the booty, they raced for the coast, keeping out of sight as best they could, looking over their shoulders every few seconds.

When Xeeka's hoodlums rounded the bend, taking turns at swigging from an outsized bottle of brandy, they had seen the fugitives running along the way three quarters of a mile ahead and let out a roar of triumph.

The sled raced toward Jethro and Zilha, who were almost out of breath. When they reached the main sledway from Noph to Zohan, the breathless pair took the right branch toward Zohan. A few moments later, Jethro looked over his shoulder again. The sled—which had needed to slow down for the curve—was at full acceleration, only fifty yards behind them.

"Zilha," he gasped, "keep going 'til they're only a few yards away. When I say 'go' dodge off into the woods."

"Keep the wick on full and smash right into them," shouted Xeeka viciously.

Jethro's lungs were ready to burst when he gasped "Go, Zilha, go!" They veered sharply to the left off the way and into the trees. The speeding sled shot past with Xeeka screaming at the sled-man to stop. Jethro and Zilha fought their way through the undergrowth between the enormous trees of the dense woodland and then dashed across a wide clearing toward the floating forest.

The sound of cursing and clumsy crashing through the trees had come dangerously close. The gangsters, fresh and eager, knew their prey were not far ahead and were desperate to get to them before they reached the sea. Jethro and Zilha got to the floating forest and stumbled straight in. Too tired to go farther, they collapsed under a bush and peered out to keep an eye on their pursuers while they got their breath back.

The gang stopped in the lush, grassy clearing with the floating forest on the far side. The gnarled mass of roots which formed the hinge was just ahead. It was almost an unwritten law that anyone who had run foul of the legal authorities or the gangs would not be pursued by either into the floating forest. Besides the danger of wild animals, there was the risk that the hinge could break at any time. The hinge took up the movement as the forest rose and fell with the ebb and flow of the tides. After a section of forest had grown much more than five or six miles into the sea, its inertia was so great that a change of tide was liable to break the hinge. It was well known that this section of forest stretched more than fifteen miles into the sea and could go at any time. An assassin returning after dispatching his victim to find twenty yards of water between himself and the shore would be condemned to spend the rest of his life on the new island. To swim would be to commit suicide. To make a canoe might delay suicide for a few seconds. To hope for the boss to send a boat would be crying for the moon.

Jethro's heart had been in his mouth as he saw Xeeka burst into the clearing and stop. The stragglers caught up to the leaders and the gang assembled in a bunch. Such a big group, so close, so little chance of escape. He lay there panting hoping against hope that they would not come into the floating forest.

Xeeka was obviously weighing the situation. There were enough of them to leave sentries to give warning if something went wrong. They were near enough to their quarry to catch them very soon, with any luck. They were well armed and should be able to face most wild animals. Jethro's heart sank as Xeeka raised his arm, pointed in his direction and shouted "Let's go!" The gang surged forward but, at that moment, a bronto lumbered into the clearing a little to their right, heading right across their path. It stopped as soon as it saw them and turned its head for a better view. The gang froze, every eye on its tail—four tons of death and destruction sticking up into the sky. It twitched with agitation. None of them waited for Xeeka to give an order. They turned, raced from the clearing, and disappeared into the trees.

❖ ❖ ❖

Jethro and Zilha had soon learned the art of survival in the floating forest. They found one or two other fugitives here and there, and although they knew better than to trust any of them, they nevertheless learned much about their new home. They found the food supply not as plentiful as on the mainland. There were fruit trees where birds and other creatures had dropped seeds which had taken root in the mixture of soil tramped in by migrating animals, decaying vegetation from the floating forest trees, and thick undergrowth and manure from the abundant animal population. But fruit was not as common as on the land and it took some searching for. As compensation, they found pools whose water was just as sweet and good to drink as the open sea. They were teeming with fish, and a net made of creepers was sufficient to bring them all they could want.

At first they had made a makeshift shelter not far from the land—a hundred yards or so beyond the hinge, the most dangerous part of any floating forest. Many animals moved from land to forest and back for a change of diet. Pools surged with rushing water at changes in the tide. The roots shifted as the tides rose and fell. They soon moved farther into the forest and made a comfortable little place for themselves close to a large pool. Their first child, Lano, had been born within a year. He was a strong, intelligent boy, the pride of his adoring parents. Their two daughters, Bedelia and Leanie had followed at two-year intervals. And now Zilha was pregnant again. But somehow Jethro didn't feel much excitement about that now. The problem began two weeks ago when he had wandered a bit further from home than he usually did while searching for fruit. He had seen Nina with Benaiah near this pool and liked what he saw. He had come back four times and waited till Benaiah was out of sight. Then he had crept up on Nina and used all his charm to persuade her to come and meet him in the moonlight.

When she had met him, just before the eclipse started, she told him Benaiah was asleep. They tiptoed to a pleasant clump of bushes, wrapped their arms around each other and settled into a guilt-filled session of stolen love, much of it in the welcome darkness of the eclipse. Then Benaiah had appeared from nowhere in a flaming rage.

And now Jethro stood with a bleeding nose, a swelling right eye, and a bloodstained knife; he gazed absently at the reflection of the full moon sinking behind the trees on the other side of the lake.

— ❖ —

11 Breakaway

Japh watched as Malala reached the reed screen, hesitated for a moment, then slipped through the curtain out of sight. The hanging reeds waved slightly before the motion died away, and the screen became still. Japh stood gazing absently at it, thinking of distant reflections fading into the blackness of an impenetrable forest.

Suddenly he felt the floor beneath him shake. Almost immediately the sound of cracking and creaking came from the direction of the land.

Malala came hurriedly from behind the screen.

"Lal! What was that?"

"I'm not sure, but I think it could be the forest breaking away at the hinge. It was full moon tonight, which means a spring tide. I'm going to wake Dad and see what he says."

Lal pulled aside her father's screen, stepped inside for a few seconds and reappeared. A moment later Malech emerged rubbing the sleep from his eyes. The floor shook again and loud cracking sounds filled the air.

"Japh I think the hinge is breaking up. We've got to get to the shore. Otherwise we'll be marooned for life. Lali, get your stuff."

Lal went back behind the screen, pulled an old cloak from a shelf, spread it out on her bed and bundled her few possessions onto it. Then she wrapped the cloak around them to make a compact bundle and tied the sash from an old robe around it.

Malech rushed into his room, reached under a little pile of clothes, pulled out a bag, heavy with coins, and stuffed it into his back-pack. He rammed two hands-full of clothes on top of it, closed the pack, and swung it onto his back.

Japh clipped his weapon to his belt and all three headed for the door. Malech grabbed his long, heavy staff and they hurried along the corridor to the forest outside.

The moon was now getting low in the sky and very little light filtered down through the dense foliage. Malech led them quickly to the tunnel near the pool.

The tunnel was awash with surging water.

"The tunnel's broken. It went through the roots of the hinge at a sandbank near the beach and that place must be gone already.

We'll just have to go through the forest. I haven't done that for a long time but I used to follow that track over there."

The going was difficult, with little light and an uneven path over twisted roots with thick undergrowth and dangling creepers closely bordering the narrow track.

As they approached the shore, the sounds of creaking and cracking grew painfully loud and the roots underfoot shifted markedly as they walked over them.

A mighty crack rang out a few yards in front of them, the roots shook and a surge of water rushed at them. The roots heaved and twisted. Lal lost her footing and fell. Malech stumbled, and jabbed his staff to the ground to prevent himself from falling. The heaving roots immediately gripped the end of the staff. He stood, unable to pull it free. Roots closed around Lal's left hand as the forest floor sank. She let out a cry. Japh grabbed her arm and tried to pull her up. He saw that her hand was caught and the roots were slowly closing up around it. Her hand would soon be crushed to pulp. He grabbed her wrist and jerked her toward him viciously. The hand came free, scraping her palm and knuckles and leaving some of her skin behind. He tried to lift her, but a fold of her robe was held by roots which had closed up around it. A surge of water rushed toward them. He grabbed Lal's bundle as the water caught it and started to swirl it away. Then he lifted her as high as he could to keep her face clear of the wave. Moments later, the mat of roots started to rise and the fold of Lal's robe came free. Japh helped her to her feet and Malech pulled the end of his staff clear.

They struggled forward a few more yards and saw open water ahead. Reflected moonlight showed shattered roots on either side of a slowly widening channel of water. The gap was already far too wide to jump. To their left, a mass of creepers stretched from the island to the shore. They were very taut and would soon break under the strain.

"We've got to use the creepers—quickly as you can, hand over hand. Hurry, before the creepers snap," said Malech slipping off his back-pack. With a powerful swing he sent it sailing over the water to the shattered roots on the shore. He grabbed Malala's bundle from Japh and sent it flying after his pack.

Japh unclipped the weapon from his belt, hurled it after Malech's bundle and helped Malala scramble over the tangled chaos toward the creepers.

"I can't grip the creepers. My hand hurts too much," said Malala.

"You've got to try. They won't last much longer, they're stretched too tight."

Japh moved in front of Malala and gripped a low branch to steady his balance. "Help her onto my back Malech. Lal, put your arms round my neck, wrap your legs round my waist. Hurry!"

He stepped up onto a broken root sticking out of the water at a crazy angle and sprang upward to the creepers. He caught a bundle of them and swung out over the water. He worked his way hand over hand for a few yards before the creepers sagged far enough for his feet to dip into the water.

"Japh, pick your feet up! There's a krono coming," shouted Malech.

Japh bent his knees to lift his feet and doubled his efforts to cover the distance to the shore. His arms were already tiring under the weight of two people and it was difficult to breathe with Malala's arms wrapped round his neck. One of the creepers in the bundle he was holding snapped. The others started to stretch. He was going uphill. That meant he must be past halfway, but the going was harder and the creepers could not hold much longer. Gasping for breath he forced one hand in front of the other.

Malech looked at the creepers, now so tightly stretched that one after another they were breaking with a loud snap. They would be gone by the time he could start across the gap. The krono had almost reached Japh. Japh struggled toward the shore keeping his feet as far above the water as he could. But that was not far enough. The huge creature opened its massive jaws wide enough to take him well above the knees.

With a loud shout Malech took a short run over the broken roots and launched himself out over the water. He stabbed the end of his staff down onto the back of the beast and pushed with all his strength. The huge body began to sink, and as it snapped its enormous jaws shut, its jagged teeth clamped into the hanging folds of Malala's robe. The wrench tore her grip loose from around Japh's neck and her hands slid over his shoulders. Desperately gripping the creepers with his right hand, Japh snatched at her wrist with the left and managed to hold on. The robe tore with a loud rip. The krono sank beneath the surface, a ragged piece of brown cloth between its teeth. Malech sailed past Japh and Malala, and crashed into the roots of the shore. He struggled to his feet, clutching his right shoulder where he had banged into a root, and hobbling on a twisted right ankle. He looked toward the struggling figure of Japh, still far from the shore, battling to keep putting one hand in front of the other.

Sweat poured into Japh's eyes; it stung them and he could hardly see the creepers ahead through the painful blur. He reached out for the next handhold and missed his grip. Their smooth progress jerked to a halt and Lal started to slip. Her arms tightened around Japh's neck. He looked up trying to see the creepers through the blur of sweat but could make out nothing. He grabbed blindly upward and hooked his finger tips around the creepers. He worked his hand around the bundle and swung forward. He felt one strand suddenly getting thinner beneath his grasp. It was about to snap. He struggled on, gasping, reaching further ahead. A creeper parted with a loud snap just behind him. Another in the bundle snapped as he took his next handhold, then all the remaining strands in the bundle gave way a few feet behind him. He swung forward. His legs splashed into the water. He pulled on the creepers as the water rose to his arm-pits. He was almost at the broken roots of the shore when he felt the sea bed beneath his feet. Two steps and two heaves on the creepers brought his chest up against the roots. Malala scrambled off his back onto the shore. She turned toward him and a look of horror flashed over her face. A gaping mouth filled with ragged teeth sped toward them.

"Japh! Hurry!" she screamed.

Malech took one staggering step toward the water's edge with his heavy staff raised. He threw himself forward, lashing downwards and landed a shattering blow onto the gleaming row of razor-sharp teeth.

Japh grabbed a broken root and heaved himself out of the water. Just behind him the surface burst into a cascade of spray and the head of a plesio shot toward him. Malala gasped in horror at the mass of jaws and teeth racing toward the middle of Japh's back. Malech had no time to raise his staff for a second blow. He could only jab the end into the gaping jaws. They snapped shut around the hard, old wood and crunched it to splinters. The massive head thumped into Japh, throwing him forward over the twisted roots.

Japh crashed to a stop against the trunk of a tree. Malech dragged himself further from the water's edge and sat down to rub his ankle. Malala hurried toward Japh and knelt beside him.

"Japh, are you hurt?"

Stunned and hurting Japh did not answer for a moment. Then he moved his body painfully, tested all four limbs, shook his head and said "No. I think I'm all right. Just need to rest a bit and get my breath back. How's your dad?"

She crossed to her father and found him rubbing his ankle.

"I'm fine, Lali. Just twisted my ankle a bit. Do you think you can find our things?"

She set off, moving slowly and carefully through the undergrowth searching for her bundle, Malech's pack, and Japh's weapon.

Before returning to the men, she opened her small collection of clothes and changed into a threadbare green robe. She retied the bundle, now almost empty, and draped the tattered remains of her best robe over her shoulder.

"There's a clearing just a few yards inland, and there's still a little moonlight shining into it," said Lal when she got back to them. "Let's move over there and find somewhere a bit more comfortable to wait for sunrise."

Japh wiped the sweat out of his eyes, got to his feet and helped Malech up.

"Hey Malech, that staff doesn't look too good anymore, you'll have to lean on me till you can find yourself another one. Are you sure you're able to move?"

"Yes. This is nothing. A bit of rest and I'll be walking fine. Pity about the staff. I've had it for years. I'd grown quite fond of it, too, like an old friend. But it'll be easy enough to find another here in the forest."

They reached the clearing, looked around to make sure there were no dangerous animals and moved to a soft grassy bank near a spring. They picked some healing herbs and Japh crushed them between the soles of his sandals. They made a compress for Malech's ankle and bandaged it up with strips torn from the remains of Lal's brown robe. Japh bound up her hand with plenty of the crushed herb mixture and they lay down to rest.

"I doubt there'll be many animals around," said Malech. "The breaking roots made such a terrific noise I'm sure just about everything will have run away—but, just to be on the safe side, I'm going to keep watch. You two get some sleep; it's still an hour or two till sunrise."

Lal lay on her back looking at the sky. "How beautiful the stars are tonight. So many of them."

"You should see them through a telescope," said Japh. "You wouldn't believe how many more there are. A telescope makes an amazing difference."

"Have you really looked at the stars through a telescope?" asked Lal.

"Yes, a few times. My brother's father-in-law is Professor Zalomo. You've heard of him?"

"Oh yes, I've heard of him. I'm sure everybody has."

"He discovered a new planet just two or three weeks ago. It's so small and far away, his latest telescope was only just able to pick it up."

"Are there people on his new planet?" asked Lal.

"No. Not a chance. There's only life here on Earth. Anyway it's so far from the sun, it's frozen solid."

"Where is it?" Lal asked, searching the night sky.

"I don't know. It might be right where we're looking now. Perhaps it's right in the middle of that black patch of sky next to those four stars. Do you see the four stars nearly in a straight line? If you looked at that black patch through Prof. Zalomo's telescope, you'd see so many stars you wouldn't believe your eyes."

"And that new planet?"

"Well, you never know, it might be right there in among

those invisible stars—but very faint. It's very far away," said Japh, stifling a yawn.

"What a lovely thought…" She remained silent for a few moments. Japh's even breathing changed to the sound of faint snoring. A half smile touched her lips and she gave up trying to keep her eyes open.

12 Jethro and Nina

The moon was sinking behind the trees. The blood was drying on Jethro's chin and his right eye was beginning to throb. He was still staring at the fading silver reflection in the tranquil pool when Nina crept from the bushes, walked silently to his side, and said very softly, "What do we do now?"

Jethro snapped out of his reverie, turned toward her and looked into her pretty face; then he broke into a painful smile and said "We live happily ever after."

"And how do we do that? Will you leave your wife to come and look after me? You surely don't think she'd welcome me into her home, do you?"

"Now what makes you think I've got a wife?"

"If you try and tell me you mended your clothes yourself, I'll know you really are a terrible liar." She put her arms around his neck, turned her face up to his, smiled, and kissed his lips. "I noticed it when you first came to me. That stitching has an unmistakably feminine touch. Your wife did it."

"Wow! What a clever little girl you are! I'm impressed… You're right. And you're also right that she wouldn't be happy to see you."

He wrapped his arms around her and kissed her hungrily. After a few moments, he pulled his head away, looked into her eyes and said, "But then, I have three children, and I wouldn't want to leave them."

"So you'll have to get rid of your wife just like you got rid of my husband, won't you?"

Jethro stood stunned for a moment. But before he could think of a reply, the forest floor began to tremble and a sound of cracking and snapping reached them.

Nina started, alarmed and frightened. "What's that?"

Jethro spun around to face the noise. "I don't know. I've never heard anything like it. It's coming from the shore. I wonder if it could be the hinge breaking. It's full moon tonight—there could be a strong tide. We might find that we're on an island in the morning."

"Oh, that's terrible! We must get to the land before we're marooned. Come, quickly. I don't want to be here for the rest of my life. Hurry!" Nina grabbed hold of Jethro's hand.

"Nina. My adorable jewel, Nina. Calm down and listen to me. I don't know this part of the forest. The moon's nearly down and it's getting very dark. You know how dangerous the forest is, even when there's enough light to see by. There's no point in dashing off half addled and getting killed when we don't even know for sure if it really is the hinge breaking. Let's go in the morning."

Nina contemplated his words for a few moments. "I suppose you're right...we'll have to wait till morning. But if it's the hinge breaking, then we'll be set adrift and we won't stand a chance of getting to the land."

Jethro stepped closer, cupped her chin in his hands and turned her face toward his. "How often have you left the forest since you came here?"

"Never."

"Neither have I. So it won't make much difference to either of us, will it?"

"I suppose not…but…"

"So let's just make the best of it." Jethro steered her away from the pool. "I want to see your little nest." He pulled her close and whispered in her ear, "There's time for love before the dawn comes."

"You men!" said Nina with a coy giggle, "You're all the same!"

13 A Capella

Next to four small stars nearly in a straight line, a dark patch of black sky seems to be coming closer. As it approaches, tiny specks of light appear. They grow bigger and brighter as the sky accelerates toward us. Or could it be that we are accelerating toward those specks of light? It's so hard to tell. Oh! They're stars! Beautiful twinkling stars. One speck becomes clearer and larger. And larger. And larger. It's certainly not a star. Oh, wonder of wonders! It's a planet!

As we draw closer, we see it slowly rotating about an axis pointing toward the sun. It has a moon revolving about the planet at just the same leisurely rate; it stays constantly over one spot on the equator.

We're getting close. How glad I am you came with me…so very glad. Oh, look! Far below us. There's a telescope!

We're slowing down. How gently we float toward the planet's icy surface. How gracefully we glide toward that gleaming instrument. How softly our feet brush the sparkling frozen gases covering the planet's rocky surface. How inviting the eyepiece, so conveniently placed for us to peep into.

Oh! Lovely! In the middle of the field of view is a beautiful blue globe with a delicate emerald tinge. And I can see a handsome, smooth, spherical moon orbiting exactly over the equator. It looks strangely familiar. Come look. Doesn't it somehow remind you of home?

Did you hear that whirring sound? The telescope moved a little. See, there's another planet in view. It's a little smaller. And such a brooding, rusty red colour. It's beautiful in an austere way, but also somehow disturbing. Come, let's turn the telescope far away from that doleful red ball and look in the opposite direction. What a strange sight! It looks like a great cloud of debris.

Where could all those fragments have come from? Could some planet once circling a distant star have exploded and been thrown from its orbit? Could two great bodies have collided in the depths of space? Look how shiny some of the fragments are! They gleam with the brightness of metal. The others look like massive chunks of rock.

Look at that big shiny one near the front of the cloud. Like a huge uneven ball of gleaming iron, pock-marked and pitted.

Many fragments flash across my view as you adjust the telescope to the far end of this amazing cloud. And, oh! What a sight! That ugly thing is frightening. Look how misshapen, like a badly formed potato with a narrow waist and one bulbous end fatter than the other. It's covered with pits and craters. Oh, see how the sunlight flashes from it! Bright rays catch its uneven metal surface and a blinding glare runs down a tortuous path from top to bottom as it twists and tumbles in a wild, rhythmless dance.

I'm afraid of that thing, but I can't look away. It's hideous— and yet beautiful. I think we should go back. Let's go back. The ice is seeping into my bones. I'm longing for the warmth of the sun. Let's go back now.

— ❖ —

14 New Island

Jethro stopped again to scan the little patch of forest around him that he could make out in the half-light. His ears strained for the slightest sound of danger against the dawn chorus of awakening birds and pteros.

It was a long time since he had gone anywhere near the hinge. Too dangerous. There was too much coming and going of animals. And the roots were different at the hinge. Stacked one upon another. Not as tightly woven together as in the rest of the forest. They grew predominantly in the direction of the shore, parallel to each other, not crossing and twining together in every direction as in the rest of the forest. Jethro assumed this had something to do with the constant movement as the forest rose and fell with the tides. It made walking more difficult. He wondered if this was just because he was not used to it. At the moment, it was even tricky on the normal forest floor beneath his feet because the sun was only just rising and the light was still dim.

There was a slight but noticeable pattern in the roots beneath his feet taking shape; they were becoming parallel to the direction he was moving. He could sense large animals nearby, and the forest ahead had the characteristic hint of light that signalled approaching a pool. He glanced round at Nina, who was scanning the track behind them. She moved her head round, eyes darting from the undergrowth to the spaces between the tree trunks, to the branches and back to the undergrowth until she noticed him looking at her.

"I think we're nearly there," he whispered. "I'm sure there are quite a few animals just ahead. Wait for me here and I'll check it out."

"No. We're in this together. I'm coming with you."

Jethro shrugged and moved forward cautiously. Smart girl this. Wide awake.

After another twenty yards, they saw the pale daylight of early morning between the trees ahead. The roots were now running almost entirely straight toward the light in front of them. They moved cautiously forward and saw a lambo standing at the end of the path. It was agitated and moved a little to the right, then to the left, then back to the right, undecided which way to go.

"Keep still," whispered Jethro, "It's so confused, there could be fireworks at the drop of a hat. It's not likely to be there very long. Lambos don't often stay in one place for more than a few minutes."

"I've never seen one with a crest as big as that," whispered Nina. "I want to get a bit closer and have a better look."

"Oh no you don't," hissed Jethro, "they've got very good hearing and we're dangerously close as it is."

The lambo took a step to the right, stopped, turned back and took three steps to the left, hesitated briefly, then continued to the left and soon went out of sight.

"Not likely to be anything ahead. Not where a lambo's been stamping around, but just keep watch in case it comes back."

They moved forward and soon reached a chaotic mess of broken roots with open water beyond. Half a mile away they could see a similar mass of broken roots on the shore, glowing soft yellow and orange in the first rays of the rising sun.

"Oh look! Over there to the right, there's a little beach between the end of the broken roots and that headland."

"Yeah, I see it," said Jethro "You know, we must have been living quite near to the end of this stretch of forest. It must have stopped at that beach, and I never knew. Did you?"

"No, I thought it went on for miles in both directions. I'm very thirsty. Let's find somewhere to get close enough to the water to have a drink."

Jethro pointed to a dark shape gliding just below the surface of the clear water ten yards in front of them. "That's a plesio. I don't think we'd better get any closer than this. We'll have to wait for a drink till we get back to your pool."

"We'd better not waste any time then," said Nina, turning back the way they had come. "And by the way, as soon as we've had a drink we'd better be on our way. You've got some work to do. Remember?"

15 Shopping

A sharp crack woke Japh and Lal at the same instant.

Japh sat up with a start. "What was that?"

They looked around to see Malech through the trees, wrestling with a thick shoot growing from the base of a big tree. He was twisting and pulling to break it free. "It's just Dad making himself a new staff. Wasn't it amazing on that planet last night?"

Japh looked a little puzzled. "Er... and which planet was that?"

"But you were with me, don't you remember? Oh! Perhaps it wasn't you after all," she said softly. "I never saw your face. But I was so sure it was you."

"Did you dream about being on a planet?"

"No... No... It wasn't just a dream..." She fell silent for a few seconds, then added, "but then, I suppose it must have been a dream. It was a bit frightening toward the end."

Japh smiled at her. "I hope it wasn't me that made it frightening." He looked at her for a moment, then dropped his eyes. After a few moments of silence he suddenly sat up straight. "We'd better go and find my sled; I sure hope your dad was right that it would be safe where we hid it."

Malech had come within a few yards but they had not noticed. He broke in with, "No need to worry, I'm sure it'll be fine. But we'd better get moving. Japh, you need to get to Zohan and buy your equipment. Lali my dear, we're going to have to decide where we're going to make a new home."

"Dad, we'll have to go to Zohan with Japh. That krono tore my only presentable robe to shreds last night. I can't go anywhere without some halfway decent clothes."

Malech looked at his daughter. His expression suggested that he was ashamed of himself for not buying her any new clothing for such a long time. She certainly looked very shabby in her threadbare old green robe.

"Come to Salem with me," said Japh. "You'll be very welcome with my family and we need all the help we can get with the boat. You really must come to Salem."

"Lali my dear, I'll go with Japh and buy you some clothes. I'm afraid to let you go to Zohan. Beauty attracts robbers quicker than gold. It would be very dangerous for you in the city."

"But we can't leave her alone here!" said Japh.

"I'll be quite safe as an old woman in the company of two strapping men," said Lal, untying her bundle and shaking out the contents.

She flicked the old cloak around her shoulders, tucked her hair into the hood, bent forward slightly and began to walk across the clearing with a hesitating step, looking for all the world like an ancient great-grandmother.

"Just look at that, Malech! Would you ever have guessed she was less than nine hundred years old?"

"Well, I don't know. It's very dangerous in Zohan. Still, I suppose you're right. We can't leave her here on her own."

They set out for the game trail. Malech walked with a limp, leaning on his new staff, but they made good progress and within a few minutes had reached the hidden sled. Japh hurried to the cargo hold to check that his heavy money pouch was still where he had hidden it. Then he opened the first-aid box and brought out a tube of Instant Skin to dress Lal's hand.

"It feels much better than it did last night," said Malala. "Those herbs work miracles."

"But it's still terribly raw. It must hurt quite a bit." Japh smeared a generous layer over the wounds. "Don't move your hand too much till this stuff sets. It'll be as good as a layer of skin till your hand heals completely; then it'll just peel off."

When Japh had put away the first-aid kit, they manoeuvred the sled to the way and climbed aboard.

Malech stared at the floating forest, now a large island half a mile from the shore.

"It's amazing," he said. "I can't make out one part of the forest that I recognise."

"Neither can I," said Malala. "Everything looks completely different."

Japh adjusted the lift control. The sled began to hum, rose two feet and hovered above the way. It turned slowly to the right, then back to the left as Japh adjusted the setting till it pointed straight down the way. He eased forward the thrust controls and the sled accelerated. The floating island disappeared from view and the sled sped between the trees of the coastal forest toward the next bend, seven miles in the distance.

Half an hour later, they had to slow down while a herd of game cleared the way two hundred yards ahead. A single sled produced enough radiation from the mesh to make almost any animal want to get out of the way. But the range was so much less than when a whole convoy was on the move that one had to be careful and not go too fast. It was half-way through the morning before they reached Zohan.

Lal insisted on going into a clothing shop on her own while Japh and Malech went on to the heavy machinery dealers. They were to come back for her when they had bought the equipment.

An unremarkable old woman walked with hesitant step to the door of the shop. As she closed the door behind her she slipped the old cloak from her shoulders, straightened up, folded it, and draped it casually over her arm in one smooth movement.

A confident, poised, attractive, though threadbare, young customer looked through the racks of clothing and picked out two robes. One was loose with flowing lines in pink with white lace around the collar and cuffs. The other was deep purple, simple but stylish, close-fitting, smart, and businesslike, very suitable for travelling.

She decided to wear the purple, and had her old green robe parcelled up with the pink one. She made a visit to the ladies room. She washed her face and spruced herself up, then returned and waited close to the window, pretending to look at more clothes, until she saw Japh and Malech approaching. Then she walked unobtrusively to the door, slipped on the old cloak, and, as she closed the door on the outside, pulled the hood over her head. She was once again a stooped old woman.

16 South Seas Shipbuilders

"You can't just give up and go back home empty handed!"

"But you heard the prices, Malech. Seventy-eight thousand."

"Couldn't you get by with lighter equipment?" urged Malech. "It's so much cheaper."

"I could buy light duty things in Salem and I wouldn't need to transport them all that way. But it's not good enough, anyway."

"What about secondhand stuff?" suggested Lal.

"And where on earth would I find secondhand equipment like that?" asked Japh dejectedly.

"At a shipyard, of course!" said Malech. "Why didn't I think of it before? All the shipyards are doing less business than they used to. Someone must have equipment they're not using. Let's try South Seas Shipbuilders; they're one of the biggest, and I used to know the manager. He was a friend of my father's. Don't suppose he'll still be there, but you never know. He was a first-rate fellow. It's only about a mile from here."

"But just a minute. I've only got thirty-two thousand. The shipyard people know what new equipment costs. Even if they do have some spare machinery, do you really think they'll let it go for way less than half replacement cost? They'll more likely want to build the thing, not sell equipment to let me go into competition with them."

"We've got to try. Come on, we're just wasting time standing here. And there are more eyes turned this way than I could want."

That woke Japh out of his mood. They headed for the dock area, moving as quickly as they were allowed down the left side of the way.

At the main gate of South Seas Shipbuilders, the gate-keeper seemed unimpressed with their story.

"More likely just wantin' to get into the yard and load up whatever they can on that sled of theirs while nobody's lookin'," he said to the messenger boy, making no attempt to keep his voice down. "I had a good mind to set the dogs on 'em. But that geezer says he knows Hovana. He's retired now, but he's one of the directors. Better just go to the office and take a message while I keep me eye on 'em."

In half an hour they entered the office of Alzan, the manager, who had taken over from Hovana three years earlier. Malala stayed well behind them. She discreetly took a chair next to the secretary's desk while Malech and Japh walked up to the manager's.

"This is a list of the equipment I need," said Japh.

Alzan scanned it quickly.

"Quite an order! What are you wanting to build?"

"A boat."

"How big?"

"About four-hundred-and-fifty feet long."

"That's big! Where do you want to build it?"

Japh's shoulders sagged. "Just outside Salem."

Alzan stood up and crossed to a globe standing near the window.

Here it comes, thought Japh.

Alzan pointed to the globe. "But that's hundreds of miles from the sea. It isn't even near any of the great salt lakes. How could you ever get it afloat?"

Japh looked a bit sheepish. Could it be that news hadn't travelled this far? Could it be that Alzan doesn't know? "Well...er ...my father believes it's going to rain quite a bit..."

"Going to what?"

"Well, er...water...falling out of the sky...quite a lot of it."

"Water wells up from the ground. Is this some kind of a joke? Are you trying to make a fool of me?"

"No. Not at all. My father's pretty sure it's going to happen."

"So he's completely out of his mind, is he? Oh...wait just a minute..."

Oh no, thought Japh. He knows. Now everything falls apart.

"…that half-witted doom and gloom preacher lives somewhere near Salem, doesn't he? Now I get it. Your father's so stupid he's been taken in by that wretched charlatan, hasn't he?"

Oh, what a let off! At least we may have a chance to get out of here in one piece.

"Or else this is some kind of scam to try and swindle a whole batch of valuable equipment from South Seas Shipbuilders. Either way, you must think I'm an utter fool. Did you really think I'd fall for a cock-and-bull story like that?"

Malala pulled back her hood and slipped the old cloak from her shoulders as she rose from her chair.

"Well, we'll see what the police make of your story when my security men have finished wringing the truth out of you!" stormed Alzan, red faced and furious.

With poise and charm Malala stepped quickly to the manager's desk, stunning in her new robe. "Mr. Alzan, I see you're far too wide-awake for my agent. Please let me put all my cards on the table, and I'll tell you the full story."

Alzan looked round startled. He had not noticed anyone but Malech and Japh enter his office, yet here was a stunning creature with the bearing and assurance of a super-model from the cover of a high-fashion magazine, talking as if she were the chief executive of a major company. He was speechless.

"My client has specified gopher wood. There are very suitable forests near Salem. I plan to have all the timber cut to size at the source of supply. The prepared timber will be transported to the final assembly point. I'm afraid I'm not authorised to tell you where that will be, but I can assure you it will not be at any port which you supply. There'll be no chance of any competition against your shipyard. Not only that, it's the only such project my client plans to undertake, and you're welcome to repossess all the machinery as soon as the project's finished."

She gave him her most dazzling smile and looked steadfastly into his eyes awaiting a reply.

Many seconds passed. Alzan was thoroughly confused. Was this ravishing apparition anything to do with those two clowns? Such a good-looking woman. And not just a pretty face; she's got brains. And charm. And a delightful figure. He wanted to get to know her better.

"We do have equipment that is not being used at the moment. I suppose I could let you have it on those conditions."

He straightened up, aware that his lascivious thoughts might be showing through his body language and continued in a more businesslike tone, "I might be prepared to let you have every-thing on this list for thirty-five thousand…with a few further considerations."

He looked at her levelly, almost daring her to imagine what those considerations might be.

Maintaining the charming smile, she held his gaze without faltering. "That's most kind of you, but I had hoped you could offer a slightly better price. After all, I'll only be hiring the equip-ment to make one single vessel."

"Just one vessel…but a very big one. I'll tell you what I'm pre-pared to do. You can have it for thirty thousand, and you can come to dinner with me tonight at the Pink Flamingo to seal the deal."

"That sounds delightful. But, unfortunately, I simply must leave this afternoon. Here's what we'll do," said Malala confidently. "We'll agree on thirty thousand, and then, when you come to repossess the machinery, I will personally show you all of the high-spots of Salem."

She turned away, leaving Alzan speechless. "Japh, please count out thirty thousand. We'll need an official receipt. Now if you'll excuse me, gentlemen, I'd like to visit the ladies' powder room."

With that, she walked gracefully to the door, unobtrusively scooping up the old cloak and her parcel as she passed the secretary's desk.

— ◈ —

17 Strategy Meeting

Alzan gazed after Malala's retreating figure for a few seconds. Had he really accepted this preposterous deal? And the thirty thousand that these two buffoons were counting out—was he really going to accept it?

But, what a woman!

He had only gone along with the proposal because of the prospect of getting her to the Pink Flamingo for dinner. Of course, the way the head waiter doctored the wine when he gave him the nod, Alzan knew it would lead to much more than just a first-rate dinner. But a business deal for some vague date far in the future?

"The strategy team will be here in five minutes, sir." His secretary broke into his thoughts.

Oh, I'd forgotten about that, he thought to himself. The realisation that he had no time to wriggle out of the deal struck him hard. I've got to get rid of these clowns right away. I suppose I have to go along with the deal. But I must find some way to meet her again soon. It'll take years 'til that huge boat's finished. And I have no intention of waiting that long.

He hurriedly wrote out an agreement, signed a receipt for the thirty thousand, and hustled them out of his office just before the team of experts arrived for what he knew would be a very important meeting.

❖ ❖ ❖

"Gentlemen," began the company's chief financial officer, "I hardly need to tell you that the figures for this year are worse than we had predicted in the budget. We've had to revise down our estimates for the coming year even further. I can't overstress the importance of finding a way out of our difficulties. I'd like to call on our team of technical experts to give their suggestions."

Subdued lighting filtered through exquisitely worked white net curtains covering the two picture windows of South Seas Shipbuilders' long boardroom. Like everything else in the room, they were elegantly and tastefully done with understated accents here and there, in an artistic style. The long, highly polished table in amber-coloured wood with unobtrusive, gently curving, and elegantly beautiful grain patterns across its surface was surrounded by chairs of the same wood. Sixteen men in formal attire with restrained colours and impeccable cut sat stiffly around the table, their faces serious and unsmiling. After the chief financial officer sat down, several of the seated experts looked from one to the other before fixing their gaze on a slim, middle-aged, balding man in the middle of the side opposite the two windows.

The head of the marine biology team took the hint, shuffled his papers, and began rather hesitantly. "Well, gentlemen, we've been studying the floating forests very carefully. We can say with certainty that their growth is exponential. Unless a major change takes place, the entire ocean will be completely covered within a hundred years. As you know, we've been studying ways to kill or retard the growth of the forests. Most of the chemicals we have found to be effective are very expensive and without major government funding there's little chance of their being feasible. Furthermore, these chemicals are disastrous to marine life and could ultimately destroy the fishing industry. Of course, the fishing interests would certainly lobby against their use.

"We've found salt very effective in killing the forests. We're confident that's why there are no floating forests on any of the great salt lakes. Unfortunately, the ocean contains almost no salt, and the amount needed to make it salty enough to kill the forests is simply out of the question.

"We've looked into diseases to infect the floating forest trees, but they are resistant to everything we've tried so far. Our studies suggest that physically clearing the shipping lanes may be the only practical way of keeping the ocean navigable. The cost will be enormous, but if the government can be persuaded to put a programme in place, it is a feasible solution."

A buzz of murmured exchanges went on for a few moments before Alzan rapped on the table. "Gentlemen, we will have general discussion after all the proposals have been put forward. Could we have the next presentation, please?"

The chief geologist pushed back his chair and stood up.

"We're making steady progress in our study of conditions under the earth's crust. We're now confident that there are enormous reservoirs of water about ten miles below the surface. They lie under a continuous layer of basalt. Our calculations show that they must have a very high concentration of salt and, in all probability, carbon dioxide as well.

"We've been looking into the possibility of breaking into these reservoirs. The pressure is certainly colossal, and if we were to break through the basalt, vast quantities of very salty water would come to the surface.

"If we could arrange for a sufficient quantity to enter the sea and make the ocean salty enough to kill the floating forest, then our problem would be solved. We calculate that to reach a high enough concentration, sea level would need to rise about two hundred feet.

"That would, of course, lead to the complete destruction of a few hundred major cities and a vast amount of land. It would mean that we'd have to relocate our shipyard. We have identified a very suitable site about a hundred and fifty miles inland."

"That raises some problems," said the Chief Financial Officer. "If we destroy too many people and cause too much economic disaster by raising sea level, we would have fewer customers than ever—at least in the short term."

Alzan looked somewhat uncomfortable. He leaned forward pushing a stray lock of hair from his forehead. "If it were to become known that we had engineered the whole thing, we could be finished. And how would you limit the amount of salt water coming from the underground chambers? Is there a way to limit flow? Can a channel be closed once it's been opened?"

The geotechnical engineer cleared his throat. "Our calculations suggest two possible problems that require further study. The first is the one you've just mentioned—how to cut off the flow when our objective has been achieved. We're making progress on that, and some promising solutions are being studied. The second problem could be more serious. The pressure in the reservoirs is unquestionably very high, and there's a chance that if our drilling procedure is not perfect, a fracture might occur in the basalt. This would almost certainly spread very quickly. If that happened, there would be no chance at all of controlling the flow. Sea level would rise very rapidly—and it would rise far above the two hundred feet that we need."

The members of the group looked from one to another, hoping for more promising proposals.

"Well, gentlemen," said Alzan after a long pause, "if no one has any further suggestions, it looks to me as if the possibility of breaking into the reservoirs of salt water needs much more investigation. At present, it sounds too dangerous. And needless to say, any further investigations must proceed in conditions of extreme secrecy."

Alzan looked toward the geotechnical team. The chief engineer nodded affirmation.

"For now, the only practical solution seems to be physical clearing of seaways. The only chance of winning government support is if all the shipbuilders and ocean transport companies present a unified front. So, as a first step, let's arrange a meeting with all the shipbuilders of Zohan to draw up a plan of proposed sea-lanes. Then we can circulate it to shipping companies and shipbuilders in other ports. Between us, we should be able to build a proposal so strong that the government will have no reason not to accept it."

"And we'd better make sure it's very convincing," said the chief financial officer. "If we are unsuccessful, we could be out of business in less than forty years."

18 Noph

It was almost sundown when Japh and four other units from the Zohan convoy arrived at the transport security compound in Noph. He manoeuvred his sled through the narrow entrance between high walls of perfectly cut sandstone blocks, each weighing four or five tons. The yellow sandstone at the top of the eastern wall radiated a warm, friendly glow where the evening sun's rays caught it. The walls lower down radiated heat absorbed during the warmth of the long afternoon. The tops of the walls were covered with sharp iron spikes. Three rows of razor-sharp blades protruded from the upper part of the huge iron door hinged into the north side of the entrance way. A dozen sleds were already parked. Their sled-men stood in a group near the exit, waiting for the latecomers to switch off and lock up so that they could leave.

Malech jumped down and helped an elderly woman passenger to alight. He headed for the gateway with her leaning on his arm. Japh walked to the office, paid the overnight fee, checked with the official about the opening time next morning, and then they all ambled to the gate. The gate moved on a wheel fixed to the side opposite the hinge; the wheel running in a curved, iron channel set into the paving. The gate was so heavy that it took three of them to pull it closed.

The transport official took a large key from the purpose-made pouch inside the sleeve of his uniform. He put it in the lock and turned it with a loud *clonk*. Then he pulled his key out of the lock, put it back into its pouch, and looked around for the guards. Two of them, in the uniforms of Total Security—their horizontal stripes making them look even broader than they really were—stood at the corner of the security compound nearest to the city centre, chatting. The third guard was fifty yards away, hurrying toward them. A small purple triangle inside a fine black ring in the middle of his chest was the only decoration on his otherwise plain silver-grey Tubal-Cainite uniform. It marked him as a member of Universal Guarding, one of a multitude of new security companies springing up in response to rapidly rising criminality.

The official gave him a vicious tongue-lashing about being late, threatened to report him to his boss, and then stormed off down the street. The sled-men snickered, made some unkind remarks, and then hurried away around the corner. Japh tapped the chastised guard on the shoulder, gave him a smile of encouragement, told him he appreciated his being there to guard the place, and set off after the others.

Japh knew Noph quite well. He had often accompanied his father on preaching trips in years gone by. He'd only been there once recently, though. Preachers in general and his father in particular were not welcome anymore—and on the last trip he doubted at times that they would get out alive. He hoped nobody would recognise him and as they approached the business district. He hunched his shoulders and bent his head, looking down at the sidewalk. He noticed that Malech looked uneasy.

"There's a pretty decent hotel just around the next corner," he said as they reached the main drag and turned toward the centre of town.

Malala was wrapped up in her old cloak, the hem of her purple robe showing below its border. Malech clutched his staff, alert eyes darting from the passersby to the dark corners of buildings, a concerned expression on his face. They passed a public works department sign warning of way-works ahead. The sidewalk narrowed where the shallow excavation of the sledway had broken into it. The excavators had obviously not taken much care, and the workmen had done no clearing or tidying before they packed up for the weekend. The disorderly hole was littered with pieces of ruined mesh, and an untidy heap of soil spilled onto the sidewalk. As they passed the works, two giants approached from the opposite direction. Nearly all the giants Japh had ever encountered were arrogant bullies. These looked no different. He moved out of their path. Malech and Lal did the same, squeezing up against the way works. The giants swaggered past without a sideways glance, deliberately taking up more of the sidewalk than necessary. Lal stumbled as she stepped on a clod of soil;

the hem of her robe caught on a piece of broken mesh sticking up from the hole and her new robe tore with a loud rip.

"Oh dear, what am I going to do," she quietly lamented. "I haven't anything to mend it with. We'll have to look for a shop."

"We'd better first check into the hotel," said Japh. "The porter should be able to tell us where to find a place."

"Lali, I'm sure you don't want to arrive in Salem in patched clothes. We can afford another," offered Malech. "That one can be mended later."

"Oh Dad, you're a treasure." Malala squeezed his arm.

"This is the place," said Japh.

They turned into the foyer of an undistinguished, but clean, hotel.

❖ ❖ ❖

Malala stopped on the sidewalk a few yards from the shop. "I think it would be best if you were to stay outside and wait for me. They don't usually take too kindly to men coming into a women's clothing shop."

Malech grumbled and Japh looked a bit unhappy, but they didn't press their objections. She headed for the door, stooped over and hesitating in her step.

As she closed the door on the inside she noticed her father moving to a place on the opposite sidewalk where he could look in through the window. The light was fading, and he was not very noticeable in the shadow of an awning. Before she turned toward the racks of clothing, she slipped the cloak from her shoulders, straightening up as she draped it casually over her arm. The shop was almost empty. Just one customer at the counter paying for a robe. Just one shop assistant taking the money—a slack-faced, middle-aged woman, who looked Malala up and down before handing her customer the change.

Lal moved to a rack of clothes. The customer left the shop and Lal noticed two men who had been standing on the sidewalk move to meet her. They were at her side before the door closed.

It would be dark soon. Too dangerous to waste time. She hurriedly selected a dark-blue robe with light-blue trim, and headed for the counter.

The assistant put on a practised smile. "Hello, Duckie, haven't seen you before. Do you live in Noph?"

"No, I'm just passing through. I had a bit of an accident," she said, pointing to her torn hem. "Do you have any thread this colour to mend it with?"

"No, Duckie, we only sell clothes. You'll want to try that on, won't you?"

Lal noticed that she looked toward the windows, then fiddled with something under the counter before she left the till and came toward her. She took her arm and led her past what appeared to be a changing cubicle to a passage next to the far wall.

"Our change room's being refitted, so you can just try it on in that room at the end there, Duckie."

She pushed her gently toward the door.

Lal walked down the passage telling herself she had better hurry. The light was now very dim and she really wanted to get back to the hotel before dark.

She went through the door, and just had time to notice it was definitely not a change room—more like a large kitchen—before the door was pushed closed behind her. A man who had been hiding behind it stepped forward, grabbed her from behind and roughly pressed a pad of damp cloth over her nose and mouth. She tried to scream, but the sound was muffled by the pad. A door on her right opened. Three men rushed toward her. Fighting for air, she gasped, inhaling a sickly sweet vapour from the soaked rag and struggled to get free. She tried to kick the shins of the thug holding her from behind but was too groggy to put any force into the kick. She tried to jerk her face away from the pad, but found she could hardly move. Malala slumped forward as a fuzzy darkness closed around her.

❖ ❖ ❖

"I wonder what's keeping her so long?" said Japh.

"She went to try on an outfit about two minutes ago," said Malech from his vantage point in the deepening shadow, not taking his eyes from the window. "She should've finished changing by now. The shopkeeper's coming to the door. She's got a key in her hand. Looks like she's going to lock up for the night!"

Japh streaked toward the shop. He reached the door as the woman pushed her key into the lock. He jerked the door open before she could turn the key. The protesting woman tried to slam the door closed. Japh was too strong for her. He pressed the door open, gently shoving the shopkeeper backwards into the shop.

"What d'you think you're doing?" she screamed. "I'll get the police! I've got an alarm in here. Get out! Get out!"

"We'll go when my daughter leaves with us," Malelch said, closing the door behind him.

The woman drew back; stunned for a moment, then she regained her composure. "Don't know what you're talking about. Your daughter ain't here. Now get out! I'm locking up for the night."

"She came in here five minutes ago. Took a blue robe off that rack. You showed her to a change room over there. Where is she now?"

The woman took a step back. Her mouth fell open and she brought her hands up to her face.

Japh crossed quickly to where Malech had pointed, saw the

changing cubicle, raced to it and looked inside. It was empty.
Malech joined him.

"When I last saw her she was walking in that direction!" He
pointed to the passage.

Japh rushed to the door at the end and threw it open, hand
on the handle of the weapon on his belt. The room was empty.

Malech hurried past him and picked up a heap of blue material from the floor. "This is the robe she took off the rack. I'm
certain of it."

Japh screwed up his nose and sniffed. "Malech, do you smell
what I smell?"

Malech caught a whiff of the sickly-scented anaesthetic. The
colour drained from his face. "Oh, no!" His voice shook with
anguish, "She's been kidnapped!"

Japh tried the room's other door on their right. It led to a
little alcove with two other doors leading from it. One opened
into a store room. They soon satisfied themselves that there was
nobody hidden there. The other door led to a narrow backstreet.
They hurried outside. Thirty yards to the right the street ended
in a cul-de-sac. To the left it ended in a T-junction fifty yards
away. They hesitated for a moment, wondering what to do.

"Most likely they'd want to get her far away as quickly as
possible. I think they'd have gone left," said Malech.

"You're right. Come on!"

They sprinted toward the T-junction. Three policemen saun-
tered across the intersection, looked at them, stopped, and drew
their weapons. The officers quickly spread apart, blocking their
path, and shouted at them to stop.

Malech hurried to the senior officer, a relieved expression
on his face. "Oh, am I glad to see you! My daughter's just been
kidnapped. Please help us to find her!"

"Well, now, that's original," said one of the loutish-looking policemen. "Never heard that story before."

"So what were you running away from?" said another. "Been trying to rob one of the shops, eh?"

"No," said Japh, "his daughter's just been kidnapped and we're trying to find out where they took her. Won't you please help us? We're wasting time; they're getting away."

"Who's getting away?" said the third policeman.

"The kidnappers, of course!"

"What did they look like?"

"We didn't see them."

"So how'd you know they exist if you didn't see them?" The burly officer grinned and gave a knowing look at the other two.

The second officer made a threatening gesture with his weapon. "Put your hands above your heads. Don't move. Kalai, get their tools."

While two of the policeman covered them threateningly, the third wrenched Malech's staff from his hand and then took Japh's weapon from his belt.

"Let's go and see what the interrogation squad can get out of you. And don't try that kidnapped daughter story; they'll give you a real going over if you try such bull on them."

The senior officer screwed up his face and stared at Japh. "Now, who have we got here? That face looks familiar. Haven't I seen you before?"

The second officer peered into Japh's face. "Yes, now that you mention it, he does look familiar. Can't put my finger on it but we'll find out at the station."

Kalai drove them forward viciously. "Get going!"

The senior officer indicated with a nod of his head that they should go left at the junction.

They set off. One policeman on their left, the other on their right, with Kalai behind, prodding them again every few seconds. Within a few paces, they reached the way close to where they had been standing only a few minutes earlier. They turned right, going away from the shop that both were regretting they had ever set eyes on.

19 The Salem Club

The starched waiter bent slightly at the waist as he removed a dinner plate decorated with the sorry remains of the chef's masterpiece of the day. He replaced it with a generous portion of crème flambé. He made a valiant effort not to look into the eyes of the young man on the opposite side of the table. Such strange eyes. One darker than the other. And those thin, hard lips. The sort of person he'd prefer to stay clear of. He turned to place the used plate on his trolley and picked up another dessert, his skin crawling under the unwelcome gaze of those smouldering brown eyes.

Rendo had never been to the Salem Club before. It was too high-class to allow any but the most successful professionals to gain membership. He was irritated by the pompous show. Even the waiters were stiff and artificial. He contemplated how satisfying it would be to reduce that crisp, stiff dummy serving their table to a crumpled heap on the floor.

Uncle Irab had invited him to a small family gathering to celebrate his fiftieth wedding anniversary. Irab had come to Salem to lecture at the university quite recently and had only a few family members there. There were only eleven people in their group.

They were at a table with a dazzling white tablecloth, crystal centrepiece, and rows of gleaming silver cutlery. Rendo's eyes followed the waiter as he left their table and pushed his trolley between the other large round tables, all decked with the same white tablecloths, centrepieces, and silver cutlery—all occupied by equally smartly dressed parties—till he disappeared through oversize double doors leading to the kitchen. Rendo glanced up at the high ceiling, with its extravagant crystal chandeliers hanging opulently over the elegant scene. Definitely not my style, he mused…but then, he supposed he could get used to it…someday, maybe…

"…and, so, I invite you all to raise your glasses to the best wife any man could ever hope to find," said his uncle, as he raised his own glass and smiled at his family around the table.

The lousy hypocrite, thought Rendo, as he shifted his attention back to the party and reached for his glass of sparkling white wine. The whole town must know about his affair with that dusky piece from the biology department. And he's only been here six months.

They started eating again. Most of the conversation was an utter bore to Rendo. While putting on a half-hearted show of paying attention to the family celebration, he started listening to the people at the table behind him.

One of them, who sounded a little the worse for drink, seemed very pleased with himself about a practical joke he had got up to with one of his junior partners. Rendo gathered that they had hired a stunning blonde hooker to go after someone.

"…wouldn't tell us what happened. Cried her eyes out. You should've seen her make-up. It was a real mess. I told her we wouldn't pay her unless she told us what happened, but she just turned and walked off, blubbering like a baby."

"So what d'you think did happen?" said another voice.

"Must've been something juicy because only two days later, he skipped town before dawn."

Rendo could not understand why they burst out laughing, but he immediately realised who it was they had sent the whore after.

He was churning inside.

That worm left two days ago.

Unannounced. With the first convoy. At first light.

How many people could have seen him go?

But now you couldn't go anywhere without hearing stories about him.

For weeks before that, it had been all about where his miserable family got their money. Endless stories about them having the devil's own luck. About their piece of land having the richest seam of gold in the world—or diamonds—or rubies. Or it was stories about their fields producing three or four times the crops that anyone else's did.

Yet everybody said they weren't interested in that wretched preacher. Didn't want to know. Wouldn't go to hear one word he preached. Then how come they kept such a close watch on every single blasted thing he and his family did?

Rendo finished off the dessert absently. It had been a superb meal. He'd hardly tasted it.

"Would you like to make your way to the lounge for coffee?" inquired the waiter. It was not really a question, but a polite indication that they had occupied the table long enough. The club was so popular for weekend lunches that another party needed theirs.

They trooped into the lounge and settled into easy chairs around one of the large, low, circular coffee tables.

Unruly laughter burst from an alcove just beyond the bar. Everyone looked toward the noise. Two characters, clearly the worse for drink, were joking loudly. Irab gave them a disapproving frown. If they noticed, they paid no attention. They guffawed again. He gave up and looked around for a waiter.

Rendo carried on, glaring at them. They were at a small table next to an artificial fire which gave a warm glow to their snug little corner without giving any heat. The alcove was almost entirely artificially lit. It had no windows, only two rich-red velvet curtains covering blank areas of wall, giving the impression of window shades drawn at night. The atmosphere was perpetual evening. A waitress brought them two new drinks and took away their empty glasses.

I've seen that fat one before, thought Rendo. Loudmouthed pig. The other one looks like a long, tall drink of water. Couldn't get two more different looking creeps if you tried. He reluctantly turned his attention back to his own table.

Irab ordered coffee and cake for the group. Rendo tried to look interested in the conversation about uncle Sheth's new business in Jeerel.

A great guffaw came again from the alcove.

"Well, that God of theirs sure made a rotten choice. Married more than four hundred years and only three kids to show for it. Ever hear of anyone married that long without at least seventy or eighty?"

Rendo glanced round. It was that loudmouthed Fatso.

"And those two sons of his. Both married over twenty years and no hint of a bun in the oven between them," said Lofty, choking with mirth.

"Bad choice for a new beginning," wheezed Fatso.

"Good choice for a bad ending!" shrieked Lofty.

They laughed again, slapping their knees and rocking back and forth in their chairs.

"What do you think of the proposal from the United Stadiums Association?" asked Chohesh, Rendo's father.

Rendo's mother, Seleesha, Irab's younger sister, brightened noticeably at this. She had been looking very bored by all that talk of Sheth's new estate agency. She had never got on with her eldest brother; she detested his wife and wanted nothing to do with either of them. But the spectacles at the stadiums were what she lived for. "I think it's the best idea I've heard for a long time," she said enthusiastically.

Irab's wife Johala looked shocked. "What! Sentencing criminals to fight each other in public! It's just too barbaric."

"I don't know how you can say it would be barbaric, dear. Consider all the atrocious things these criminals get up to these days. It would serve them right," said Irab. "And they don't have to be sentenced to fight each other—they could fight against animals instead."

Chohesh put down his cup, leaned forward over the table, and looked straight into Irab's eyes. "But I think you're overlooking something. Why do you think the Association proposed the scheme?"

Irab looked slightly surprised. "As a deterrent for criminal activity, of course."

"I should jolly well think so," said Seleesha. "Nowadays there's no deterrent at all. The worst that ever happens to crooks is they spend a few days in jail till their cronies bribe the authorities to let them out."

"What can you expect after years of treating the victims of crime as criminals and the perpetrators as unfortunate victims of circumstance?" said Johala.

Chohesh nodded and turned to her encouragingly. "But they gave another reason, too, remember?"

"Well, yes, it would be an incentive scheme for the police," said Irab.

Seleesha hurriedly swallowed her last mouthful of cake. "Great idea! Those lazy useless cops need something to get them off their backsides."

"But why do they have such a dismal record of convictions at the moment?" demanded Chohesh.

"They're so corrupt the crooks have them all in their pockets. They hardly even pretend to catch criminals these days."

"Exactly!" said Chohesh.

The expressin on Seleesha's face showed that she didn't grasp what Chohesh was driving at. "Well, if the bonus is big enough, they'll catch them instead of taking the bribes."

"Don't you believe it! It would be much easier just to frame unsuspecting innocents and carry on getting bribes from the crooks as well."

"Oh, I don't think there'd be much chance of that happening," said Irab.

"Well, I do! And what about policemen using it for settling personal scores?"

Irab looked slightly puzzled. "And what, exactly, do you mean by that?"

"Well, just suppose there was a policeman who got it into his head that you were messing about with his wife..."

Rendo hastily brought his cup to his mouth to hide an involuntary grin. He glanced round to see if others were grinning, too. He almost burst out laughing when he noticed how uncomfortable Irab had suddenly become. His wife looked decidedly edgy, too. Go to it, Dad. Sock him another one below the belt.

"Just think how easy it would be for that policeman to get you out of his way. If his colleagues would get a nice big bonus for getting you convicted and sentenced to the stadium, I don't think it would be too hard to find a couple of them to agree on a story. Suppose they came up with a corpse and swore blind they'd seen you commit the murder."

Lofty's loud, inebriated voice broke into their stunned silence. "Only hope they've got is the unmarried one."

"Not much chance of anyone wanting to get hitched to him," said Fatso.

Laughter pealed from the alcove again.

Seleesha, looked thoughtfully across the table at Rendo. She was worried about the fire burning behind his eyes as he glanced toward the two drunk men in the corner. Such a fine, strong, sturdy son—and good-looking, too. It wasn't his fault his eyes were two different shades. Not surprising he was a bit less friendly than most of the other children; they had teased him terribly at school. How unkind people were to her little lamb. Oh! People just didn't understand him. She had even heard no-good scandal-mongering gossips saying he was a bully. Well, such people were just jealous of him. Yet, you never know who might pick on him and go telling lies to the authorities. "When you think about it," Seleesha broke the silence, "the Stadium Association's plan might not be such a good idea after all."

"Did you know that, as of yesterday, they've instructed the police in Noph to try it out as a pilot scheme?" asked Chohesh.

"And if any girl did marry him, her dad would murder her before she could get into his bed!" Lofty bellowed, nearly rolling out of his chair.

Rendo was seething.

He glared over his shoulder at Fatso and Lofty. He turned

his thoughts to getting them to some place where he and his buddies would give them something else to talk about.

20 Dusk Encounters

Japh looked sideways at Malech, whose face was a mask of misery. He was just opening his mouth to try and say something comforting when another vicious prod in the back made him stumble.

"Save the jawing for the kind and considerate gentlemen you'll meet in a few minutes at the station."

The other two policemen grinned.

"Yeah, save your breath. You'll need it."

A chuckle ran between the three of them.

"You never know, might need all the breath you've got for fighting a tyrano."

"Just a little one, of course."

The three laughed again.

"If you're very good, cooperative little boys, they might even give you a skull-buster to defend yourselves with."

"And don't think of concocting another story between you before we get there. Just keep your big mouths shut," said Kalai, giving him another brutal jab.

As they approached a crossroad, a stifled scream sounded from their left. A moment later a second, louder scream suddenly choked into a strangled sob.

"Well, what have we got here?" said the senior officer. "This might be a case of us having to look the other way for a moment or two."

They came to the crossroads and saw two separate scuffles going on thirty yards up the side street.

In the first tussle, two men held a teenage girl with her arms behind her back while a third fastened a gag around her mouth. In the second, an even younger girl, already gagged, was being lifted off her feet, kicking violently, while a man with a long scar down his cheek tried to grasp her ankles. A moment later, he succeeded and twisted her legs till she gave a muffled cry of pain and stopped kicking. Then both groups hurried toward a side street and disappeared.

"Hey! That's my sister's kids!" shouted the senior officer.

"You're joking!"

"No, I mean it. Come on! Let's get after them!"

Kalai dropped Malech's staff and sped off after the other two officers. He stumbled at the curb of the intersection and Japh's weapon slipped out of his hand. He hesitated for a moment; half turned as if in two minds whether to go back and pick it up, cursed under his breath and raced after the other two policemen.

Malech stood rooted to the ground. Japh dashed forward, picked up his weapon, grabbed Malech's staff, thrust it into his hand, took his elbow and steered him back the way they had come. "Don't run. We don't want to get arrested again. Just try to walk quickly without looking suspicious."

They reached the intersection and turned left, thankful to be off the way and out of view if the police should come back. They got to the T-junction where they had been arrested and stopped.

"I think they'd stick to the backstreets. Probably not go to the main way," said Japh.

"I think so, too. Best chance is straight on."

They followed the narrow street round a curve till they came to a crossroad. They looked each way. It was a drab, dirty part of town that Japh had never seen before. The streets were little more than alleyways between slummy older buildings. They stood, not knowing which way to try. All three choices seemed equally uninviting.

"Oh, why was I such a fool? To suggest going to buy clothes! I should have known better. In a place I've never even been to before. What an idiot!" Malech sounded desolate, almost in tears.

"It's not your fault, Malech. I should never have let her go into that shop alone."

"But what on earth are we going to do?"

"There's one thing we can do. We'd better pray."

❖ ❖ ❖

The atmosphere in Luke's was hot and steamy. It wasn't the first time Caro had been there.

What a dump! Don't know why anybody would want to come here. There he is. Right sozzled. And in a fighting mood, too.

"You never did neither."

"You calling me a liar, then?"

"Well ain't you?"

"That's fighting talk, but you're such a lily-livered..."

"Hey, Esdras! Easy man, time you was out of here. We're on first go tomorrow. Come on."

The drunken men slouched around the table next to the window turned to see Caro coming from the doorway. He stopped, gripped the back of a chair and gave the drunken hulk opposite him an angry stare.

"Well, what's it to you how long I stay here, then? Go on back to Dora's and leave me alone!"

"D'you think I's wanting to fight bandits all by m'self, and you with a hangover asleep on the floor? Come on, we got to get out of here. We's late as it is. Nearly dark. Place'll be crawling with thugs soon. Come on. Right now!"

Esdras started on a string of curses, but they dried up as a

grey pallor came over his face. He suddenly looked very ill. He
struggled to his feet and started forcing his overweight frame
toward the aisle. Caro noticed a movement in the street through
the window. He glanced at the figures hurrying by, but they were
gone before he could get a good look.

By the time Esdras had squeezed his way past the chairs
around the crowded tables he was looking very sick.

"Hey, Caro, I'm going to throw up. Better get outside quick,"
he groaned.

❖ ❖ ❖

"There are three ways to try. I'll go left, you go right, and if
we don't find anything we'll come back and try straight ahead."

"No, Malech. It's too dangerous to split up. We stick together.
Let's first try straight on, then we can come back and try the
other two."

The backstreet wound through a dingy, dilapidated slum.
It was almost dark. There were few people. They tried to stop
and ask one or two if they had seen anything of Malala, but the
scurrying inhabitants were obviously afraid, and hurried off as
they approached, pretending not to hear their question. A hundred yards from the crossroads, three thugs appeared out of a
doorway, knives in their hands. Malech jumped back and half
raised his staff. Japh had his weapon in his hand in a flash. The
thugs stood their ground. One put two fingers into his mouth
and gave a shrill whistle. There was the sound of approaching
feet. Malech and Japh glanced at each other; then they began
to retreat quickly. They were thirty yards away when they made
out three more thugs arriving to join the group at the doorway.
They hurried away in the semi-darkness and got back to the
crossroads.

"We're too late, Japh. The light's gone. We don't stand a chance in the dark. Oh, why did I ever suggest that she buy a new robe?"

"Stop it, Malech. I told you it's not your fault. We've got to keep trying. Let's take the alley to the left."

Japh tried to sound hopeful. In his heart, he knew their chance of finding her had faded with the daylight, but with Malech going to pieces with grief he just had to get a grip, force the pace, and hold everything together.

They set off down the alley. It seemed deserted, but a faint sound of chatter and movement could be heard somewhere ahead. They pressed on for thirty yards and saw light from the window of a dingy tavern. Two figures were outside, dimly lit by lamplight spilling from the open door. Malech clutched his staff; Japh's hand went toward his belt. They approached watchfully.

"Excuse me. Have you…" Japh stopped as one of the figures bent forward and began to retch. Japh saw the gleam of a pool of vomit in front of them. This fellow must have been throwing up, off and on, for quite a while.

"That's what comes of drinking at dumps like this. Don't you know they always cuts the booze with surge?"

"Ugh…oh…well, you don't think guards make enough to drink at the President, do you?"

"Try boozing a bit less then."

Japh felt sure he recognised the voice. "Is that you, Caro?"

"And who's that, then?"

"It's Freeloader by the sounds of it," said Esdras.

"Well, whadaya know, so it is. Hey, what's you doing at a crummy hole like this?"

Japh came close and stood next to Caro, who tightened his grip on his hulking friend's shoulders as Esdras leaned forward to retch again.

"We're looking for a woman who's just been kidnapped. She

was wearing purple and she had an old beige cloak with her, but she might not have been wearing it. Have you seen anything that might help us?"

"No, ain't seen no women along here. I only came twenty minutes ago to get Esdras out of this here pub."

"Should've come earlier. I might not be feeling so rotten if you'd come a bit sooner. Couldn't tear yourself away from Dora's till you'd no money left, could you?"

"Ain't my fault you can't keep away from the booze. And I can still stand when I've gone through my money. Not like some I knows around here."

Esdras retched again, but this time there was nothing left in his stomach and he choked painfully.

"I suppose it were a woman on that stretcher. Had long enough hair. Hanging right down it were. Didn't get a good look though."

"You saw a woman on a stretcher?"

"How long ago?"

"What was she wearing?"

"Which way did they go?"

"Hey, wait on a bit, can't answer you both at once. I saw four chaps carrying a stretcher just after I got into the pub about twenty minutes ago. Saw them go past the window. Didn't get a good look at whoever it was what was sick, but I did see long hair hanging down."

"Where did they go to?"

"They was going that way, but I didn't see where they went."

Japh and Malech peered into the gloom down the street, winding its away into pitch darkness.

"Thanks, Caro, thanks a lot. Come on, Malech, they've got a twenty minute start." Japh and Malech set off down the street.

"They went down that alleyway just up there," called Esdras

groggily, "I saw them when we came out of the pub. I was feeling so bad I wanted to shout and ask them to come back for me but I threw up right then."

Japh fumbled in his pocket while he hurried back to the doorway of the pub. He pulled out two coins and pressed them into the hands of the guards. Then he and Malech ran toward the alleyway.

❖ ❖ ❖

"Well, Doc. What's the story?"

"You're in luck with this one. No STDs at all. Not surprising really. She's a virgin."

Manahon looked very surprised. "What! She don't look young enough. She ain't a preteener, is she, now?" He turned toward Pandy, Roon, and Ashon. "You hear that, fellers? Just keep your hands off or I'll cut them off—and it'll be more than just your hands I cut off. They pay double for virgins. Nearly treble in Nopo and Jeerel. Even more in Asahan. None of you's going to touch her. Right?" Nobody broke the silence. Manahon turned back to the small middle-aged man next to him. He was dressed in casual clothes, but he looked out of place. His clothes were too clean and neat to fool anyone that he came from this part of town.

"Thanks, Doc."

"And by the way, after today my fee's going up. Double. Two of my colleagues from the hospital got fired and struck off the roll for doing this. The risk's becoming too high."

Manahon grimaced. Why did things have to get so difficult?

Since RAK hit the scene, two years ago, it had become impossible to sell a girl to any self-respecting brothel before their medic had certified that she was RAK-free. Even private buyers had started insisting on a certified check up before handing over their cash. Since they were paying for an examination, they usually got the medic to do a test for some of the other sexually transmitted diseases at the same time. Almost fifty different STDs now. Sixty years ago, there were only two.

Why did things have to get so difficult?

It was not worth the risk and expense of smuggling a girl to a distant city only to find that she had RAK and was unsaleable; or had one of the other incurable STDs and would fetch a price hardly big enough to cover the expenses.

And now those expenses would be even higher.

Manahon cursed under his breath.

"Hey boss, did you hear that? Sounds like someone at the door," said Roon.

Silence fell in the squalid, ill-lit room.

A sound of scraping came from one of the skirting boards. It stopped as abruptly as it had started.

"Just a rat," said Pandy.

Manahon listened intently for a few more seconds. The scraping sound came again. "Yeah, plenty of them." He turned to the doctor and pulled out a small bag from his pocket. "Here's the money, Doc."

"You'd better check there's nobody in the street before I go out. I don't want to be seen leaving this place by anyone who might go telling stories. That's what happened to my two colleagues."

"Roon, check the street? Give us a whistle when it's clear."

The burly thug headed for the door, picking up a skull-buster from a shelf next to the kitchen on the way. He unlocked the door and stepped outside. Almost immediately there was a loud thwack followed by a dull thump. Ashon and Pandy straightened up, looked at each other for a moment, then raced for the arms shelf.

❖ ❖ ❖

When Roon unlocked the door, Japh, who had been standing with his weapon in his hand and his ear pressed to a crack in the wood, pulled back and flattened himself against the wall.

Even though it was almost dark, Roon spotted him immediately. In one well-practiced movement, he jumped clear of the doorway and swung his skull-buster above his head. Japh lunged, but Roon stepped skilfully to the side avoiding the thrust and aimed a crushing blow at Japh's head.

Malech smashed his staff into Roon's temple with a resounding thwack. Japh threw himself to his right, but he was not quick enough to dodge the skull-buster. It caught his left shoulder a glancing blow. Roon crumpled to the ground, Japh staggered backward, stifling a cry. He stood for a moment, dazed and hurting. Malech charged through the door. Japh pulled himself together and leapt after him.

A burly thug grabbed a skull-buster from a shelf, another was right behind him. Malech raced toward them with his staff raised. A third man with a long knife in his hand ran toward them. A fourth was behind him, half hidden by the other thugs. They were outnumbered, two to one.

Malech lashed down with a powerful smash at Pandy's head, but he ducked expertly and swung his skull-buster up to block the blow. Ashon reached the shelf and grabbed a weapon. Japh rushed toward them. Pandy swung his skull-buster in a smashing blow toward Malech's head. Malech desperately raised his staff and charged through the blow. Japh lunged and ripped open a gaping rent in the thug's throat. Pandy's legs buckled under him. The skull-buster glanced off Malech's staff, slipped from the thug's failing grasp, and smashed into Japh, knocking the weapon from his hand and sending him sprawling to the floor.

Dazed and hurting, Japh came to a jarring halt against the

wall. He looked up to see Manahon stabbing down at him with his long, curved knife. Japh propelled himself off the wall toward Manahon's legs. He struck the thug's bended knee and knocked him off balance. The knife thudded into the boards where Japh had been lying and Manahon tumbled to the floor next to it.

Japh jerked round looking for his weapon. It was under the arms shelf. He scrambled on all fours toward it and saw Ashon lashing down at Malech. With his back against the wall, Malech tried to raise his staff to ward off the blow. Japh kicked out at Ashon's leg and caught him a vicious thump on the knee, throwing him off balance and spoiling his aim. Malech managed to dodge the badly aimed slash and jumped away from the wall swinging his staff upward for another blow. Japh grabbed his weapon from the floor as Manahon lunged toward him. Japh sprang back, raising his weapon just in time to catch Manahon's hand and send his knife spinning across the room. The thug staggered backward clutching his bleeding hand.

Japh turned to see Ashon raise his left arm to ward off Malech's blow. The clout broke his forearm with a loud crack. Bellowing with pain he lunged at Malech's chest. Japh lashed out at the hoodlum's throat, almost severing his head from his body, and he crumpled to the floor. Behind him, Japh heard movement near the arms shelf. Manahon grabbed a weapon with his undamaged left hand and while Japh turned to face him, he swung it upward for a slash at Japh's head. Malech jumped forward and smashed his staff into the side of Manahon's skull. He staggered back and fell to the floor unconscious.

Japh and Malech looked around for the fourth man they had seen as they rushed in. He was kneeling on the floor with his hands clenched in front of his face. They stood panting, gingerly rubbing their bruises for a few seconds, scanning the room for hidden gangsters. Then they approached the kneeling figure, who broke into a fit of trembling and stammered out a plea for mercy.

❖ ❖ ❖

Manahon clawed his way back to consciousness through a painful red haze. He lay crumpled in a heap on the floor. He reached for his head. It felt as if it were bursting. Blood streamed from a gaping wound above his left ear and from a long, deep cut in his right hand. He looked around the room. The fellow who had hit him stood with feet apart, head turning uneasily from side to side, staff in hand, ready to whack anything that moved. Ashon and Pandy were lying in pools of blood on the floor. Doc cowered on his knees, his hands to his mouth, eyes round as saucers. The other man was bent over the woman, untying her bonds.

Manahon pressed hard around the cut on his bleeding head. Must get these wounds stitched up…going to bleed to death at this rate. The younger man finished untying the woman and lifted her onto his shoulder. She groaned. Must be coming around. The man carried her to the door and went out. The staff-wielding fellow followed close behind him.

"Doc…Doc," moaned Manahon. "You've got to help me. I'm bleeding to death."

The pathetic little figure got slowly to his feet and looked around the room. Horror was written all over his face. He cautiously picked his way across the floor, careful not to step in any blood, and quietly slipped out of the door.

21 Lano's Island

Nina was not very popular as stepmother to Zilha's children. They had always got away with cheek and disobedience to their mother, but Nina delighted to wield a cane at the slightest excuse. Nina soon bore Jethro a son, Jed. She spoiled him rotten and paid very little attention to her stepchildren.

Lano resented Nina even more than his sisters did.

He had been six years old when his father failed to come home that unforgettable, terrifying day when the forest became an island. His mother had gone looking for him the next morning, leaving Lano to take care of the girls. He never saw his mother again. And his father arrived home later that day with this woman.

Lano spent as little time as possible at home. Ostensibly he went looking for fruit in the floating forest, but he actually spent his time exploring, watching the animals, learning about the forest and its inhabitants. He became expert in every aspect of forest craft. He could flit among the trees like a ghost, climb nimbly to the highest branches, hide in the slightest cover, sense the approach of danger long before its exact nature became apparent, and imitate the sounds made by almost every creature in the forest.

At fifteen, with his voice broken to a deep baritone and soft fuzz starting to grow on his chin and upper lip, a sudden spurt of growth made it clear he would soon become a powerfully built young man.

He was sixteen when he spent his first night away from home.

He left home early, after a beating from his stepmother for something Bedelia had done. He did not betray his sister. Not so much out of love or loyalty to her, but mainly because of stubborn contempt and a strange satisfaction in proving that his stepmother was being unjust, yet again. He smouldered with rage. He often contemplated breaking Nina's neck. He knew he was strong enough to overpower her easily. But he was still in awe of his father. His mind played over all sorts of plans to kill her without his dad being able to find out.

Lano made his way quickly through the forest, past pools he had discovered years ago, then past pools he had discovered quite recently, and then into a part of the forest where he had never been before. He crept close to tyranos and brontos, lions and buffalo, delighting in his ability to get perilously near to them without their noticing him. It was nearly sunset before his resentment abated enough to think of going home. By then it was obvious that he would not be able to get there before dark. He was thirsty and decided to press on to the pool which he sensed was not far away. He would drink, look for some wild fruit to eat, find a safe, cosy nook to sleep in, and go home the next day.

Then he heard sounds that stopped him in his tracks.

Voices.

The shrill giggle of a little girl. The deep rumble of a grown man. Then a woman's cheerful call of encouragement.

Lano had only ever seen two people apart from his own family—two crotchety old fogies, Baba and Karo. They lived a few miles from his home. He had not seen them often—they were suspicious and unfriendly and made it very clear they did not like children. Lano was both afraid and excited by the sound of these new voices. Would they be hostile? Would they try to beat him? Or would they be friendly? Maybe they'd even let him stay the night with them? He crept toward the sound, confident of his ability to approach undetected.

A family sat in a circle on an open patch of roots which had been made smooth and level. They were eating their evening meal and chatting together. Lano's eyes roved from one to the other till they stopped, riveted on the face of a young girl.

She must be as old as me. Oh, what a face! What a lovely body! What gorgeous legs!

"Daddy, tell us a story," said a young boy sitting next to the girl Lano was gazing at.

"Tell us about the animals fighting in the stadium!"

"Tell us about the professor and his planets!"

"Tell us about the water falling out of the sky!"

"You've heard all my stories, so many times. Aren't you tired of them?"

"No, tell us again!"

Lano was throbbing and tingling. Something bubbled up inside him. He had never imagined feeling anything like this before. He just had to get closer to that girl! He had to get close enough for her to see him. How he ached to have her face right in front of his. How he hungered to touch her. He crept forward, gazing at her, willing her to look up and see him.

"Why did that man think there was going to be water falling out of the sky?"

"How did the water get up there?"

Lano moved in closer, no longer trying to remain hidden.

❖ ❖ ❖

The mother of the family looked around the circle with a smile of contentment. How much better it was here in the floating forest than it had been in the city all those years ago, constantly dodging the police, constantly dodging the people they had robbed. Constantly having to find new ways to dispose of the booty. Oh, how fortunate that after they killed that stupid old couple who woke up at the wrong moment, the police had chased them and they ended up here! Now life was so simple. Only wild animals to be wary of—and they were predictable.

One just had to learn how to keep out of their way, and they were only too happy to leave you alone. And these dear, lovely, priceless, precious children—eagerly listening to their dad telling them yet again about that crank from Salem and his tall tales. She beamed with pride as she glanced from face to eager face.

Until she looked at Asa.

Asa was not listening. She was staring out into the forest with a strange look on her face. She was tense and on edge.

The woman followed Asa's gaze into the forest. She suddenly froze. Her mouth fell open. She wanted to scream but the sound strangled in her petrified throat.

There was the face of a young man! A young man staring at her daughter! Staring at her Asa!

22 One Day in Salem

"Come in."

"Hello, Dad! Oh! What's that you're doing?"

Malala crossed the small room to the table where Malech was touching up the letters he had been painting on a poster board. She ran her eyes over his work and read out loud, "Ultimate crime. Babies murdered, mothers scarred for life."

Malech put down his brush. "There, that'll do. It's finished."

Malala bent slightly and blew gently on the wet paint of the last few letters. "Beautifully done! You're going to put it outside that new clinic aren't you?"

"That's right. It opens at nine. I want to get there by half-past eight."

"If you fix it to a wall or a pole, it will be taken down and thrown away before anybody gets to read it."

"Yes, Lali my dear, I've thought of that. I'll hold on to it so they won't be able to just throw it away."

"Dad, I don't know…that sounds too risky. And what about the work on the boat? We've still got so much to do."

"Yes, I know there's still a lot to do, but the major timber work's finished. Yesterday I prepared the last of the planking. Shem and Sarai should have that fixed by mid afternoon. They've made amazing progress. In fact, they've done the job in less than half the time I'd thought it would take. And do you know why? It's that magneto-hoist Japh made for them. Works like a dream. You really did marry a very ingenious chap, you know."

"Daddy, you don't know the half of it. He's an absolute dear as well as a genius."

"Tomorrow I'll start helping you two lovebirds with the caulking. But I've simply got to do this today. I'll never be able to live with my conscience if I just stay here and do nothing."

"But Daddy, it really is very dangerous in Salem. You will take care, won't you?"

"Yes, Lali, my dear. I'll take my staff with me. It's never let me down yet. And anyway, I know in whom I've trusted so far. I'll carry on trusting Him till the end."

"Dad, you're a saint. You're very precious to me and to Japh …and to the whole family. Do be careful. Please!"

Malech put his arm around her shoulder and smiled down at her beautiful face. How fortunate he was to have such a gem of a daughter! He kissed her lightly on the forehead. "I'll be back for supper this evening. Have a lovely day."

Malala turned and left the room. Malech tested his poster to check that the paint was dry. Then he tucked it under his arm, crossed to the door, took hold of the staff leaning against the wall in the corner, stepped outside, and closed the door gently behind him.

❖ ❖ ❖

"I say we just storm the place, do the lot of them in and get the gear."

"And what if we can't work out how to use the gear?"

"So what if we can't. We're only losing trade 'cause the dumb junkies prefer that new twist. If they can't get it, they'll be back to the Diamonds right away."

"If we can't make it, someone else will. Then we'll be back with the same problem again."

"Why not just snatch their chemist."

"How?"

"Dead easy! Haven't you seen that new doll at Queens of the Night?"

"Oh yeah! She's stacked!"

"Like the twin peaks of Avilah!"

"That's the one. Irresistible! It won't cost the earth to rent her for an afternoon. We just send her after him, she brings him to Fareno's pad, and we're in business."

"Hey! Why my place?" It was the first time Fareno had spoken. As a newcomer to Salem, and an even newer recruit to the Diamonds, he mostly kept his ears open and his mouth shut unless he was spoken to.

"Because there's not much chance he knows your pad. That's why."

"Everybody in that gang knows most of us and where we hang out. Can't take him some place he's clued into. He'd smell a rat straight off."

"Cut and run before he's in range."

"I still say we go for a raid. If we get their chemist and do nothing about the rest, they'll be on our backs with a hit in no time. Even if it's only him they take out, it'll scrub our plans and we'll be back where we are now."

"Why not snatch him and do the raid straight afterwards?"

"Now you're talking" said Tob.

A chorus of approval went round the room and the meeting became a hubbub of individual exchanges for a few moments.

Tob was the leader of the Diamonds. He was a striking figure, only slightly above medium height but powerfully built. His head was shaved completely bald. His black beard was thick and bushy. This helped to make him look older than his mere forty years and he had adopted the style for that very reason. He accentuated the baldness of his head by rubbing oil into his scalp each time he shaved it.

Tob pushed back his chair, noisily scraping the floor. The hubbub faded as he stood up. "I'll go and see Elishama at The Queens this afternoon. I'll see what I can get the price for that doll down to."

"Hey, look at the time, you guys. We need to hit the road. There's that unfinished business with Zakes and Rephaim."

"And after that, we'd better do some long-range scouting on the chemist."

The gang headed for the door.

❖ ❖ ❖

"It's my body. I've got the right to do what I want with it."

"Young lady, where did you get the idea that it's your body?"

"Of course it's my body!"

"I know you're going on inside your body, but did you design it yourself? Did you manufacture it yourself?"

"I don't know what you're talking about!"

"Do you even know how it works? Do you know how your liver works? Or your kidneys? Do you even know how your eyes see or your ears hear?"

"You're confusing me!"

"And even if it were your own body, your baby's not part of it. Your baby's living in a different body. And his body's only attached to yours by a cord for the short time he's inside you."

"You talk such tripe!"

"Perhaps—but you're still listening. And do you know why? You know it would be wrong to go in there. You know it will be on your conscience for the rest of your life if you kill your baby."

"I'll have a bawling brat to look after for more years of my life than I can put up with if I don't."

"You'll have a child to pour your love into, a child who could give that love back to you multiplied many times over."

The young woman hesitated for a few indecisive moments, then hurried to the door of the clinic and went in.

Malech sighed and turned his poster toward the passing pedestrians. A girl and her mother were heading for the clinic. The mother scowled at Malech and walked in front of her daughter, trying to block her view of the poster. Behind them Malech could see a bunch of men about fifty yards away. Looked like a gang of spivs—trendily dressed, rebellious expressions, truculent gait. The mother and daughter swept past him deliberately keeping their eyes turned away. He swivelled to keep his poster facing them. The girl glanced back, a worried expression on her face. He smiled encouragingly at her.

❖ ❖ ❖

"Hey, I've seen that creep somewhere before."

"Who? That jerk with the poster?"

"Yeah. He's from my home town."

"Hey, Fareno, you told us only the hardest kind of rocks come from Zohan."

"The wettest kind of drips, too, by the looks of it."

The gang snickered.

"Oh! I remember who he is. He's a preacher. A stinking, homophobic bigot."

"We don't want anymore of that kind here. Old Doom and Gloom's enough for one town."

"More than enough!"

"Much more than enough! I don't know why somebody hasn't wiped him out yet. It's years and years he's been spouting his rot!"

"Well, we should at least take this creep out before he starts with his fundamentalist clap-trap."

"He has already. Just look at that poster."

"Ultimate crime. Babies murdered. Mothers scarred for life."

"They're all the same, those narrow-minded religious jerks. No respect for a dame's right to choose what she does with her own body."

Tob was walking next to Fareno in the middle of the gang. He gave him a nod. "You guys up front head straight for him. When we get there, split down the middle, half on his left, half on his right. Right?"

"Right!"

❖ ❖ ❖

Malech watched sadly as the mother and daughter reached the door. The girl turned to look at him with a worried expression on her face. Her mother pushed her inside. Malech turned back to face the street. The bunch of hoodlums was almost upon him. Heading straight for him. Too close to think of moving out of their way.

Malech looked at the faces of the men. They studiously avoided looking at him. Some were gazing at the sign over the door of the abortion clinic, some were looking across the street, some were staring into the distance beyond him. Not a glance at him or his poster. He thought of letting go of the poster with his right hand and grasping his staff, clasped between his body and his left forearm.

The men came within three yards, seemed to notice him for the first time and moved aside, some to his left, some to his right. The urge to drop the poster and grab his staff was very strong, but it was definitely too late, there were men all around him. He would be very hard-put to defend himself if they turned nasty. His heart pounded. He glanced left and right. They seemed to be just walking past. No sign that they meant him any harm. From the corner of his eye he noticed a movement on his left—a fellow with a shaved head and bushy black beard moving his hand toward his belt. Instinctively Malech let go of the poster with his right hand, grabbed his staff and started to turn toward the fellow. He could see that right hand, coming up from the belt, gripping a long, double-edged knife. Malech had started to swing the staff to knock the weapon out of his hand when he felt a stab of pain in his right side. Although half paralysed, his unthinking reaction was to turn toward the jab. But before he could turn far enough to see Fareno, whose knife was plunged into his side up to the hilt, a bolt of white-hot agony shot through him. Tob's blade struck upward from below his ribs and straight into his heart.

23 Reunion

"Well, what d'you know! If it isn't Caro. You on first convoy?"

"Looks like it, don't it? I'm on a Superswift with sled-man Taban. All the way through to Zohan," said Caro, looking very smart in a brand new uniform. The thin black and purple stripes running over his shoulder and down to the waist were unscratched.

The brass stipe between them glinted in the early morning light. "Well, well, so am I. Just like old times, eh?" In contrast to Caro's smartness, Esdras looked decidedly scruffy. His uniform was too tight over his bulging beer belly, and it was pitted and scratched from years of use. The thin brass stipe of the company colours was so tarnished it looked almost as dark as the black and purple ones. Two days ago, his supervisor told him to polish his uniform but, so far, he had not got around to doing it. "So what made you leave Total and come back to the old firm?"

"You know how it is with women. My old dutch kept making such a fuss about me being away for a month or more at a time. Total don't care how long you're away. Last trip, we got to Uz and there were a convoy heading for Jeerel what were short of guards, so they sent me along. At Jeerel they was short for Antinopo. Went on like that till Tarshish and that's about as far from Salem as you can go. Didn't get home for nearly three months. I weren't the only one what quit."

Caro looked at the sleds parked around them. "I heard there's only ten in the convoy."

Esdras looked uneasy. "I sure hope you got it wrong, Caro, the gangs always seem to know when there's a weak convoy coming."

"You can bet your boots it's the transport officers what tips them off. Haven't you noticed how prosperous they seems to be nowadays? And what happened to your idea of becoming a sled-man?"

Esdras rubbed his chin. "Well, the manufacturers never did cotton on to retractable wheels, did they? Maybe Freeloader's got a patent and they're waiting for it to expire."

"More likely the sled-men's union threatened them. Here's a Superswift just coming in. Let's see if it's ours."

As they began to thread their way through the sleds parked

untidily outside the transport office, Esdras tapped Caro on the shoulder and pointed toward two rapidly approaching figures.

"Well, look at that. Speak of the very devil! It's Freeloader. He's heading for our rig."

"And just look at that floozy with him. That's what I call a real peach!"

"Keep your eyes to yourself, Caro, I can see the ring on her finger from here."

"Don't see birds like that around much these days, too dangerous. I wonder what Freeloader's thinking of, bringing her with him."

"Well, thugs aren't up at this time, are they? Sun's hardly up yet."

Caro gazed lustfully at Malala, swinging easily along next to Japh, till Esdras caught his arm.

"Hey, just look at this! Ulm! Haven't seen you for ages. You going all the way to Zohan?"

They stopped at an old, rather battered sled and shook hands with the sled-man.

"I got sick. More than two months. They laid me off after one week, rot their miserable guts. I'm hanged if I'll work for them again. Rather drive an old tub like this. Only going to Noph. Coming back straight away."

"This outfit will do the same, you know. They'll lay you off if you gets sick again," said Caro.

Ulm looked past the burly pair. His expression hardened. "Hey, just look at that!"

"What?" said Caro and Esdras in unison, turning to look in the direction of Ulm's angry stare. He was looking at Japh and Malala, who had reached the big Superswift and were heading toward its sled-man.

"So what's Old Doom and Gloom's kid doing here?"

"You don't mean Freeloader's one of that lot do you?"

"Course he is. Do you mean you can't recognise those scum?"

"Never got round to looking them up and checking them out," said Esdras.

"I'm not so sure I knows what Doom himself looks like," admitted Caro.

"You must be the only people in Salem that don't!"

"Anyway, we'll see you at the recharge," said Esdras as they started moving toward the Superswift. Japh was talking to Taban. They saw him hand over an envelope and some money. Just before he turned to leave the sled they heard him say, "Alzan will give you double that when you deliver it."

As Japh walked past the end of the Superswift, he noticed Caro and Esdras with scowls on their faces ambling toward the sled. He looked away, but a moment later a puzzled expression crossed his face. He looked again at the two guards and stared at them for a second or two. Recognition broke over him. With a smile he gripped Lal's arm and steered her toward them.

"Esdras and Caro!" Japh stopped in front of them and held out his right hand. Neither made any sign of taking it. His smile widened and he dropped his hand to his side. "Oh, I see you've found out who I am."

They grunted.

"For a long time I've wanted to thank you for your help in rescuing the long-haired lady from those stretcher-carrying thugs. Let me introduce that very lady, my wife, Malala."

Both hard scowls softened somewhat and the guards mumbled vague pleasantries.

"And I've been wanting to talk to you about coming with us on the boat. I know you haven't got time now, the convoy will be leaving soon, but when you get back won't you come over? You know where our place is. We'd love to have you over for dinner and explain everything to you. Time's running out. I truly mean that. Time's running out. Please say you'll come."

"Yes. Please say you will," added Malala, "we really do want you to come. There's room for you on the boat. We're very grateful for the way you helped us."

Caro and Esdras glanced at each other. They looked puzzled and their hard scowls had completely evaporated.

"Well, that's very kind of you," said Caro. He could not keep a smile from creeping over his face. "Maybe. When we get back from the next trip."

"Yes, maybe we will," said Esdras.

"It was great to see you both again." Japh smiled and held out his hand. This time Caro glanced at Esdras, hesitated for a moment and gripped it firmly. Esdras followed suit a few moments later. Japh and Malala turned and hurried away toward the exit.

"They don't seem such bad folks. But we'd better watch it. You know we'll be pariahs and outcasts if we really do go to their place for dinner."

"You know I always thought Freeloader weren't a bad sort."

"Yeah, he's all right."

They looked around to see if anyone had noticed them shaking Japhs' hand. There did not seem to be any hostile stares. Maybe nobody had been watching.

"Pity he didn't he give me that letter to deliver," said Caro. "I could have done with the money."

"He watched you last time, didn't' he? Knows perfectly well you'll be straight off to Pink Lady or Teeny Teens as soon as we get to Zohan. And never a thought for his letter till you're broke."

Caro scowled, unable to think of a cutting reply before Esdras continued. "Still, I suppose even you'd be more reliable than the post office. I wonder if anyone ever uses them anymore."

"They'd have to be soft in the head. Them crooks in the sorting office opens every letter to look for money, so I've heard."

"It's not just money. I've heard they're more interested in letters to use for blackmail."

"And I heard of one postmaster what had an agreement with a paper recycling firm. Sold them every second bag."

They rounded the front of the rig and approached the sledman.

"Hello. Caro and Esdras. We're on a Superswift to Zohan with sled-man Taban." Caro held out his authorisation. Taban looked it over carefully, held his hand out for Esdras's and examined that one just as thoroughly. He recognised both men, having seen them on numerous sleds over the years, but one had to be very careful these days. The more he saw of people, the more he believed that nobody could be trusted anymore. Superswift always used their own in-house guards. Taban had no faith in security companies.

Before he finished studying their authorisations, three guards from Total Security arrived and stood in line, papers in their hands. Taban handed Caro's and Esdras's back to them and took those from the new arrivals. The Total men stood fidgeting in their dark uniforms. Faced with only black and purple rust-proofing as an alternative to the plain matte silver-grey of standard Tubal-Cainite, all the security companies used the same colours. Total's scheme was broad horizontal bands which made their burly guards look even broader. It was not a very popular design with the guards—the dark bands soaked up the sunshine and made the uniforms a little more uncomfortable in the warmth of midday than those of most security firms.

Caro pulled Esdras aside and muttered under his breath "There's at least two guards on this rig already. I just heard them, they's in the cargo bay checking the stuff. And here's five more of us. Where we going to sit? Not enough seat belts for so many guards on a cargo sled, even a big one like this."

"D'you think they got wind of a show?" said Esdras.

"Just scared of being in a convoy with only ten sleds, more like," said Caro.

"You're not all on this rig," said Taban after finishing with the authorisation papers. "Three sleds that were supposed to go on later convoys have been rush-loaded to come with us. Just wait here while I go to the office and tell them. The other rigs should be here in a few minutes."

❖ ❖ ❖

When Taban got to the office, there was an army officer talking to the transport official and two men were standing in line. The slack-jowled civil servant appeared to be trying to keep a straight face, but looked distinctly uncomfortable.

"Of course you can go with any convoy you like, but you might have let me know yesterday. How can we plan things properly if sleds just turn up without notice?"

"We only got our orders yesterday evening. And anyway, what planning do you need for an extra sled? I'd have thought you'd be only too glad of a squad of soldiers going with such a small convoy."

"Well, er, yes. Of course…you'll want to be right up front."

"No. We'll take up the rear," said the army officer as he headed for the door.

The transport official turned and looked at the well-dressed, sharp-eyed fellow next in line with a somewhat preoccupied stare.

"We're sending an extra passenger unit. More interest than

we expected in the martial arts refresher course in Noph. They're all armed, so we qualify for the maximum discount."

"Paying cash?" asked the flustered official after an awkward hesitation.

"Yes," said the snappy dresser, counting out coins onto the desk.

Next in line was an overweight fellow in the colourful uniform of Salem Dew. "We got an urgent message from Noph. Running low on whisky. We're sending two extra units."

Taban got the impression that the official was not feeling very well when he told him that three extra Superswift sleds would be joining the convoy.

❖ ❖ ❖

The sun was not yet high enough to be visible through the foliage, but the day was already warming up. Twenty-two men were heaping large branches across the way right at the apex of a bend. Another man, a burly mass of muscle and bone with an untidy black beard and piercing, fierce black and very bloodshot eyes, directed operations.

Cush felt the sweat running down the back of his neck and cursed under his breath. He wrinkled his nose and sniffed. Why should he care if the men made snide remarks about his smelly hair? None of them were particularly keen on taking a bath more than once or twice a month. They were all a bit high. Why should he care about the unusual smell from his sweaty hair? But he did. And he'd run out of soap and deodorant. Sure hope there'll be some in this convoy. He arrived at the pile of branches at the same time as Suvaner, a strapping young fellow he got on well with. "I don't like it," he mumbled under his breath. "This is the way we used to work before the convoys wised up. Every guard in the business must've practised a hundred times for a crack like this. Much safer to hit 'em hard when they're goin' fast."

"Yeah, but look what a mess it makes of the loot."

"Better off with only a quarter of the loot than only a quarter of the gang left alive."

"Oh, come on, man, only ten in the convoy, an' Pashahn's plan ain't the same as they'd be used to."

"We used to hit the first sled and work back for the very good reason the guards are every bit as good with a weapon as us. You've got to hit 'em with at least four to one to get it over quick. If you give the other guards time to form a squad, it's big trouble. We'd get the first sled wiped out in ten seconds flat, then go for the next, and the next. It's the last few, where the guards have time to group, where the real fightin' comes. Pashahn's idea of hittin' in the middle and workin' forwards and backwards at the same time means we got to split in two. Some sleds these days got four guards. There goes our four-to-one advantage."

Cush had become so worked up that he was no longer speaking in an undertone. He heaved his branch onto the pile and turned to go for the next. His way was blocked by the intimidating bulk of Pashahn, whose wild, black, bloodshot eyes knifed into him. Pashahn's lips were twisted downwards in a vicious sneer. Both thumbs were thrust into his belt, and the fingers of his right hand stroked the sheath of his long dagger.

"You the big man 'round here, then?" he demanded.

"No, Boss. Sorry, Boss, didn't mean no harm, Boss."

"Watch you tongue, Cush. Or I'll cut it out. I give the orders and nobody's going to put doubts about them in the minds of my men. Got that?"

"Yes, Boss. Sorry, Boss."

Pashahn's right hand shot out and caught Cush a blow which sent him sprawling and broke one of the few teeth left in his mouth. Most had been knocked out years ago when he'd been in a high-speed crash. He'd been the only survivor…the end of the famous Elrod gang. He'd come out of it with four broken ribs, a broken arm, a broken leg, multiple lacerations, and a few intact teeth. He'd set the arm and leg himself and miraculously survived. It had been nearly a year before he joined another gang. He walked with a limp, which had made Golt wary of letting him join, but he proved such a skilled sled-man and such a cunning fighter that he was soon second in command. Then last year, after ten years of good pickings, Golt got himself killed along with most of the gang in a raid that went wrong.

Cush had only been with Pashahn for a few weeks. As he picked himself up, tenderly fingering his throbbing jaw, he was thinking he wouldn't be with this outfit much longer. He'd skip as soon as they put in at a city. He'd look for a gang with more brains at the top. Or maybe he'd start his own gang.

"They're coming!" yelled a voice from near the start of the curve.

Cush dashed to join the rest of the group assigned to the rear half of the convoy. The other half, with Pashahn leading, were on the opposite side of the way. They were forty yards back from the barricade. They guessed that was where the middle of the convoy would be when it came to a stop. Pashahn's group were to hit the fifth sled and work forward. Ebanah's group were to hit the sixth sled and work backward. Crouched down in the undergrowth, keeping out of sight, none of them had a good view of the convoy. The hum of electric circuits grew louder as the convoy approached, decelerating for the bend. The sound suddenly changing to a whine as thrust controls were thrown into full reverse. Then, when the leading sleds went by, there came the hiss of cargo bays scraping on the ground as lift was reduced to help with braking.

When the sleds were almost at a stop, Cush leapt to his feet with the rest of the gang and dashed for the one directly in front of him. It was a big Superswift, sure to be at least three guards, maybe four. He saw Pashahn's group streaking toward the sled alongside and somewhat ahead of the Superswift on the opposite side. A passenger tub. He didn't like that. It takes time to wipe out the passengers, valuable time in which guards can get organised.

His attention snapped to the Superswift as his group reached it. Suvaner was the first to make a spring to board it. He missed his footing and one of the guards ripped him open with a well-practised thrust. Before the guard could pull back his weapon Cush jabbed his long, thin blade through the guard's throat just above his protective uniform and ripped the life out of him.

In next to no time, the gang was all over the sled. But another attacker was killed and yet another wounded before the rest of the guards were slaughtered. Not the way it should be. Golt's gang wouldn't have botched it like this. Nor would Elrod's. Cush saw the sled-man dive for a fallen weapon and made a thrust at him. Just at that moment he heard a startled cry from Ebanah. As a reflex reaction, he looked up and pulled back his weapon to the ready. He took in the scene at a glance and froze, terror clamping his chest like a vice. Sweat poured from his head and streamed down the back of his neck.

Everything was wrong. He was looking at eleven sleds. There should have been only four. A large band of guards were forming into a phalanx. A whole squad of soldiers was running toward him. They had almost reached the Superswift. He turned and saw Pashahn's group. They hadn't even killed all the guards on the passenger sled yet. And the passengers were all armed and fighting like trained soldiers. Half of Pashahn's group, together with some of the convoy men, were on the ground covered in blood.

Cush jumped down and streaked toward the forest.

He had almost reached the undergrowth before a stab of pain shot through his back. Vision disappeared in a burst of fireworks. His feet caught in a clump of bramble and he toppled forward. Flashes like sheet-lightning hammered the back of his eyeballs. Between the flashes were faces. Faces of guards he'd killed. Faces of passengers he'd killed. Faces of gangsters he'd killed. Faces with mouths wide open, shrieking in terror. Faces with blood streaming from gashes in shattered foreheads. Faces pleading for mercy. Faces screwed up with hatred. Faces he saw every night before he had downed enough booze to get to sleep. Then, just before he hit the ground, all the lights went out.

24 On the Wings of Love

Oh, look! There between the stars! Haven't we seen that dull red ball before? Years ago, didn't we see it through a telescope? But now we're racing toward it, speeding as on the wings of eagles. How marvellous it is to be out here again amidst the breathtaking beauty of the night.

How enchanting to glide so gracefully, suspended among the constellations. Hovering over this strange red planet. It doesn't look like a good place to live. Dust and rocks and those huge frozen lakes. One might have expected there to be some vegetation around them. But it all looks so dead!

A mighty explosion just south of the red planet's equator throws up a cloud of shattered rock. A crater, fifty miles in diameter, starts to come into view through the thinning dust. The next impact throws up an even bigger cloud, and spreading dust begins to obscure the planet's surface. Two smaller impacts in quick succession add their contribution. It is soon impossible to see anything but billows rising from an all-enveloping dust cloud.

An enormous gleaming mass of metal, pitted and cratered, hurtles past.

Oh, look! We've seen that before, too! How fortunate it missed the planet! But see the expanse of debris hurtling past. Innumerable fragments! There must be millions. And over there, far, far away in the distance, that burst of light. Did we not see something like it years ago? Why, yes! I remember sunlight snaking down the gleaming surface of that huge, twisting, tumbling, misshapen mass of metal. How terrible it looked. Beautiful, but terrible!

But why so silent, my precious one? Oh! Are you really my beloved? I remember, last time, I never saw your face. How strange that I can't see it now.

Such a strange radiance—such glorious radiance—but fading with the stars, speeding toward the dawn, fading with the darkness, fading gently away—fading, fading, fading.

25 University

Johab let himself into the observatory, crossed to the power panel and pushed up the main switch. Wall-mounted discharge lamps brightened slowly to reveal the telescope room, clinical, forlorn, and deserted. Johab was always first to arrive, but the hollow ring of his footsteps echoing down the hall still gave him a creepy feeling along the back of his neck. Today the sound was slightly different. There was an urgency in his step as he walked to the battered old table and put down his briefcase next to one of the straight-backed wooden chairs. That new girl from Noph had joined Irab's group and tonight would be her first time at the telescope. He hoped she would arrive early—well, at least before Mathian—so he could show her the ropes. He went over in his mind exactly what he wanted to say for the fourth time since leaving home that evening. He patted his hair straight, practiced holding his shoulders back and pulling his stomach in, and launched into his speech for the fifth time.

But the new research student came on the same outer-ring rapid transit sled as Mathian, and they walked in through the door together.

"Hi Johab, this is Leisha."

Johab felt his knees turn to water when Leisha came forward beaming at him with a radiant smile. Her even, perfect white teeth made a stunning contrast to her dark complexion and big black eyes.

"Glad to meet you, Johab."

"Oh...hello...er...what a pleasure...er...can I show you the telescope?"

"Why yes, that would be very much appreciated. I've been looking forward to seeing Prof Zalomo's masterpiece."

"Oh yes, it's a beauty." Johab sounded a little bigger and almost managed the first half of a smile. "Prof invented the three-stage telescope more than a hundred years ago. This is the fourth version, and it's so good most people think it's almost perfect."

"The original was the reason Salem's astronomy department became so famous." Mathian showed no intention of leaving Leisha to Johab for the evening, and he stayed close to her side. "The world's top astronomers almost fought for appointments at Salem just to work on it. Our department's definitely the best in the world."

Johab started to demonstrate the telescope's drive mechanism. "Some of the best staff have left to head departments at other universities. The new replacements aren't as good as those who left."

"Well, I don't think it was such a great loss with most of them. Religious cranks just like Zalomo," said Mathian. "I'm glad I'm not in his group, I don't like all that God stuff he keeps spouting. At least the university's stopped hiring people like that, so it will soon be a thing of the past."

"I wanted to join his group, but there are too many in it already," said Leisha.

"So did I," said Johab, "everybody wants to be in his group, but they don't allow more than ten. And, anyway, I think there are quite a few who think he's right about God, even if not many admit it."

"People like that have a much better attitude to women," said Leisha pointedly, "not like today's liberated men—just looking for sex with no responsibility."

"Well don't forget that male headship is an inseparable part of their package deal," said Mathian.

That brought Leisha to instant silence and attention switched back to Johab's explanation of the drive system.

When the demonstration was over, Leisha turned to Johab, "So how did you come to be with Irab?"

"I didn't know enough to choose between any of the supervisors so I opted for the smallest group. I thought I'd get more personal attention."

"And does Irab give lots of personal attention?" Leisha looked Johab straight in the eyes, the answer seemed important to her.

Johab desperately wanted to say something clever. But gazing into those deep, dark, limpid pools, his mind became a dizzy, whirling blank.

"Unfortunately, I can't say he does," Mathian broke in, "and

I must admit, there are other shortcomings in Irab's group, too. In most of them, the supervisor and the assistant arrive early to get everything set up in good time."

The sound of loud banter outside drew their attention to the door, which swing open a moment later. An intimidating figure stepped in, looked toward the research students and barked "Mat, come and give a hand…" He stopped in mid-sentence when he saw Leisha. His cold, two-colour stare softened and the hint of a twisted grin crossed his thin lips. He continued in a more friendly tone, "there's equipment to bring in."

Mathian hurried to the door and the pair disappeared outside.

"Who was that?" asked Leisha in a subdued whisper.

"That's Rendo, the assistant, he's Irab's nephew. And that's the only reason he's an assistant, I bet nobody else would employ him. Mind you, I don't think he actually wants employment, he only works two nights every fortnight—when Irab's team is at the telescope. He's got a gang, and I think he just comes here so he can say he works nights at the observatory if the police call him in for questioning."

"Oh, I see. The police will never bother to check up on how many nights a week he actually works."

"Of course. But do be careful, he's very dangerous."

Their whispered exchanges stopped abruptly when the door opened again and Irab, Rendo, and Mathian came in with a packing case between them.

Irab and Rendo almost always arrived on the last transit sled of the day and today was no exception. The night was well advanced, and much observing time lost by the time the latest version of Prof Zalomo's spectro-analyser was eventually set up and ready for testing.

"Right. Johab and Mathian, try this thing out on the lakes of

Mars, it should be able to confirm once and for all whether they are frozen water or not. Leisha, come with me, I want to explain our research program to you in detail." Irab walked to the table, sat down at the head, indicated the chair on his left for the young woman, and allowed a self-satisfied smirk to settle over his face.

Johab and Mathian went through the lengthy testing procedures for the optic cables connecting the spectro-analyser to the telescope. Satisfied all was as it should be, they set the drive controls to bring Mars into view. Johab fiddled with the focus for a few seconds.

"I can't get it in focus. The eye-piece must be fogged," he grumbled, unscrewing it from its mount.

"There's nothing wrong with the lens," said Mathian after both had peered through it. "Let me see if I can get it to focus." A few moments later, he sounded much less confident. "There must be something wrong with the telescope."

"Oh don't say that, we're supposed to take a whole lot of measurements tonight and it's getting late already. Let's try the scope on something else."

"Good idea, Saturn's high enough in the sky for a good view."

Johab set the controls for Saturn and it came into the field of vision bright and beautiful, its rings forming a stunning halo around it. "Nothing wrong with the telescope. Must be something wrong with Mars. Let's have another look."

They took turns peering at Mars. The sound of Rendo's snoring rose from the corner furthest from the door, where three easy chairs were placed around a small table littered with astronomical journals.

"There's no sign of the great lakes" said Mathian. "No sign of anything, Mars is just a fuzzy red ball."

"We'd better get Irab to come and have a look."

They turned to the table. Irab was smiling smuggly, leaning forward, and speaking confidentialities to his captive audience.

❖ ❖ ❖

"So what's happening on Mars, Irab?"

Irab looked round, careful not to spill the overfull, steaming mug from which he was just about to take the first sip. "Oh, hi, Tubal. Come and join us."

Tubal put his mug on the low table and drew up a chair. There were only two other people at the table in the corner of the tea room furthest from the door—Irab, from the astronomy department and Elian, from philosophy. Elian, a tall, handsome, dark-skinned young man who somehow made everything he wore look like the height of fashion, came once a week to give a lecture on the philosophy of science. Four postgraduates sat at a table near the urn; the other two tables were littered with empty mugs.

"I've got three research students who've been keeping a close watch throughout the night. Of course, the way Mars turns, it's not much more than half the surface we've seen, so we're not sure the same kind of thing is going on over the whole planet. Since the bright spots have disappeared and the colour and brightness of the surface have changed, I think the most likely cause is a planet-wide storm raising a huge dust cloud."

"Could a storm be so big it affects the whole planet?" Tubal sank back into the low, comfortable chair. "What about volcanoes?"

"Well, we haven't ruled them out, but it would mean a sudden outburst of activity over all the area we can see. Even if there were really big ones, it would need about twenty or thirty erupting all at once. We never saw anything in the past that made us think there might be more than two or three volcanoes on the whole of Mars."

"But I don't remember ever hearing of a storm raising a major dust cloud, either."

Irab was drinking from his mug and before he could respond, a slight curl came to Tubal's lip as he added, "And what does Professor Zalomo have to say?"

Irab hardened his expression to one of obvious distaste. "Ugh! He suggested a bunch of meteorite impacts could be kicking up clouds of dust but, as far as I'm concerned, the idea of a huge number of meteorites striking at once is just clap-trap. After all, we're not sure we've ever witnessed even one meteorite impact on Mars. I think he ought to keep his half-baked ideas to himself. What does he know about planets?"

"Yeah, I know what you mean. He came down like a bronto's tail on my nebular theory of planetary formation. It was a damned good theory, too."

"I don't think I've heard of your nebular theory, Tubal," said Elian, speaking for the first time. "Tell me about it."

Tubal looked sideways over his mug at the philosopher. He didn't think very highly of philosophers. He didn't think very highly of most people. But he enjoyed airing his own ideas. He set down his mug so that he could use his hands to emphasize his words, leaned forward in his chair, and began in a subdued version of the bombastic style he used in his lectures. "I propose that the planets condensed from a spinning disk of gas and dust. Over a very long period of time, dust particles collided and stuck together. Gradually, the largest agglomerations of particles had sufficient gravity to attract the material around them and become planetesimals. These, in turn, attracted one another and eventually coalesced into planets around the central mass of gas that became the sun."

"Sounds promising," said Elian. "Why didn't Zalomo like it?"

"He wanted to know what happened to the angular momentum of the sun, and how some bodies in the system could end up spinning the wrong way. He also wanted to know why I thought particles bumping into each other would stick together, rather than breaking into smaller pieces. What a loser he is! Rejecting a perfectly good theory just because a few points need a bit of firming up. Refused publication in the departmental research bulletin till I could give plausible answers to his objections."

"Well, you should've expected that. It's no secret he believes the planets, the sun, stars, and everything else were created—woof!—just like that, in a puff of smoke," said Irab.

"I hadn't heard of the puff of smoke theory, but you're right; he's a religious freak. Shouldn't be allowed in this department at all, never mind be head of it. There's no place for religious fundamentalists in astronomy—or anywhere else in science."

"Well, it's true that idea's out of fashion," said Elian, "but until just a few decades ago, most scientists—and just about everybody else for that matter—used to believe in divine creation. It's a philosophically defensible position, you know, even if it isn't popular anymore. And it's hard to see how the whole subject of origins can be anything other than metaphysics anyway. Can't go back in time and make observations, can we?"

"So, you're a creationist, too?" said Tubal in a tone halfway between incredulity and scorn.

"No. I just try to keep an open mind. It's a position that's never been disproved."

"A scientist should look for naturalistic answers, not cop out and bring in The Big G whenever he can't find a solution."

"What if there isn't a naturalistic solution? What if there really was divine creation?" said Elian, putting down his empty mug. "But I must leave, gentlemen. Pity, just when it looked as if things might be getting interesting. I've got a lecture at the physics department in ten minutes." Elian picked up his briefcase and strode purposefully toward the door.

Tubal and Irab sat silently watching him till he had disappeared down the corridor.

"Another narrow-minded bigot," sneered Tubal, taking a sip from his mug. "Wonder if anyone else at this university still thinks like him."

"I'm afraid so," said Irab. "Why else would Zalomo still be head of department?"

"I don't see why Zalomo should be able to control the bulletin the way he does. He determines who gets anything published, which, in effect, determines who gets well-known enough to stand any chance of promotion," said Tubal in a sullen undertone, casting a glance toward the research students, now putting down their mugs and preparing to leave.

"Pity he's still got a long time till retirement. He's not much older than six hundred."

"And there's little chance of advancement till he's gone," said Tubal lowering his tone and watching the research students leaving the room.

"We're stuck with him for another century, at least."

"Unless something were to happen to him," murmured Tubal, glancing round to make sure no one else was in the tea room.

Irab lowered his voice. "What sort of thing did you have in mind?"

Tubal dropped his voice till it could only just be heard by Irab leaning over the table toward him. "Suppose he were to go to the observatory to take a look for himself and give some expert advice to your research students. Not as part of a team working all night, but just for a consultation. Just for an hour or so around midnight. Not many people around after midnight. Not many, except thugs, that is. He might just happen to run into a couple of cutthroats on his way home."

"Hmm... As it happens, I've got a nephew working as an assistant who could make that more than just a possibility," said Irab, ominously.

❖ ❖ ❖

"Come in."

The door opened and a radiant smile peeped round the doorpost.

"Hello, Dad. Are you busy? Can I talk to you for a few minutes?"

"Sarai! How lovely to see you! Please come in and shut the door. I'm busy with a new problem, but that can wait. Seeing you is much more important. I've half an hour till my next lecture. Oh, that looks good!"

Sarai set down a freshly baked pie on the desk. "I did some baking today and I made this specially for you. I know you like strawberry pie, and our crop has been exceptional this year— they're so sweet and delicious. You'll love it."

Professor Zalomo bent toward the pie and breathed in the delicious aroma. "Ahh! This smells wonderful."

"Dad, we're busy with the pitching, and it's nearly finished. You wouldn't believe how much pitch it takes for just one coat. We've given it three coats, but Japh insisted on one more for the outside. Shem looks like burnt toast already. I'll hardly be able to recognise him when he's finished with his pitch sprayer."

"You've a good husband there, Sarai. I never told you, but I was worried sick about you marrying one of the rogues of Salem. It's hard to find a man who isn't a scoundrel these days. Make sure you appreciate him—even if he does look like overdone toast."

Professor Zalomo got up and went to the door of his secretary's office. "My daughter's paying me a visit, would you please put the kettle on?" He turned back to Sarai. "I'm so glad the work's nearly finished. I've heard rumours that the riffraff in town are planning some sort of sabotage."

"They're getting worse all the time. Lal's still grieving over what they did to her father. He was such a kind man."

"Such a disgrace that the reports all spun the story to make it his fault. Hardly a word of criticism for the thugs who killed him."

"Not one of them was arrested."

Professor Zalomo's secretary brought in a tray with two cups, a tea pot, and a jug of milk. She set the tray on his desk with a smile, nodded to both, and returned to her office without a word.

"He was such a good influence on Japh. I couldn't get over the change in him when he got back from Zohan."

"Yes, you're right, he seemed very downhearted for a while before he went."

"Actually I was afraid he was going to crack under the strain of being an outcast, but he came back from that trip a changed man. And you know, he seemed to get even stronger after Malech was murdered."

He poured a little milk into each cup and picked up the teapot.

"I know what you mean, Dad. It's almost as if he realized Malech wasn't afraid to die for what he believed, so he shouldn't be afraid either."

"I hope he doesn't go the other way and become foolhardy. But I don't think he will, he's a very sensible young man."

"Lal's so concerned she refuses to let him go anywhere without her. She says if anyone kills him, she wants to die by his side."

Professor Zalomo handed her a steaming cup. "Well, that's a bit melodramatic, but I can see her point. And he'll probably be extra careful knowing she's at risk, too."

"It's really getting very dangerous in Salem, Dad. That's why I'm here. I came to ask you to get ready to come and join us. You will come, won't you? You said you'd come."

He took a sip. "Yes, my dear, I'll come, but only at the last minute. I'm needed here at the university. The students need someone to present an alternative to the godless humanism they're being pumped full of. Besides, I'm busy with a problem that's just cropped up. Something very strange is happening on Mars and I'm trying to find out what's going on."

Sarai, who had been one of his most promising students before marrying Shem, was immediately interested. "What's happened? Do tell me!"

"We don't really know. We do know that the bright patches, which we think are lakes of frozen water, have disappeared. The whole surface—or at least, as much as we have been able to see so far—has dimmed and changed colour. By far the most likely explanation is dust being thrown up into the atmosphere. The problem is we can't see what kicked up the dust. The most popular theory at the moment is a huge storm, but storms need convection, and that needs heat and I can't see where enough heat could come from—certainly not from the sun. We're in one of the cooling stages of the solar cycle. The other popular idea is volcanic activity, but the pattern's all wrong. The dust's been kicked up everywhere and it would need an incredible arrangement of volcanoes erupting all at once. Personally, I think the most likely cause is multiple meteorite impacts. I think a number of them bombarded the planet over a period of at least a day. Mars rotates once in just over twenty-four hours, and I suspect the group was so spread out, it took more than a day to go by."

"Has there been anything like that in the past?"

"No. That's the big weakness with my idea, but I do have the shadow of a reason for my suspicion. Four days ago, Mars passed in front of a star. I was hoping to find out something about the star and something about the atmosphere of Mars at the same time. While I waited for the star to reappear on the other side, I saw what I'm sure was a very faint light winking on and off very slowly and irregularly. It was some way from Mars, and I think it could have just been at my yellow spot. That's why I could see it even though it was so faint and I wasn't looking for it."

"Let me guess what it might be," said Sarai. "What about a long, thin body turning end over end. You could only see it when its long side was reflecting sunlight."

"Sarai, my girl, you should've carried on with your studies. I didn't think of that until two days ago, after some of the research students reported the funny things happening on Mars. Actually, as soon as my star reappeared, the winking light dropped out of my mind and I never even mentioned it to anyone on my team. Then I thought of the explanation you just gave. I've been doing some calculations. Assuming it was not much further away than Mars and it has a similar surface to the Moon, to be visible at all it would need to be about a hundred and fifty miles long and at least forty wide."

"And would a body that big hitting Mars explain the dust?"

"No, I don't believe it did hit Mars. There would have been such an explosion that debris would be thrown up so violently we would have seen it coming from the impact site. But it struck me as too much of a coincidence that dust should be thrown up so soon after I saw that winking light and guessed it might have been part of a cloud of meteorites, some of which did strike."

"Well, it would be interesting to see if you can spot it again."

"Yes, I can hardly wait for my team's turn at the observatory next week. If I can find it again, I want to plot its position and work out a trajectory. Fortunately, Irab invited me to go along for a couple of hours tonight and give his team some advice on what they're doing. I might just be able to spend a few minutes trying to spot my elusive little light."

26 Island's End

Lano was bored.

Life with Asa had been sweeter than he could have ever imagined.

For a while.

Now that she was pregnant, he looked forward to having a child. That should give some new interest to life. But, for the moment, something was lacking. He missed the excitement he had found in exploring the forest when he was a free agent. And Asa didn't really have much conversation. She talked enough. More than enough…but had nothing really interesting or challenging to say. Lano was becoming restless. He sat staring out over their pool, watching the sky getting lighter behind the trees as the sun prepared to put in its appearance. Lano hardly even noticed that Asa was speaking to him.

"Lano, you're not listening to me!"

"Oh! Yes. Well, I was listening. But I've been thinking I'd better go and look for some more fruit trees. When the baby comes, we'll need to have a really good food supply."

"But there's plenty. We've never gone short."

"Yes, but he'll soon be a big strong chap and he'll need lots to eat. I'd better go and make sure."

"But he will be very small for years. He won't even start to eat fruit for a year or two."

"Yes, but when he does, I want to be sure he'll have plenty. I'm going to have a look around. I'll be back soon."

"Oh, Lano, don't leave me. Let me come with you."

"No. I can go much quicker on my own. I won't be long."

He got up, strode off into the forest and disappeared from view.

Five minutes into the forest, Lano was jubilant. It was the first time he had been alone for a long time. Too long. Asa had been at his side constantly since they had been married. He revelled in the freedom to do whatever he wanted to do. He could sense animals nearby. He listened. Stegos. He moved silently in their direction, hugging the cover of the undergrowth, alert for the slightest change in the direction of the breeze, eyes darting from the trees ahead to the forest floor in front of his feet, avoiding anything which might make a noise when he trod on it. He soon spotted them. Three young ones whose plates had barely started to change from the dull olive drab of babyhood to the iridescent colours characteristic of their sex. He edged forward toward the biggest, the only female, till he could see her head, low down next to the ground, chomping her way through the lush undergrowth, seeming to have no preference for thorns, ferns, flowers, or creepers. His eyes followed the line of her body with its plates sticking out left and right, arching far above the tallest undergrowth and down to the tail resting on the ground. He moved to his left and slid forward till he could have touched the sharp spikes on the end of her tail. What a thrill to come so close to death and slip away without her even knowing he had been there!

He moved around the stegos and headed into the wind, covering ground quickly and easily, heading eastward through unknown territory, alert for signs of dangerous animals, watchful for the almost imperceptible lightness between the trees in the distance that signalled a pool.

The sun—which was just visible now and then where tall animals had stripped enough leaves to let the sky show through—had passed its zenith when Lano began to feel hungry. He climbed a tree to collect a handful of the tenderest leaves, came down and walked along eating them, keeping his eyes open for wild fruit. He spotted dabs of red bird droppings full of black spots. After following them for thirty yards, he came to a mulberry tree laden with sweet, ripe fruit.

Lano began to feel a bit guilty. He loved his exploring, but it was getting late. Asa would be getting worried. He'd better go back. But not yet. Just a little longer. Just one more pool.

Between the trees ahead, he could sense a slight brightness before he was sure he could really see it. But this light seemed different. As he advanced, the brightness seemed to spread a long way on both sides. It must be a very big pool. And there was something different—an unusual pale green glow. He stopped, conscious that something was wrong, but not sure what it was. His eyes darted from the mat of roots in front of him to the spaces between the trees, to the branches above him. The branches seemed lower than usual—only just above his head—not just on a tree here and there, but all of them. He noticed that the tree trunks seemed thinner than normal. And he heard a strange noise in the distance—*whooshshshsh*.

Lano crept forward. He was now alert for anything out of the ordinary and noticed that the roots were narrower than usual. They did not have the gnarled look of the forest he knew so well. And they were unusually clean. The compacted dust of decayed dung, animal remains, and leaf mould, which usually left only the top of the root visible, was largely missing, but there were plenty of patches of dung and newly fallen twigs and leaves. The roots looked somehow young. Another faint *whooshshshsh*. He stopped to strain his ears for a clue as to what it might be. He sensed a slight movement of the forest floor beneath his feet. He could see definite signs of light behind the trees, but it was that eerie, pale green lightness. New situations could be dangerous. And this must be a pool the likes of which he had never seen before. Unforeseen threats could be lurking. Better be very careful. He slipped from one patch of cover to the next, gliding noiselessly as a ghost. The branches were now so low that he had to bend to walk under them. The trunks were only half their usual diameter. There was an unfamiliar smell in the air. He heard another *whooshshshsh*—much closer this time and the forest floor rose and fell perceptibly a moment later. A few steps further, and he was in a new forest. The roots beneath his feet were thin and wet. Small gaps between them allowed water to seep up from below. The sky was visible between the branches not far above his head. Branches grew from the young trunks only a foot or two above the roots. He pressed forward carefully, the mat of roots deforming beneath him at every step. Another *whooshshshsh* made him start. The sound came from just a few yards ahead and almost immediately the roots rose and fell very noticeably, the young trees all around him shook. He stepped forward holding onto the trunk of a sapling no thicker than his arm. The roots were now only just big enough for him to stand on, with gaps between them where the water showed through. He pressed forward and emerged from between saplings barely taller than himself to a sight that astonished him.

Roots trailed off into clear water. Shoots springing up from the roots carried pale green leaves which were like miniatures of the leaves he knew so well. Beyond them was a breathtaking expanse of shimmering blue water, and in the distance a dark-green mass stretching as far as he could see in either direction. The crest of a wave made its way over the water toward him. As it reached the roots just in front of him, it broke over into a white froth of bubbles. It made the *whooshshsh* sound he had heard several times, and lifted the roots so sharply he almost lost his balance.

Lano stood transfixed gazing at the scene. The sparkling blue sea stretched so far he could hardly imagine the world could contain so much water. The dark-green expanse in the distance, he soon deduced, must be another forest. And the enormous expanse of sky was vastly larger and more majestic than the patches of blue he had seen so often above the forest pools.

He was about to turn reluctantly away from the magical view and head back to Asa when he heard a shout far away to his right. He turned toward it and listened intently. The shout came again, and then came the faint but unmistakable sound of men singing together. They sang a few words then stopped for a moment, then sang a few more words and stopped again. On and on went the song. Lano wanted to hear the words. He wanted to see who was singing. He hurried back into the part of the forest he knew so well and skirted the unfamiliar belt of new growth next to the sea. He could no longer hear the distant singing, but he made his way swiftly in the direction the sound had come from.

Playing games with the animals had completely lost its attraction. He gave them all a wide berth and continued on his way as quickly as he dared. He had covered well over a mile when he heard a faint shout somewhere ahead. He hurried on and soon heard singing again. But this was a different song. Slower, with more syllables in each line and longer pauses between them. And there was only one man singing. But in the pause at the end of each line came a chorus of "Yaahh" from many men. Lano was soon close enough to make out the words. He stopped to listen but they made no sense to him.

The first mate's sloshed and the bosun's drunk –
Yaahh
The coxswain's paralytic on his bunk –
Yaahh
But when the coastguard's come, they're still gonna lose –
Yaahh
We'll drown 'em like rats in a tub of booze!
Yaahh

He shook his head, gave up trying to understand what these strange words meant and crept forward toward the lightness ahead that told him he was approaching a pool.

Old Doom and Gloom can rant and rave –
Yaahh
About a fire beyond the grave –
Yaahh
But we've better advice than that old scum –
Yaahh
Light a fire in your belly with a pint of rum!
Yaahh

Lano pressed himself against a trunk and peered through a screen of creepers hanging from the branches above. He could hardly believe his eyes. This pool was unlike any he had ever seen. The roots at the water's edge were not smoothly eaten away, they were uneven and split. They looked as though they had been chopped with an axe. But the really astounding thing about this pool was the enormous object floating in it.

The rich and famous, the mighty fine –
Yaahh

Sit down to dinner with a glass of wine –
Yaahh
But men like us, all fine and dandy –
Yaahh
Drink like lords from a barrel of brandy!
Yaahh

Lano could not see the singers; they were hidden behind that huge wooden structure taking up most of the pool. He backed into the trees and moved round to the left. He was soon in the younger growth where he did not feel so confident. He moved more carefully, taking extra care to remain invisible, keeping the floating giant just in sight between the trees. The pool stretched all the way to the area where water could be seen between the roots. When Lano came to the end of the great monster, he had to watch carefully where he planted his feet. The roots were only just big enough to stand on. He edged toward the pool.

Old Gloom's so full of his story 'bout water –
Yaahh
He's only got three sons and not one daughter –
Yaahh
But we make dozens of snotty-nosed brats –
Yaahh
'Cause we get our urge from the whisky vats!
Yaahh

Lano peeped through the screen of leaves and saw the singers. They were in three groups; each group pulling on a thick rope. At the end of each line of their song, they all heaved together, let out a lusty *Yaahh,* and moved a foot or two backward. Between Lano and the singers, a channel of water stretched from the pool to the open sea. With each pull on the ropes, the channel opened a little wider.

Just one more pull will see us through –
Yaahh
Just one more pull and that will do –
Yaahh
But don't let her go till we've made her fast –
Yaahh
Then we'll all have some grog before the mast!
Yaahh

When the ropes had been tied to something out of Lano's line of sight, the men let go of the rope and made their way toward the main body of the forest. They were soon hidden behind the floating monster.

Lano went back the way he had come and continued going round the pool toward the other side. He found a clump of cover with a good view of the area where the men had congregated. He was amazed at the number of people, he was amazed at the size of the cleared area where they were gathered, and he was amazed at the buildings behind them tucked in among the trunks of the trees.

The men were spread over a wide area of clearing, each talking to a woman, most of whom had children at their heels. Lano's eyes strayed over the scene till they stopped at a big hulking brute of a man and the most stunningly beautiful woman he could ever have imagined. He stared, not breathing, heart thumping, something inside him contracting into an aching knot. The hulk scooped her into his arms, kissed her passionately, and then turned toward the floating monster. He walked to a long ladder leaning against its side, shouted a command and started to climb. The other men left their women and followed him up the ladder and out of sight onto the huge thing.

When the last man had reached the top, the ladder was lifted up and disappeared from sight. Then the monster began to move slowly through the channel toward the open sea. As soon as it was beyond the channel, someone Lano could not see untied the ropes. The floating saplings which had been pulled aside moved back toward their normal place and the channel was soon so narrow that no hint of the ocean could be seen.

Lano stared at the marvellous, divine young woman. He tracked her movements through several conversations with other women, some encounters with squabbling children, and finally to a hut between the trees. It was nearly sundown. He should have been home with Asa by now, but the fleeting thought of Asa was a distasteful annoyance. He had to find a way of talking to that goddess. And soon. He glided between the trees till he came to the back of her hut. He moved closer and found a crack to peer through.

— ❖ —

27 Final Observations

There it is. Very faint, and visible for only a second or two, but unmistakable. Why haven't the research students spotted it? Or have they seen it, thought it unimportant, and just not bothered to report it? Admittedly it's right at the edge of the field of view—only just visible—but surely someone should have noticed it. Ah, there it is again. Definitely brighter this time. Irab should have picked it up. It's his postgraduates that have been studying Mars, and they've been at it since long before the dust cloud. They should be so familiar with that part of the sky that something unusual should stand out like a bronto. There it is again, even brighter this time. Nobody worth anything at all as an astronomer could miss that. But why would the brightness change so significantly? Perhaps it's not only much longer than it is broad, maybe it's flattened, maybe it's in the form of a flake. It's possibly twisting as well as tumbling. Then sometimes the wide face of its long side reflects the sun, and sometimes its narrow side. There it is again, much dimmer this time. Quite understandable that they'd miss a glint as faint as that.

Professor Zalomo withdrew from the eyepiece with a concerned expression on his face. He noticed the anticipation in the research students' faces. He glanced at the table where Irab was hunched over some papers.

"I believe there is something which could possibly throw some light on the problem. It's quite clearly visible, and I'm a little surprised that either you haven't noticed it or haven't thought it significant enough to mention."

The postgrads' faces fell. They glanced at each other and looked back to Professor Zalomo.

"Just take another look and see if you can see anything at all out of the ordinary. Oh, and by the way, where's the assistant? I haven't seen him since I arrived."

"We haven't seen him either. I think he must be sick or something," said Matthian.

Zalomo walked over to the desk. Irab seemed to be deliberately trying to avoid him. Odd! Irab had invited him especially to come and give some advice. One would have expected him to be hovering around attentively.

"Irab, I think there could be a clue staring us in the face, I've just asked your students to take another look. It might be as well if you did, too."

Irab looked up from his papers. He looked flustered and on edge.

"Is something wrong, Irab?"

"Why, no! No, Professor. Nothing at all! I've just got some admin work to do—time allocations for the telescope and such things. Sorry. I've been a bit preoccupied, that's all."

Zalomo noticed that Irab tried to smile and appear nonchalant. He failed on both counts. "Isn't that part-time assistant, what's his name…Rendo, supposed to be on duty tonight, Irab?"

"Oh! Yes. He sent a message that he's sick tonight. I got his note too late to arrange for a stand-in," said Irab.

Professor Zalomo had the uneasy feeling that Irab was lying to him. His manner was very strained. He seemed to be in a state of nerves. He left Irab sitting at the table and went back to the telescope. Johab was peering into the eyepiece.

"Well, I suppose it could look a bit fuzzier than last night. But that doesn't help at all. If it's a storm, it just got stronger. If it's volcanoes, they just erupted again."

"Maybe we should do some measurements on the fuzziness. We can compare it to what we find next time," the new girl suggested.

Zalomo shook his head sadly. Narrow thinking, narrow observing—confined by blinkers. He and his colleagues seemed somehow to have failed to instil that enquiring spirit, that passion for being ever alert to the new and unexpected that was the mark of a real astronomer. As head of the department, he assumed responsibility for that, of course. What could he do to remedy the situation? He'd leave them to keep searching, and tomorrow he would call them in for a lecture on expanding their horizons and being ever alert to the possibilities of the unexpected. How disappointed he would be if they hadn't spotted it by then! He picked up his hat and walking stick, tested the stick's handle, walked to the door and let himself out into the night.

The midnight air was cool. He drew in a deep breath and

enjoyed the smell of wet grass hanging in the stillness. The crescent moon was more than halfway down toward the horizon. The stars were bright but the moon would soon be so low it would be difficult to see the path. It was a good half hour's walk to his home. He set off briskly, his thoughts wandering over the possibilities of that strange winking light.

He rounded a bend in the path and glimpsed a slight movement close to one of the trees in a little grove of poplars not far ahead. His pulse started to race. Better be careful. There could be robbers around at this time of night. His eyes scanned the path before him. Perhaps he'd better skirt round to the left of the grove. He quit the path and was soon entangled in brambles. What a pity! No way here. He unhooked himself and moved back to the path. He knew the area to the right to be wet and marshy. A number of springs rose there, and the area was quite level. He tested the surface. His foot sank easily into the soft ground. He'd have to stick to the path. He brought the shaft of his walking stick to his left hand, twisted the handle with his right to release the catch. He checked that the blade slid easily within its wooden encasement.

With ears straining for the slightest sound and eyes darting from tree to tree, he passed the first poplars in the grove. Moving smoothly and quietly he advanced along the path, going silently over his mental check list. Centre of gravity low. Knees slightly bent. Feet apart for stability. Weight evenly placed on the balls of both feet. Ready for movement in any direction. A scraping noise to his left! He slid the blade silently from its sheath and turned to see a dark shape appear from behind a tree. A ray of moonlight glinted from the knife in the hand of the figure gliding toward him. Zalomo lunged. The thin, straight blade of his sword-stick passed effortlessly through the attacker's throat.

A gurgling gasp broke the silence. The man dropped his knife, clutched at his throat, and sagged to his knees. Zalomo pulled back his blade and turned toward a noise of snapping twigs to his right. He slashed at the barely discernible figure bearing down on him and felt his blade slice into the bare flesh of the attacker's neck. Then a searing pain stabbed the middle of his back. Another shot into his left side. Held by a strong grip on the knife in his back he was unable to turn. In an agony which made every movement a supreme effort of will, he raised his blade and stabbed backward over his shoulder. A shriek and then a stifled curse broke out behind him. His sword-stick was wrenched from his failing grip. Another bolt of pain slammed into his back and his legs began to buckle.

Zalomo saw the ground rising to meet him as he slumped forward. Then the pain faded away and he began to lift upward. He could see a body sprawled on the ground. Four men with knives in their hands were looking down at it. Floating higher, he could see three other men lying crumpled up in the undergrowth. In another moment, he was among the branches of the poplar trees and both the living and the dead were hidden by leaves. After a few more seconds, he was above the trees looking down on the grove…so peaceful…so beautiful in the moonlight. And there below him was the lush countryside, with moonlight glinting on scattered patches of water. How much water there was! Myriads of little springs and tiny pools, each catching a bundle of moonbeams for a moment, each holding part of that reflected crescent for a shimmering instant before passing it on to the next, while the image in its entirety sparkled away toward the town. Even Salem looked strikingly lovely in the stillness of this wonderful night. And there above the town, those stars he had come to know and love so well. The crescent moon was pure and pristine in its silver loveliness. And above the moon were more of his old friends, the stars. There were the Pleiades! Had they ever looked so beautiful? And above them? Oh! He had never seen a light like that before. Such radiance! Growing so quickly! Such radiance! Filling the whole sky! Such glorious radiance!

28 Telina

"You'd better talk very quietly; it would never do if one of the other women were to hear you. And there are four men who've been left behind on guard duty. Now, I want to know how you got here."

"I came through the forest."

"But that's impossible! What about the tyranos and brontos and lions and things?"

"Oh, it's easy to avoid them if you know how. Snakes are more of a problem than the big animals—some snakes are so well camouflaged you have to be a bit careful. But you get used to spotting them. You have to watch out for the velos, too, but they're quite small and all you have to do is get into a tree. They can't climb and they soon go off to look for something else."

"I don't know if I believe you. I've never heard of anybody going more than a few yards into the forest. What's your name?"

"Lano. And what's yours?"

"Telina."

"Telina. Such a beautiful name for such a beautiful woman. It suits you."

"Don't try your flattery with me, I've dealt with men before. Now why did you come here?"

"I heard the singing and came to find out what was going on."

"The singing? Oh the shanties. They always sing shanties when they're pulling together."

"I didn't understand the words."

"Tabin, the shantyman, makes most of them up as he goes along."

"What does 'the first mate's sloshed and the bosun's drunk' mean?"

"It means they'd drunk too much booze and couldn't even stand up anymore."

"Who'd drunk too much? And what's 'booze' anyway?"

"Whisky, brandy, rum, and stuff like that. Haven't you ever drunk alcohol?"

"No. Never heard of it."

"Well don't try it. It's a curse. You never know what people will do when they've been drinking."

"And what was that great thing that they all climbed onto?"

"You mean the ship? Wow, you really don't know much! Haven't you ever seen a ship before?"

"No. Until today I'd never seen enough water for such a big thing to float on."

"That's not even a big one. It's the big ones they go to rob."

"You mean there are others? I spent an hour looking out over that huge expanse of water and I didn't see anything like it."

"Of course you didn't. You can only see a tiny bit of the ocean from one place. It goes on for thousands of miles. A signal came from one of the lookouts thirty miles away. There's a big ship coming. Ganoobo and the men will get into position to attack it before first light."

"Who's Ganoobo?"

"He's the captain… He's my husband."

"I saw him...I saw him kiss you. I was very jealous. Do you love him?"

"I...I...well...I used to. Yes. I mean no. I used to. I left my first husband for him. Well, that is, I left his dead body. That was before I knew how mean and ruthless Ganoobo is. And anyway, I wanted children. But it looks as if the only thing he's going to give me is RAK."

"I could give you children."

"Oh, yes. And how do you know that? You don't look old enough to have any to prove it."

"Asa's just about to have my first baby."

"Asa? Is Asa your wife?"

"Yes."

"Well you'd better go back home and take care of her and your kid."

"I'd rather take care of you... And what's RAK?"

"You really don't know anything, do you! It's a disease. A very bad disease. It kills you in a couple of months. You die in agony. There's no cure."

"But why should Ganoobo give it to you?"

"Well, you see, when they rob ships, they throw all the men overboard. They get snapped up by the kronos and other hungry things. The women they keep to sell to the traffickers. It's usually a few days before the traffickers come to load them up and take them away. Ganoobo and the men give them a really bad time till the traffickers come. I've sneaked up and watched them through a chink in the palisade. It's disgusting. And it's only a matter of time before he gets RAK from one of them. Then he'll give it to me and we'll both die. Horribly."

"If you come away with me he won't be able to give it to you, will he?"

"He'd come and kill you. And me as well. He'd kill you very slowly and you'd wish you'd never been born. I've seen him kill people he had a grudge against."

"He'll never catch me. I can move through the forest so that nobody can find me. I can get within two yards of a tyrano or a bronto without them even knowing I'm there. I could teach you how to do it too."

"Hush!"

"She's got a man in there, I heard them talking."

"You sure about that?"

"Dead certain. And it's not one of our men, either."

"If we bust in there and there's nobody, we'll be in big trouble."

"There's a man in there with her, I tell you. I had my ear to that door for half an hour."

"All right, Ben, let's go."

Lano was on his feet in an instant. In a flash, his eyes scanned the hut by the dim light of the smoky lamp. Then he leapt toward the corner furthest from the door, where the branches making up the frame of the roof were furthest apart. He tore through the thatch as the door crashed inwards and in a moment he was outside. He turned to stretch out his hand to grab Telina, but a shaggy bear of a man had her wrists in the vice-like grip of his huge, hairy hands. Lano ducked as a knife hurtled toward him. It lodged itself in a roof timber half an inch above his head. He risked another glance into the room. Shaggy bear was dragging Telina toward the door. Two men were only a few feet away, rushing toward him. He grabbed the handle of the knife, wrenched it free from the wood, dropped to the ground and raced through the darkness toward the forest.

29 Dream Boat

"I just gotta get a snort."

"Why?"

"Oh, I don't know. But I just gotta get a snort. I'm feeling real bad."

"How d'you get one?"

"Tob gives me one when I tell him what he said."

"Look, there's a man coming."

"Hey, that's him. That's Old Doom and Gloom."

"Really? You're not kidding? He doesn't look like I thought he would. I thought he'd look like a monster. I thought I'd be so scared I'd wet myself."

"Agh, no. He's just a half-witted old fogy. Comes and stands out there every day and spouts his piece. Then goes back to hammering and messing about with that whacking-great big thing over there."

"How does he know there's anybody listening? I can't see anybody, and I'm sure he can't see us behind this bush."

"Well, I can tell you there's a whole bunch of people hidden away. Half the kids in my school come every day. There's so many people who're too scared to come and listen themselves, they get us to come. Then we go and tell them what he said."

"Why are they scared of him? He doesn't look scary to me."

"I think they're afraid other people would think they're interested in what he says."

"But they are! Otherwise they wouldn't send the kids to listen, would they?"

"Oh forget it, I don't understand grown-ups. They're all just as nuts as Doom and Gloom."

"But if half the kids from the school are here, who's in class?"

"Hardly anybody."

"But what do the teachers say?"

"Oh, they don't care, and, anyway, they're usually too drunk to notice. But be quiet, he's just about at the place where he stands and speaks."

The two boys, crouching behind a juniper bush, fell silent. A noise came faintly to their ears. They turned their necks to see where it came from. The sound came rapidly closer—and louder. Large animals were walking purposefully in their direction. Hannumith grabbed his little brother by the shoulder and hissed, come on, let's get out of here. They stood up. Twenty yards away were two brontos...coming straight toward them! Amos screamed and stood rooted to the ground. Hannumith snatched his little brother's arm and dragged him behind a huge gopher tree. The brontos ignored them and strode straight out from the forest and into the clearing. They headed for that huge lump, black and shining under a brand new layer of pitch.

The brontos passed within a few yards of the man, who appeared to be utterly amazed. If he had planned to speak, as he usually did, then he must have changed his mind. From their cover behind the tree, they watched him start to follow the brontos. They had looked terrifying at a range of less than twenty yards, but from a distance the boys could see they were actually small, as brontos go. Must be only young ones.

From their left came a scream, then the sound of scrambling through the undergrowth and a boy came running in their direction.

"Hey! Jerry! What's up?" hissed Hannumith.

The fleeing urchin looked toward the voice, saw them, and raced to the tree.

"There's two wolves! They nearly got me!" panted Jerubbaal,

looking back to where he had come from.

"There they are!" said Hannumith pointing toward the clearing. Two wolves had just emerged from the forest and were loping across the clearing, heading after the brontos.

The man stopped following the brontos and stood staring at the wolves. Then his attention shifted. The three boys followed his gaze and saw two antelope slip silently out of the forest and follow a few yards behind the wolves.

"Hey! Hann! Did you ever see anything like it? Do you think those wolves can't smell or something?"

"I don't know, Jerry, but this is weird. I don't like it. I'm getting out of here. Come on, Amos."

They started to move away from the clearing toward the town but covered only a few yards before they heard another noise in front of them. Two stegos came into view between the trees. They were walking straight ahead, not looking to right or left. The boys dived behind a big, old tree. The stegos ignored them and tramped on toward the clearing.

❖ ❖ ❖

"And who's this, then?" The thin lips barely showing through Tob's bushy beard took on a well-practiced smile to match the well-practiced friendly tone of his voice as he squatted on his haunches to bring his bald head down to the little boy's level.

"It's my little brother, Amos, sir."

"Ah! Now that's a nice name, isn't it? Amos! And how old are you, Amos?"

"Six, sir."

"Six! So you're a big chap now. Old enough to have a snort now and then, eh?"

"No, sir. I've never had a snort."

"Well, well, they say there's no time like the present. How

about trying one now?"

"Oh, no, sir. I don't think I'd better."

"Now what makes you say that, Amos?"

"My mother wouldn't want me to, sir."

"Oh, well, you expect that don't you. Mothers are always spoilsports, always wanting to stop you having fun and enjoying yourself. But now that you're a big chap you should start thinking for yourself and making decisions on your own, shouldn't you?"

"Well, I don't know if I'd like it, sir."

"But it's nice…very nice. You're sure to like it. Hann likes it. Don't you, Hann? Just give it a try."

"I don't know…I really don't think I'd like it, sir."

"But how can you know if you've never tried it? It makes you feel so good! As if you were walking on air. Floating above the housetops. You'd like that wouldn't you? I'm sure you'd like it. But you'll never know just how nice it is if you don't try it, will you?"

"No, sir."

"Of course you won't. So let's just give you a shot…There, that's the ticket. In just a few minutes, you'll be soaring like a bird."

Tob stood up. The smile and the friendly tone evaporated. "Well, Hann, what was the story today?"

"He didn't say anything, Sir."

"What? You don't expect me to give you a snort for a story like that do you?"

"But it's true, sir. Two brontos came out of the forest just when he was going to start."

"Two brontos!"

"Yes, sir. They nearly trampled Amos and me to death."

"Did they go and squash Old Doom and Gloom instead?"

"No, sir. They just walked right past him and went to that big black thing they've been making."

"Are you spinning me a line? If you are, I'll break your miserable little arm and chop your fingers off, one by one."

"No! No, sir! It's the truth, sir! And then two wolves came. They nearly ate my friend, Jerry, but he ran away and hid with me and Amos."

"Do you think I don't know that wolves can run a whole lot faster than little boys? You're lying. I don't like being lied to!"

"But it's true, Sir! And they didn't chase Jerry, they went straight for that big black thing. And then two antelope came, and two stegos. And the stegos nearly walked right over us and we got scared and ran away."

"And did they all go toward that thing Old Doom and Gloom and his lot have been making?"

"All of them, sir. And please, sir, can I have my snort, please, Sir?"

Tob dug into his pocket and brought out a packet, dispensed a frugal dose and gave it to the cowering child.

"You'll have to pay for the next one."

"But where will I get the money, sir?"

"Well, now. You'll have to come to my place and we'll have to have a little chat about that, won't we?"

"Oh, uhm…I don't know, sir. Er, well, if you say so, sir."

"And now you'd better be running along. Beat it!"

"Yes, sir."

Hannumith took Amos' hand and tried to lead him home. His little brother was in a daze, eyes glassy, staring into the distance. Hannumith put his arm round his waist, supported as much of his weight as he could, and together they stumbled down the street.

Tob watched the urchins till they turned the corner and disappeared from sight. He stood, agitated and uncertain for a few minutes. Then, after looking around to make sure nobody was watching, he set off toward the forest.

❖ ❖ ❖

Shem began to give up trying to understand what was going on. When the animals had suddenly started to appear from the forest and walk into the huge doorway, he had been amazed, afraid, and relieved all at the same time. His fears at having large and potentially dangerous animals like brontos, mammoths, tyranos, and sabre-toothed tigers in close proximity in a confined space changed to deepening amazement when one after another they quietly squeezed into their pens, and, without even sampling the food which it had taken so much effort to collect, went to sleep.

Walking around the pens of sleeping animals, the silence seemed almost unreal. The animals were so still, and breathing so quietly, Shem wondered at first if they were still alive. He went close to one or two and satisfied himself they were.

He had not even finished checking the second of the three levels before he began to lose concentration. His mind wandered to the family quarters on the deck above. His step slowed and he felt drowsy. He turned for the stairway wondering why he felt so sleepy. Reaching the family quarters, he found his father at the table filling in his diary and his mother stowing crockery in a cupboard stuffed with straw.

"Hi, Dad. The animals all seem to be in a very deep sleep. I'm feeling drowsy myself."

"It looks as if your mother and I are the only ones not feeling tired. Go to bed. The others have already turned in."

Shem found his wife dead to the world strapped into her narrow bunk just below his own. *Funny that Japh should have insisted on making such a secure system for keeping us pinned down. Anyone would think we were in for a very rough ride.*

Still, he might just be right. He tightened the buckles. Japh has a knack for things like that—always making things—and they usually work better than you ever thought they would. How could we ever have built this great barge without him? He sank back onto his pillow. Strange how soft and comfortable the bed feels today…

He drifted into sleep.

30 Alzan

"…for the use of South Seas Shipbuilders equipment, which has worked faultlessly. Only pitching remains to be done. We expect this to take three months. When it is finished, we do not know how much longer we will be at the site. I would therefore suggest that you arrange for the equipment to be collected as soon as possible. The site is easily visible from the sledway from Noph a mile and a half before reaching Salem.

Yours sincerely,

Malala

P.S. The bearer has been paid two…"

The beginning and the end were unreadable because of dense, rust-coloured stains.

"This mess. Is it blood?"

"Yes, sir. Sorry, sir."

Alzan took the letter to the bright light of the window, tried again to make out the remainder, gave up and read the legible part again.

"When did you receive this?"

"Just over three months ago, sir."

"Three months! Why did you take so long to deliver it? Do you expect me to pay you anything for stale news? Three months! You dolt! What were you playing at for three whole months?"

"Sorry, sir, my convoy was ambushed and I got injured. Quite badly, sir. Spent two months in hospital. Confined to bed for three weeks at home after I got out. Only went back to work last week, sir."

"Then why didn't you give it to someone else to bring?"

"The man who gave it to me made me promise to deliver it personally into your hands, sir."

"Man who gave it to you? What was his name?"

"Japh, sir. Used to know him quite well. We went to school together about ninety years ago." Taban had noted the change in Alazan's tone and manner. He might be able to get his delivery fee after all. He had been promised four days' wages. Worth trying for, even if the letter was now irrelevant, stale news.

"Was he alone when he gave you this letter?"

"No, sir, there was a young woman with him." He noticed Alzan's stifled reaction and decided on a gamble. "An exceptionally attractive young woman, sir."

Alzan opened the top drawer of his desk, reached inside and brought out a gold coin. He passed it to Taban and indicated with a gesture that the interview was over.

Taban hurried out, trying to suppress the grin which covered his face. Almost a month's wages! Must have really touched a chord.

❖ ❖ ❖

Alzan stood staring blankly at the letter.

"Malala."

How strange he had never been able to find out her name.

"Malala."

Music on the tip of his tongue. Music ringing through the corridors of memory. The name on the official receipt was 'Japheth Ben Noah of Salem.' He remembered with contempt that fellow and his foolish talk about water falling from the sky. Lots of information available on his father. Crank of the first order. Still prophesying doom and disaster after all these years. The very worst kind of religious nut. Should have been put out of the way long ago. I ought to have realized that stupid oaf Japh was his son—I would never have agreed to them taking the equipment if I had.

And the older man who had known Hovana. Malech. Another religious nutcase. Dropped out of circulation after upsetting a gang with his fundamentalist preaching.

A deep pocket had access to any police file in the archives. But without a name he had got nothing on Malala. Not the slightest lead on the woman who had haunted his dreams for twelve years. She had disappeared without anyone having even seen her. Except his secretary. And her description made him wonder if she had actually seen her at all. Must have been too busy preparing for the strategy meeting to see straight. And now? Did he have the time to wait for an information search on her? No. He'd already waited too long. Must leave immediately after the meeting.

He had arranged to take Sunella, his latest mistress, to dinner at the Gilded Lily that evening. He sat down and wrote a note apologizing for the fact that he had to go away on urgent company business, but would see her after he got back. He took a small, beautifully wrapped parcel from the bottom drawer of his desk, slipped it into his pocket, hurried to the door behind his secretary's desk, and went through to the boardroom, where she was arranging a tray with glasses and a water jug.

"I have to leave immediately after the meeting and I'll be away for two weeks. Please have this note delivered. And as soon as you've finished preparing for the meeting, I want you to arrange for our newest sled, our best sled-man, and the four best guards in the company to be ready to leave in time to catch the last convoy for Noph."

"Certainly, sir. The team should be here within ten minutes. I'll just get the file, then I'll see to it." She left the room, brought in a thick dossier, put it at the head of the table and then left, closing the door to the office behind her.

Alzan made his way to the picture windows on the other side of the room. He pulled aside one of the net curtains just far enough to get a clear view of the courtyard outside the main entrance. He grunted at the sight of fifteen colourless, expressionless, smartly dressed men who had just alighted from two passenger sleds and were ambling toward the security man guarding the door. He took his seat at the head of the table, opened the file, and glanced at the agenda.

❖ ❖ ❖

"And you're quite sure that Geo-Drilling Inc. cannot be traced to South Seas Shipbuilders?"

"Absolutely certain. The company's registered as having five shareholders, three of them never existed, the other two are dead, and neither of them ever had connections with any ship-building company. We set up Geo-Drilling through a small holding company registered in Tarshish, which also has no living shareholders on the register. It's impossible to trace them to us."

The atmosphere around the highly polished table was more tense than Alzan could ever remember. He looked at the amber wood, and his eye followed the line of an exceptionally curvaceous pattern in the grain. For years that curve had taken his thoughts to the woman he would soon be setting out to see, but he forced himself to put her out of his mind and focus on the business at hand. He looked up at the chief financial officer. "And what about our new location?"

"We've bought the land for our new shipyard in the name of another holding company—which also cannot be traced to us. Just before the rising sea level begins to threaten our yard, we'll advertise for land on a worldwide scale. We'll only buy the new land from our holding company after a number of negotiations for other sites have failed. We'll make sure that competing interests outbid us for other, suitable looking, but lower-lying sites. There will not be the slightest suspicion that we had made preparations in advance. Er…perhaps I should point out that there's been a slight change in plan concerning land for the drilling site. The geotechnical team has indicated that their requirements are not as they had initially indicated."

Alzan stiffened and shot a hard stare in the direction of the geotechnicians. There was a decidedly edgy look to the team. They fidgeted and glanced uneasily toward their senior man. Alzan's tone was soft but icy. "Oh? What's all this about?"

The chief geotechnical engineer cleared his throat. He seemed to be trying to look unconcerned, but his embarrassment was clear to see. He nervously brushed a lock of hair from his forehead and began to speak in a louder but less confident voice than he usually used. "At our previous meetings, we had made only preliminary calculations. We now have more reliable data to work with. Our latest analysis shows that if we drill a hole large enough to raise the sea level within a reasonable time, we could face a number of difficulties. One is that if we allow the water to just escape out of the borehole, it will shoot out so quickly it will be blasted very high into the air. It might even go into orbit. The jet would be visible from many miles away and the authorities would be on to it very quickly. We'd thought we could get over this by shooting the jet into an energy dissipater, but we've found more problems with this than expected.

"The best solution will be to drill our hole in the sea bed, and have the discharge a long way below water level. If this were done in the open sea, the turbulent water bubbling and splashing up would also be visible from miles away, so we propose drilling under one of the floating forests."

"And do you have a suitable floating forest in prospect?"

The chief financial officer, who was the second cousin of the engineer and was clearly trying to cover for him, broke in. "We've found the perfect location not far from Antinopo. It adjoins a large tract of neglected, unused forest next to the sea. The tidal range is exceptionally low. The belt of floating forest is more than two hundred miles long and almost twenty miles wide—and it's very unlikely that its hinge will break within the next fifty years."

"And are we sure we can buy that land?"

A wry smile stole across the CFO's usually expressionless face. "It's as good as settled. Another little company that has not the slightest connection with us is busy fixing the deal right now—and the price is a giveaway."

"You mentioned other problems, what are they?" Alzan turned to the geotechnical team again.

"The water will be shooting out of the drill-hole so quickly that it will cause rapid erosion unless we line the hole with a very strong, wear-resistant casing. The jet of water will produce a huge frictional force trying to lift the lining out of the ground. We've designed a special Tubal-Cainite casing which screws into the rock around the drill hole. We had to re-engineer a micro-vibration/ultra-torque impulse driver to screw the casing into the rock behind the drill. We've completed testing and we're now confident the system will work."

"If it has to be made of T-C-ite, it must be very expensive!"

"True," the chief financial officer broke in. "The cost is enormous, but if it's the only way to stop the firm going bankrupt, I don't see that we have any option."

"I suppose you're right. Oh, and how do you close off the flow of water after our goal is reached?"

The geotechnical engineer almost smiled. He looked as if a load had been removed from his shoulders. He was obviously relieved that the embarrassment of his team's former miscalculations had passed off so easily. "When we get within two miles of the target, we'll stop drilling with the large-diameter machine and attach the final length of casing just above the sea floor. It has an integral valve unit with a completely unobstructed bore when the valve is open. We'll collapse the drill-head and withdraw it through the casing. The remainder of the hole will be done with a smaller diameter drill, working through the middle of the large-diameter hole. When the sea is salty enough to kill the floating forests, we'll send in a diving team to build a protected access on the sea bed so they can get to the valve and close it."

"Hmm... It sounds as if the system could be approaching feasibility at last. How soon can you start?"

"As soon as there's agreement to move ahead."

Alzan looked around the table, scanning each face for some sign of concern or some clue to a question or a doubt. "There's just one thing that bothers me. How do we make sure that the drilling team doesn't let the cat out of the bag? It's essential that nothing goes any farther than this room."

The geophysicist allowed the hint of a grin to curve the corners of his mouth. "When the drill gets close to the water-chamber, the last layer of rock will disintegrate into the borehole. The drill head will be blasted up through the casing and a quarter mile diameter of floating forest above the borehole will be shattered by the impact. The drilling camp and everyone in it will be destroyed."

"But what if some of the team are off duty? What if they're fishing or something—maybe a few miles away from the camp?"

An awkward silence settled over the table and sixteen men glanced from one face to another until the marine biologist spoke up in his usual gentle voice. "The entire area will be fenced off to keep trespassers out. After the last delivery of casing sections, the only further access would be occasional food deliveries for the drilling team. It would be quite easy to arrange for a cage containing a dozen or so velos to be dropped off just inside the entrance gate a day or two before we expect to break through. The cage could have a remote release mechanism. If there are any survivors, they wouldn't be likely to get past a pack of velos that haven't eaten for a day or two."

After a few moments of silence, Alzan scribbled a note in the file, looked up, glanced from one expressionless face to the next and sat back in his chair. "Well gentlemen, I think we should start as soon as possible."

Grunts of approval echoed round the room. Alzan pushed back his chair, stood up and indicated that the meeting was over. In less than a minute, all of the colourless, expressionless men had shuffled out of the boardroom door.

Alzan left for home.

❖ ❖ ❖

"Oh, hello, darling! I didn't think you'd be home so soon."

"Well, my dearest, a very important meeting's just cropped up. Top secret. I can't even tell you where it will be. Vital for the future of the business. Got to pack a few things and run. I'll be away for at least two weeks."

"Oh no! I'll miss you so much. Two whole weeks!"

"I'm sorry, darling, I'll miss you terribly too, but you know how the business works."

"I'll pack some food for the journey."

"Oh, thanks, darling. Whatever would I do without you? You're a real treasure."

— ❖ —

31 Pirates Cove

"Here they come!"

Fifty pairs of eyes looked toward the tower sticking up five feet above the highest trees. The seaward side of the tower was camouflaged with leafy branches, but the side toward the clearing was bare, and the lookout, leaning over the rail nearest to them, stood out sharply against the bright morning sky.

The place burst into action. Women bustled about sprucing up their children. Two men emerged from one of the huts with the bound and dishevelled figure of Telina between them. They carried her to the middle of the clearing and dumped her roughly on the ground among a group of women. Then they joined the other two men who had been left behind on guard duty and headed for the new growth at the ocean's edge.

"Well now, we'll soon see what Ganoobo thinks of his woman playing around with strange men, won't we. Ha ha ha. He's got a way about him, has Ganoobo."

"Oh, yes, Missis Holier Than Thou, I've seen him vent his ill humour on my Jeroboam. Right vicious he is. It'll serve you right to get some of it yourself."

"It'll serve you right if he sells you to the traffickers."

"Ha ha ha ha ha!"

"Look! There they are!"

The women turned toward the sea. The tops of masts and derricks could just be seen above the trees. They listened to the noise of men clambering down the ladder, then they followed the sound of their joking and cursing as they made their way toward the ropes. Shantyman Tabin's familiar voice broke into song and the forest beyond the pool began to shake.

> *The merchants put their boats to sea –*
> *Yaahh*
> *Thinking their profits are certainty –*
> *Yaahh*
> *But men like us have got other ideas –*
> *Yaahh*
> *We turn their smiles to sobs and tears –*
> *Yaahh*

The channel opened a little at every heave. After a dozen or so verses, the passage from the sea was wide enough. The ropes were tied off and the ship was brought through to the pool.

"What you got?" shouted one of the women.

"Bales of cloth, brandy, a hundred thousand in gold, and a whole lot more," shouted one of the men leaning over the rail.

"And twenty-three that we'll have to teach their new profession," smirked a vicious-looking fellow with a long, ugly, puckered scar running down the left side of his face.

The ladder appeared and was lowered from the deck. Men started to scramble down it. A moment later, a group of women were hustled up from below decks and prodded toward the ladder. One of them rushed forward to the rail, grasped it with both hands and screeched in a loud voice, "You're all a disgrace to mankind! That man from Salem was right when he said this generation deserves to be drowned like rats. And you people deserve it even more than most. You deserve to…" Ganoobo's fist smashed into her face, breaking her jaw and knocking out half a dozen teeth. The woman collapsed to the deck, blood oozing from her shattered mouth.

"Now, if anyone else wants to do some preaching, you can have your say after you see what happens to people who don't behave exactly the way I want them to. Bring them here."

The remaining women were pushed roughly to the rail. They looked down to see a narrow strip of water between the ship and the roots of the floating forest.

Ganoobo grabbed the bleeding woman's hair in his left hand, lifted her till her toes were barely touching the deck and ripped away her robe with his right hand. He bent down and grasped one ankle, lifted her effortlessly over the rail and dangled her, head down, two feet away from the side of the ship. Blood poured from her mouth, splashing into the water below. Blurred shapes could be seen under the surface. An ugly head appeared for a moment and sank silently below the water. A deathly hush settled over the scene. Ganoobo waited till every face was turned toward him, then, after a long, dramatic pause, he let go of the woman's ankle. She fell toward the pool screaming.

In the ferocious blur of foam, teeth, and jaws, it was hard to tell if the woman actually reached the water before she was torn to pieces. The commotion lasted only a few seconds. Then the ripples faded away while the spectators on the shore and on the ship looked on in awed silence.

❖ ❖ ❖

"Here they come!"

Lano froze. He had been working his way from hut to hut, trying to find chinks to peer through or listen at. But he still had no idea where Telina was. He heard a bustle of activity on the far side of the buildings and slipped back into the forest, taking care not to cross any open ground visible from the observation tower.

Lano had not slept at all the previous night. When he reached the forest he had stopped, tense and scared. To move further in among the trees in the darkness would have been suicide. To stay where he was would be to risk being caught by the thugs. He stood not knowing what to do, clutching the handle of his knife, ready to attempt defence if an animal suddenly rushed at him, listening to the sounds of the night. From the camp came sporadic voices and the creaking and slamming of doors, but he could not detect any sound of pursuit. As his eyes adjusted to the darkness, he made out the branches of the nearest trees by faint starlight reflected from the roots and the mirror-like surface of the pool. He moved slowly toward one of the trees and warily climbed into its branches, tense and alert, fearing the strike of a snake at any moment.

He had spent the night constantly watching for thugs creeping up on him from the camp, his eyes straining to focus in the darkness on the forest floor below. Every few minutes, a dim shadow had seemed to move and his heart had thumped so loudly he wondered how the thugs could fail to hear it. Each time he thought he heard a movement below him, he had tightened his grip on the knife, ready for a fight that he knew he would never win. And the thought of snakes or predators stalking him through the pitch blackness of the surrounding branches had been a never-ending worry.

When the first light had eventually seeped in among the trees, Lano had climbed thankfully down to the forest floor. As the light improved, his confidence returned and he circled the camp, observing the buildings, the watchtower, the watchman, and the open spaces, trying to find a clue as to where they had taken Telina.

After the lookout's shout, the camp had sprung to life. The sound of frenzied activity gave him a renewed sense of urgency. He glided round the edge of the forest until he was beyond the buildings and could see everything going on in the clearing. His eyes scanned the scene till they stopped abruptly on the bound figure of Telina in the middle of a group of women pointing and jeering at her. The two men he had seen dragging her away the previous evening were walking toward the young forest next to the sea.

How could he get to her without being seen? She was in the middle of the clearing. The lookout had a perfect view of her. At least a dozen women surrounded her. What chance did he have now? Armed with a knife, he should be able to deal with quite a lot of unarmed women. They might very well run away from him if he brandished it threateningly. And with all four men in the forest, he should have a few seconds to free Telina before the watchman's cries could bring them back again.

He studied the camp resenting every precious second. The closest he could get to her without being seen from the watchtower would be behind one of the huts quite near to the base of the tower. A clump of trees between the tower and the huts had not been cleared away and it should give him good cover. He moved back a little further into the forest and hurried round toward the tower.

> *The merchants put their boats to sea –*
> *Yaahh*
> *Thinking their profits are certainty –*
> *Yaahh*

Lano stopped cold. There must be about forty men joining in with their "Yaahh." Forty armed killers like the thugs who had nearly got him just a few hours ago. His heart sank as he pressed on behind the huts toward the clump of trees near the tower.

"What you got?" called a female voice somewhere ahead of him.

Lano crawled on his belly out of the trees and into the shadow of a hut.

"Bales of cloth, brandy, a hundred thousand in gold, and a whole lot more." Lano reached the end of the hut and peeped out to see the speaker leaning over the rail.

The ladder was lowered over the side of the ship and men clambered down it. Soon there were a frightening number of people in the clearing. Lano looked despairingly at Telina, thirty yards away. Most of the women had moved toward the boat, and only two or three were between him and her. But at least twenty burly, armed men stood within ten yards of her. Lano eased forward till he could just see the extreme edge of the watch-tower and peered up toward the lookout. He was leaning on the railing watching the proceedings on the ship. His only chance would be to move slowly and smoothly enough so that the lookout would not notice a sudden movement from the corner of his eye. Lano pulled back behind the cover of the hut, stood up, and snatched a few handfuls of thatch from the roof. He slipped back into the clump of trees and cut several tough, thin creepers. He tied a few bundles of thatch to various parts of his body as a makeshift camouflage and crept back to the corner of the hut.

A woman on the ship was shouting. The onlookers seemed shocked and amazed. He saw Ganoobo stride toward the woman and smash his fist into her face. Then he picked her up, ripped off her robe, and held her over the side of the ship. Everyone crowded forward for a better view of the proceedings. Lano's heart leapt. Telina was left there in the middle of the clearing completely alone. He rose to a crouch and started moving smoothly toward her. Halfway there and no shout from the lookout. With his heart pounding, knife gripped tightly, he hurried softly and silently across the bare roots. He reached Telina just as a shrill, terrified scream plummeted toward the water. He whispered a warning to be quiet and slashed the cords binding her hands. He darted round to cut her ankles free, lifted her to her feet and pulled her toward the hut he had come from. They were almost halfway to the hut before the lookout gave the alarm.

Pandemonium broke out behind them. Pirates barged women and children aside, bumping and trampling them in their frenzy to give chase. The camp was a turmoil of shrieking women and terrified children, shouting and cursing men, and the pounding of feet over the cleared roots. Lano and Telina reached the trees with the nearest pursuers forty yards behind them.

"Stay right behind me, and put your feet exactly where I put mine," Lano raced toward a dense clump of undergrowth. He ducked expertly between the creepers, slid between the thorny bushes, and dodged around the tree trunks like a wraith.

"Oh!… Ah!"

Lano looked round to see Telina yards behind him struggling with creepers, tearing herself away from thorns. The crashing of the pursuers was frighteningly close. Lano dashed back, pulled Telina free and draped her over his shoulder. "Just keep still and hold tight" he hissed and set off away from the rapidly approaching commotion.

"That's them!"

Lano dodged for the cover of a bush. A knife flashed past his head and thudded into a tree five yards in front of him.

With Telina on his shoulder, it was difficult to go quickly. He had to take extra care to avoid being caught in the dangling creepers and to stay a little further away from the thorns. With the extra weight, he could not run at anywhere near his usual speed. The crashing behind him came closer. He scanned the forest ahead desperately trying to think of something. Without looking behind him he could hear they were now only twenty yards away. Just to his left he could see a narrower than usual gap between the trees. He headed for it, hoping against hope. From almost ten yards away, he saw the beautiful camouflage pattern he was looking for. He raced straight toward the giant mottled viper curled at the base of one of the trees. Just in time to avoid a strike, he dodged round the tree and then back to the line he had been on. He glanced round to make sure the pursuit could see him. There they were, only fifteen yards away. The two fastest runners—one with a green bandana, one with a red cap—were heading straight for him, machetes in their hands, triumph all over their faces. He raced on.

Lano glanced round when he heard the shriek of pain. Green bandana crashed to the ground with the viper's long fangs deep in his leg. Red cap swerved to one side, stumbled, caught himself, and danced toward the thrashing heap looking for an opportunity to chop the snake in half without maiming his friend. Lano slipped silently into the foliage and hurried on. Shouts and screams behind him intensified as the rest of the pirates stumbled into the snake-fight and then faded as he sped away through the trees.

32 Prelude

Caro glanced at the countryside speeding by. The convoy was racing through a wide plain of lush pastureland dotted with pools of water and occasional clumps of trees. Sheep and cattle grazed under the watchful eye of their herders. He swung his attention back to the sleds in front of him. Nineteen of them, and there were another five behind. Shouldn't be much chance of robbers trying to take on this convoy. Good job. He wasn't sure he would be much use if there was a hit. He clutched at his groin as a jab of pain made him flinch. He thought again about how little time he had left. Even in his new uniform, with its broad black and purple horizontal bands he was beginning to look thin. It hung around him, creased and baggy. The firm would fire him soon—within a day or two it would be obvious that he was too ill to be an effective guard anymore. And to think he'd only been back with Total Security for two months.

Ironic that Total had come to him with an irresistible offer because they were desperately short-staffed. More than half of their guards had died of RAK. And within three weeks of joining them, he had started showing the first symptoms himself. What a pity he hadn't taken Esdras's advice. He'd tried to keep away from Dora's, but simply couldn't resist that stunning olive-skinned beauty who'd arrived a few months ago. He'd never had any practice at saying no to his lust. Should've taken Esdras a bit more seriously. Such a pity he was gone. He owed Esdras a three-month lease on life. Esdras had taken that place on Taban's Superswift and let him go on the one right next to the army sled. He'd been a good buddy, had Esdras. One of the best. A good fighter, too. He'd taken out one of that mob and crippled another before they broke his head wide open.

Pain pricked him again. He tried not to wince too much. He'd noticed Uzza the sled-man looking at him with a concerned expression on his face. *He suspects, I know he does. He's seen enough of his guards go down with RAK already. Still, it might not be such a bad idea to be reported at the next stop. Sure to be sent home.* Total Security was up to its old game of sending guards off wherever there was a need, no mater how far from home. He was very far from home now, nearly at Tarshish. Nearly on the opposite side of the world from Salem. By the time he did get back, he might be unable to stand anyway. After that would come a few days of non-stop suffering and then it would be all over. RAK didn't take very long.

A twinge came and subsided, came back more strongly and faded away. Caro thought of his wife. She'd just started showing the first symptoms. He was sorry she would die too. Not really her fault. She'd been a good wife. Better than he deserved. But then, she was no angel. He'd known for more than a month she was messing around with that young lout from three doors down while he was away. She's probably with him right now. Well, serve him right. He'll be next.

Another jab of pain made him wince. He pressed his groin and turned his face up to the sky biting his lip to stop himself crying out. A white streak was flashing silently across the sky. He'd never seen anything like it. It was very high and moving very fast. In a few moments it faded into the unbroken blue of the midday sky.

Caro was puzzled. He was wondering what on earth it could be when a searing bolt of agony hit his lower abdomen. He clutched at the pain and struggled to hold back a moan.

❖ ❖ ❖

Bedelia and Leanie hated it when their father went out collecting wild fruit. Their stepmother always waited for Jethro to disappear before picking on them. Since Lano had married that nice girl Asa and left home nearly two years ago, things were even worse. Nina had only two children to vent her spite on, and there was just as much of it as there had been when there were three of them.

"Let's get out of the way before she finishes combing Jed's hair. We can go to the other side of the pool and hide till Dad gets back."

Leanie needed no second invitation. They slipped behind a tree and made their way carefully through the forest. Bedelia touched Leanie's arm lightly and stopped, pointing to the right. They kept perfectly still. A rhinoceros ambled through the trees twenty yards away and disappeared as quickly as it had come. A few seconds later, the girls resumed their journey to the far side of the pool.

They reached their favourite place, where a very large tree leaned over the water. Their pool, like the others they had been to, was nearly circular. The host of small creatures which fed on the roots of the floating-forest trees needed tranquil water and sunlight. They lived only around the rims of floating forest pools. Forests still anchored to the land sometimes had them along the most sheltered bays of the coast, too. Usually the roots were eaten back at a rate only slightly quicker than the forest grew. If a root projected into the water it received more than its share of sunlight and was eaten back quickly. But here, their favourite tree leaning far over the water had shaded a knot of roots which now projected several feet beyond the rim of the rest of the pool. It was easy to climb the sloping trunk and reach the thick, low branches where they could lie on their bellies looking down into the water, completely hidden by leaves and invisible from the shore.

Leanie pointed to a shoal of brightly coloured fish that appeared from under the roots on their left. They swam swiftly toward the projection under their tree and disappeared. A huge turtle materialised from the depths, reached the surface, took a mouthful of air, did an elegant turn, and with a few graceful strokes of its flippers, vanished into the abyss. Around the rim of the pool they could see hundreds of fish feeding on the crustaceans which lived in the roots. Occasionally a big fish would emerge, grab one of the crustacean-eaters and melt away again under the forest. From directly under their tree, a huge shoal of silver fish emerged and swam away from them toward the middle of the pool. A white streak flashed down from their right. The streak hit the water and from the splash a fish-eagle rose with a struggling fish in its talons. It flapped away to the trees out of sight.

The afternoon passed quickly. There was never a dull moment looking down into those crystal-clear depths. They could have happily stayed till the sun went down, but when they heard their father call, they climbed down and started for home.

After a few paces, they stopped to look back fondly across the pool. There were birds and pteros circling overhead watching for the right opportunity to snatch an unsuspecting fish. Suddenly they saw something they had never seen before. A brilliant white streak flashed above the pool and disappeared. A moment later, they heard a deafening crack and a roar from above their heads. They were looking at each other in amazement when the boom of a huge explosion thirty miles away shocked them into action. They turned and set off for home moving as quickly as they dared. Before they had got very far, the forest began to shake and the roots beneath their feet began to move rapidly upward. A frightening creaking and groaning filled the forest. Panic-stricken animals appeared from nowhere and began to rush about in confusion. Here and there tiny gaps opened between the twisted roots and jets of water squirted up. After the tsunami had passed under them, the mat of roots settled back again. Leanie lost her balance and stumbled. Her left foot slipped from the root she was standing on and came up hard against a gap. Before she could regain her balance, the roots closed up around her foot. She screamed in agony. Bedelia shouted for her father, who came running to help. After a few seconds of trying to pull his daughter's foot free, he ran back home for his axe.

The rocky chunk of meteorite, a hundred yards long and forty wide had vaporised many tons of water when it ripped through the floating forest and smashed into the ocean beneath. The superheated steam blasted a huge section of their island into the air. As Jethro chopped frantically to free his daughter's foot, the forest roared with the sound of shattered remains of roots, trunks, branches, animals, and fish smashing down through the leaves.

Jethro freed Leanie from the roots and lifted her into his arms. Her foot was crushed and bleeding. He carried her gently home as big drops of water started to fall from the sky. He looked up in amazement. Such a thing had never happened before. He had an uneasy feeling about it, something was nagging at his memory. Leanie was sobbing in pain. Jethro turned his attention to comforting her.

❖ ❖ ❖

"Irab, I've just had a telemessage from the minister of information. He's panicking about two reports that have just come in. One's from Tarshish. Two independent observers reported a glowing streak very high above the Earth. It appears to have been a meteorite which grazed the atmosphere and passed on into space. The other is from a ship three days out from Antinopo heading for Zohan. It looks as if a major meteorite struck about fifty miles to the east of it. It landed in one of the islands of floating forest. There was an enormous explosion."

"Oh, sheol! Was the ship damaged?"

"No, they were very lucky. The tsunami wasn't big enough to swamp them, but it might have been if the forest hadn't acted as a damper. If it had landed in the open sea, we might have had a major disaster."

"Yes, I'm sure you're right. It could have been very serious."

"But look here, Irab, the minister's furious that there was no warning. How could it happen that you people didn't publish an alert? Surely you should have spotted something days ago."

"Well…er…none of our teams are studying meteorites…we haven't been looking for them."

"What! Isn't anybody here keeping their eyes open for something important or dangerous these days?"

"There's been a lot of reorganisation in the department since Professor Zalomo's death. We really haven't got back to normal yet."

"Well you'd better get someone onto it right away. The minister's certain to ask if there are anymore meteorites approaching and if I can't give him the picture, somebody's head's going to roll, I can tell you!"

Professor Jonadab, dean of the faculty of sciences, strode off down the corridor with a stern expression on his face. For many years he had had a very good relationship with Prof Zalomo, and it had always been a pleasure dealing with the astronomy department. But this Irab fellow who'd been given charge of the observatory since Zalomo's unfortunate demise, that was another matter. Jonadab's dealings with him so far led him to believe Irab was slack and conceited. Hardly the man to maintain the prestige of Salem University's famous astronomy department. Everything was going to pot.

Jonadab crossed the quadrangle, entered the physics building, and climbed the stairs to the faculty offices hoping against hope there would be no urgent message from the minister of information waiting for him.

33 Nemesis

Caro was gazing glassy-eyed at the sled in front of him. He'd hardly slept the previous night. He'd been barely able to walk to the sled this morning. Uzza had made some snide remarks that removed the last shadow of doubt—he knew all right. He'd definitely be reported this evening. What was he going to do? They'd probably pay him off there and then and leave him to make his own way home. The lousy swine!

Caro's eyes strayed over the lush farming land beside the way. Fields of tall grain waved gently in the soft breeze. Rows of vegetables were impossibly green in the bright sunlight. Orchards were teeming with apples, plums, and peaches. Avenues of trees lined the tracks to cosy farmhouses. Then his thoughts started wandering, jumping from one thing to another. He thought fondly of his wife. They'd been together for almost eighty years. What a pity he'd beaten her so often. Such a pity he hadn't told her he loved her for decades. He suddenly wanted to tell her how much he appreciated her, and say he was sorry for the way he'd treated her. He would—just as soon as he got home. He thought of Esdras again. He'd always carped at Esdras about his drinking—but at least he'd died an honourable death, fighting bandits, not rotting away from inside, suffering the agonies of RAK. He thought of the strange streak in the sky he'd seen yesterday. He looked up to see if there might be another. He scanned the unbroken blue above him for a few seconds and spotted a bright white dot slightly in front of the sled, well over to the East. Looks as bright as Venus—but you only see Venus after dark! Funny! It's getting bigger. Cor blimey! It's nearly as big as the moon!

For one minute and seven seconds Caro stood gaping at the rapidly expanding ball of light. By the end of that time, every guard, passenger, and sled-man in the convoy had been frozen, petrified, with their eyes riveted to it for what seemed to each one like a lifetime.

A sled just behind Caro's had drifted across the way and spun off into a corn field. No one seemed to notice. All attention was riveted on the approaching bright ball, so big it covered more of the sky than one could focus on at once. Caro could make out pits and craters on the metallic surface. Another sled began to spin. Mesmerised by the terrifying sight, the sled-man's hands remained unmoving on the controls as his neck swivelled to keep the body in view. The sled smashed into a tree. Sleds throughout the convoy drifted across the way. Nothing seemed important anymore except the heart-stopping nightmare racing toward them. One sled after another crashed into each other as distracted sled-men's concentration became completely fixed on the rapidly approaching mass.

Caro hardly even noticed the stab of pain in his groin which struck just before the enormous body began to glow. A blast of wind hit the convoy before the white-hot mountain of pitted metal smashed into the ground a few miles to the left of the sledway. The forest, the sleds, the sledway, the sky, and everything else vanished.

On impact, the massive body disappeared in a blinding flash, brighter than a thousand suns, as its entire five-and-a-half-million-million tons of metal evaporated. Fifty million-million tons of the earth's crust evaporated with it. The shock wave radiating from the impact crater flattened every tree and building within six hundred miles and killed every living creature for another three hundred beyond that. A thousand-million-million tons of the atmosphere were blasted out into space, never to return. The heat radiating from the explosion cremated the bodies killed by the shock wave and ignited shattered forests for a thousand miles. Debris hurled into the air from the four-hundred-mile-diameter crater rained down for thousands of miles. Scorching whirlwinds with temperatures of hundreds of degrees and moving at hundreds of miles per hour sped away from the crater, causing vast devastation. Earthquakes of stupendous power raised tsunamis up to three miles high, which raced across the ocean at almost the speed of sound.

But perhaps the most spectacular consequence of the arrival of this six-mile-diameter meteorite was the breaking open of a crack through ten miles of basalt. A crack that spread rapidly, zigzagging north and south at four-thousand-five-hundred miles per hour until it encircled the globe.

❖ ❖ ❖

If Alzan's sled had been heavily laden, the driver would have needed to turn up the current slightly, since they were climbing a gentle slope. A pedestrian might not have noticed, since the slope was very gentle and very even.

It was unusual to see a solitary sled in these dangerous days but at the last toll station all the other sleds in the convoy, being heavily laden, had needed to recharge their batteries. Alzan was impatient to be on his way and with only ten miles to go and four well-armed company guards onboard, he felt justified in pressing on without the convoy.

He was tingling with excitement. Only three more miles. He felt the little package in his pocket and drifted into reverie again.

There had really been no rush to repossess the equipment. Business was no longer booming. Every year the orders were fewer. Every year there was a little less work for the equipment still in the yard. All because of those floating forests, he thought bitterly. It would be so easy for the government to put in a programme to clear the seaways. The shipbuilders had put so much effort into devising a perfectly workable plan. But these days nothing got done without bribes, and to get the sea-lane clearing project under way would mean paying millions to each of half a dozen ministers of state. Shipbuilders were no longer in the strongest of positions to pay such bribes. They were having to tighten their belts. The sled manufacturers could afford to out-bribe those same ministers to block the scheme. The tougher things got for shipping, the better for sled manufacturers. Soon just about everything would have to go by sled. Yes, it's the sled manufacturers who are expanding production lines and coining in the profits. They're the ones who can buy the officials these days.

He thought of the meeting he had just chaired. It would take time to get their plans into operation. Even at full speed, drilling would take a couple of years. And you never know what unforseen problems might delay things. Just a few setbacks and the company could be bankrupt before they broke through.

But then he remembered the present in his pocket, a magnificent necklace with matching earrings. White gold, inset with diamonds, sapphires, rubies, and emeralds. So tastefully done. Such skilful craftsmanship. So stunningly beautiful. If a shipbuilder can't outbid a sled manufacturer for a statesman's bribe these days, he can at least still afford a gift fit for a queen. A smile came to his lips. In his imagination he could see himself settling that lovely necklace around her neck, he could see her look of appreciation, he could see her in his arms. He could see…but he suddenly awoke from his daydream.

There, not half a mile away, was an enormous ship, black and shining under a fresh coat of pitch. But what a strange craft, a huge barge. No drive plates, no cargo derricks, nothing that one would expect on a normal ship. This must be the vessel that his equipment had been used to make. But what madness to build it here! How on earth could this huge boat be moved to a port?

Then he noticed strange things going on. A fellow waving a flaming torch was addressing an enormous crowd. Next to the ship a huge pile of dry brushwood had been heaped and the torch-wielder made a great show of bringing his torch toward the tinder. The crowd was loving it, roaring with delight, clapping, cheering, and waving.

The tinder must have been very dry. Within a few seconds of the torch being thrust into the wood, there were flames taller than a man. The torch-bearer hurried away from the blaze and turned to watch as the flames spread rapidly toward the boat. The cheering of the crowd died away as the blaze became a fearful roaring inferno. They looked on in awe. Those in the front of the crowd pressed back from the searing heat.

Alzan screamed at the sled-man to put on more speed. Anger and fear raged within him. What if Malala was in the boat? What if she was not, but that maniacal crowd intended to turn their attention to her after the boat had been incinerated? What if she had got away before the mob arrived? How would he find her? He opened his mouth again to shout for more speed.

His words were drowned by a deafening *thwack!* which swept from north to south on their left. Looking toward the sound, he saw, far to the north, jets of water bursting from the ground in rapid succession. Incredibly powerful jets shooting water so high that it disappeared into the blue haze of the sky above him. The advancing line came within a mile and raced on rapidly to the south. He turned to follow the amazing spectacle and saw another line approaching from the southern horizon, racing straight toward him. Alzan shouted to the sled-man to get out of the way, but the new line of fountains was approaching so fast that even if the sled-man could have heard he would not have been able to take evasive action. A jet erupted directly below the sled and punched it toward the sky. Alzan was thrown to the floor next to the side-rail. He saw a crack in the ground below the sled breaking open at an astounding speed. From the crack, jets of water shot up. The crack, with its roaring jets, was racing toward the other line of fountains. The new line ran into the first with a deafening impact which hurled water at enormous speed in all directions. A water-spout smashed into the sled, throwing Alzan clear. He hurtled toward the ground screaming.

34 Upward in the Forest

"I wonder if Baba and Karo would know how to treat this." Jethro was binding a new poultice of leaves onto Leanie's foot. "If this goes septic, she won't survive."

"And we won't survive if we try wandering off to see those miserable old fogies with the animals all stirred up like this."

As if to underline Nina's words, the sound of breaking branches came toward them, rapidly getting louder. A few moments later, they could see huge shapes approaching beyond the screen of creepers and low branches around their den. Two young brontos had left the well-beaten track and forced their way between the trees. Their heads, high in the foliage, could not be seen, but their massive bodies and powerful legs were a terrifying sight. They pushed the trees aside, trunks bending, branches breaking. They came within a few yards and crashed past, snorting and bellowing, and disappeared into the forest.

"Jethro! That was close! What are we going to do? I'm scared stiff! The animals are out of their minds."

"They've been thrown out by that upheaval. It's not surprising. It sure scared me."

"What if it happens again? It might be Jed that gets hurt next time."

"We'd better make sure the kids stay close. And another thing—we'll be safer in the hammocks. The way the roots moved, it's not surprising Leanie's foot got trapped. And we'd better rehang them. I saw Jed's and yours got pulled tight when everything bucked upward. We ought to change things around so each is strung from only one tree like mine and the girls'."

"And we'd better make them a whole lot stronger, too. We should cut some more creepers and double everything up."

"We can get some extra for straps to tie ourselves in with."

"Bedelia, look after Jed while we go and cut some more creepers. Don't let him wander off to play. You've seen how wild the animals are today—they might crush him before he could run away."

Leanie was soon bound loosely but securely in her new hammock, moaning faintly. They taught Jed how to tie himself in. Bedelia, being older, wanted to do her own tying in her own way.

They talked about Lano. Whether he and Asa might have been hurt, and if they were taking adequate precautions against a repeat performance. Since they lived two days' journey away, not far from Asa's parents, they would just have to try and stop worrying about them and go to see them when things were back to normal again. Jethro was particularly concerned about Asa, since she was nearing the time to deliver his first grandchild.

The night passed uneventfully, and Leanie even managed to fall asleep. In the morning, they discovered that many of the animals in the neighbourhood were still agitated. The family cautiously collected some food for breakfast and remained close to home.

Bedelia was again given the job of making sure that little Jed did not run off to play. She was beginning to tire of her chore when she heard her stepmother scream. Looking around, alarmed, Bedelia saw a strange sight. Instead of the trees on the other side of their large pool being outlined against the blue sky, they were now framed by a rapidly rising green background. A background which she recognised as being made up of trees—but very small and far away. She stood staring in unbelief at the astounding sight of the distant forest rising higher and higher into the air.

Nina came running, followed closely by Jethro. Bedelia snapped out of her stupor and jumped for her hammock.

Jethro picked up his son and strapped him in. Nina swung herself into her hammock and fumbled frantically with her straps. She glanced up toward the pool and screamed in terror. Jethro made for his own hammock, but before he could tie his straps, the forest around them burst into deafening creaks and howls. Water shot up from the pool. A terrifying roar pounded their eardrums. The world leapt into action, rocketing toward the sky.

35 Stadium

When Tando returned to the lounge of the Pink Lady, he expected to find his cronies waiting for him. But his session in the Battery had taken longer than he thought—much longer. Tando loved his work in the Battery and time just slipped by. It was such a pleasure to break the girls the boss brought in. This one had been some kind of a religious nut, with old-fashioned ideas about morals, right and wrong, and other such nonsense. Well, she shouldn't give the boss anymore trouble. He had a self-satisfied grin on his face as he entered the plush, sensuously decorated, softly lit room and looked around for his buddies.

The lounge was empty.

"Hello! Where's everybody gone?" he called. There was no answer.

Then he looked at the clock and cursed his over-indulgence. "Half-past already! I'll have to run."

At the door, he scanned the street nervously. His cronies had taken the sled. He didn't like the prospect of walking even one block alone, and the stadium was four blocks away. But he was in luck—the muggers had all left for the stadium, too. Leaflets distributed throughout the city had convinced just about everyone that today's event was not to be missed. Not that many people ever did miss a session at the stadium.

He joined the crush of latecomers at the long bank of turnstiles. Like many thousands before him, he cursed the cashier. Double the usual entrance fee. It said nothing about that on the leaflets. But for the largest trico and tyrano ever seen at any stadium within a thousand miles, almost everybody paid up despite their grumbles. The minimum stake was also doubled. Since you could not get in without a betting slip as well as an entrance ticket, and since the nonrefundable admission was paid before reaching the betting booths, Tando was really feeling swindled by the time he reached the stairs for the upper gallery. How could he choose between the trico at five to four on and the tyrano at seven to five on when he had not even seen either? He should have got there earlier. But then, he thought to himself with a grin, he wouldn't have missed his fun in the Battery, even for a good look at them in their cages. He liked tricos, so that was where he put his money.

Like all the other seating, the upper gallery was full, but Tando thought that this would be the most likely place to find somewhere to squeeze into. The stadium was always packed. Today it was bulging. He joined hundreds of others sitting illegally on the steps between the rows of seats. He noticed a group of five or six giants in the seats just ahead. He stayed clear of giants as much as possible; you could never tell when they might lose their temper and vent their anger on anyone who happened to be in their way. Still, he had never had any trouble at the stadium. Huge crowds stood around the arena. The air resounded with bawdy songs and puerile chants. Tando, like everyone else, had already forgotten the hole in his pocket and was loving every minute.

Two huge cages were brought in on oversize cargo sleds. The crowd roared.

The trico, furious and frightened, rammed the bars of his cage again and again. The crowd roared.

The tyrano, ravenous after five days without food, bellowed. The crowd roared.

The trico's cage opened first. Electric prodders shocked the beast to a hasty exit. It stood staring at the strange sight as the sled glided away with its cage. It turned around searching for a way of escape. Its back was turned when the tyrano was prodded from his cage fifty yards away. The tyrano saw the trico immediately. He looked around for an easier meal.

When the trico saw the tyrano it stopped turning and eyed it warily. It was a big one. It would need watching. But at the moment it was stomping away, toward the crowd of people.

Tando howled happily. The tyrano was trying to catch a spectator! He'd never seen that before. This one was so big it could nearly reach to the level of the lowest seats in the bottom gallery! Watching the terrified spectators cringing back from those enormous jaws less than a yard away was nearly as good as watching a fight! Tando whooped with excitement.

It took twenty minutes before the tyrano gave up trying to reach the crowd. Bellowing angrily, he now looked again at the trico. Five days without food can make a big difference to a tyrano's estimation of what it can tackle. He started to move toward it. The trico stamped its front foot several times. It lowered its head pointing its three long, strong, sharp horns menacingly straight toward the tyrano. The crowd roared.

The tyrano had apparently dealt with tricos before. It knew better than to rush onto the three deadly horns. Tando found himself yelling at the trico, "Keep facing him! Turn, you stupid lump! Yeah, that's the stuff. Stick him in the belly!"

But the trico missed. The tyrano, after running round to the left, had feinted and dodged back to the right. He reached round the trico's great, flared, armoured collar and snapped at the unarmoured flank. But he had to reach so far that he was off balance, and before he could tear off a lump of flesh, the trico twisted his huge bulk far enough to jab his front horn into the tyrano's forearm. The tyrano staggered back without letting go. The trico bellowed in pain as flesh tore way. He rushed forward while the tyrano was regaining his balance and landed a vicious stab just below the ribs. The tyrano was driven to fury by the pain of his wounds. He jumped to his right and snapped at the bare patch on the trico's flank. But the armoured collar kept him at bay and his teeth only just raked the raw wound before he had to stagger back to avoid another thrust.

The angry, bleeding, hurting animals were circling each other when the first shock shook the stadium.

The animals did not appear to pay much attention.

The spectators did.

The stadium, built to the minimum standard the contractors

could get away with, and which was now seriously overloaded, swayed alarmingly. At the second, stronger quake, the structure collapsed. Spectators tumbled screaming into the arena with broken beams crashing down around them.

The tyrano backed away from the trico and ran toward an easy meal. He snapped up a terrified, screaming young woman. The next mouthful was a man pinned down by a fallen beam and unable to move. After that, with the edge taken off his hunger, he became more leisurely, biting off a head here, an arm there.

The trico, meanwhile, seemed bent on venting his anger and frustration. He surged toward the struggling mass of humanity, trampling them underfoot and butting them with his horns.

Tando was terrified. His section of the stadium was still standing. It was joined to the main staircase on the West side. The building inspector, who had a grudge against the contractor for shortchanging him on a previous contract, had demanded an exorbitant bribe for that staircase. It had been cheaper for the contractor to build it to the specifications. It withstood the earthquake. A section of stands attached to it were swaying, but still standing.

Tando could see the havoc the animals were causing. He recognised Pagaled, his fixer, fleeing the tyrano. His leg was broken, he stood no chance. His head and upper torso disappeared into the huge jaws. The lower torso fell to the ground gushing blood. Tando went cold, he would need another fix within two hours. Where would he get his dope now with Pagaled gone?

People scrambled past Tando making for the staircase, but he stood transfixed. The trico was stamping toward a young woman screaming in terror. Her hip had been smashed by a collapsing column which knocked her into the arena. Now she was trying to drag herself along clutching tufts of grass with her slender fingers.

Tando had seen her often. Such a beautiful girl. He had often dreamed of what he could do to her in the Battery, but she was always with tough gangsters, so if his boss ever got hold of her, she probably wouldn't need much softening up. His heart went out to her as the trico angrily stamped her to a bleeding pulp.

A huge hand grabbed Tando's shoulder. The first of the giants had reached the aisle in his flight toward the stairway. The others were close behind. Tando blocked their way. The next instant he was hurled into the seats beside the aisle. As he tried to regain his feet, a searing pain shot though his right leg. It was broken. He slumped into a seat.

The blast of a very distant but enormously powerful impact shook the stadium. Half of the remaining structure collapsed. Tando was thrown against the back of his seat. Pain stabbed his broken leg again, he clutched it, unable to move. For several minutes, his eyes took in the catastrophe around him—the shattered stadium with its hordes of injured, those still able to move viciously fighting their way to the exits, and the two huge animals, dripping with blood, killing indiscriminately, trying to escape.

A wind sprang up suddenly and quickly strengthened to a howling gale.

Tando's attention jumped to the skyline.

It was moving.

Upward.

A distant roar could be heard above the screams of the crowd and the howling wind. Tando stared in disbelief at the great black mass rising into the sky. When the horizon disappeared underneath it, he realised with a start that he was looking at a wall of water. A mountain of water more than a mile high. Water completely filled his field of vision. It raced toward him at hundreds of miles an hour. Water seething and boiling and roaring so loudly that every person in the stadium was frozen motionless staring at it.

36 Danudin

Danudin was not paying much attention to his father's cattle. They were grazing on the tall grass at the foot of the only rock outcrop for many miles around. The lush pasture that covered the rolling hills stretched as far as the eye could see, but Danny liked to bring the cattle to this particular spot because there was a cave in the outcrop. There was something thrilling and romantic about a cave. Besides, he had discovered a wonderful hiding place inside it. If the former owners of his father's cattle were to come here looking for them, they would never find him there. If it should happen that the former owners were from one of the raids where his dad and his elder brothers had needed to kill a few people, it might be a very good thing to be in a place where vengeance-seekers would not find him. But Danny was not thinking about his cave at the moment. He was watching mammoths grazing less than three hundred yards away.

Danudin was fifteen years old, small, with olive skin and jet black hair. The second to youngest in a family of forty-eight, he was proud of his responsibility for the cattle. He was proud of the fact that he had already been allowed to take part in three robberies. He was also proud of his family's rural existence. Many country families had moved to the towns and cities in search of more excitement and easier livelihood. But his family had remained. He loved his father with devoted passion. His dad was the best cattle thief in the world. For more than a hundred years, he had made a luxurious living by stealing cattle and he had not once been caught. If his dad said the country was best, then only a fool could want to live in one of those thug-infested cities. Mind you, he had heard the older boys talking about thrilling things that went on in the great stadiums. Sometimes he thought he might get to a city just to visit the stadium—but he would only go for a day and come straight back. After all, there were no cattle in the city, and his ambition was to be as great a cattle thief as his father.

His dark eyes wandered over the landscape—lush rolling grassland with clumps of trees scattered here and there. He cast a quick glance at the cattle and returned to his mammoth watching. Amazing how quickly they were cropping the huge patch of bluebells which had looked so beautiful just yesterday. Amazing how their trunks could reach out to a clump of grass or flowers, pluck it, and swing it up to their mouths in one smooth, swift movement. Of course, there were plenty of lesser animals grazing near the mammoths, but Danny had no eyes for them. Those amazing tusks! And each one's so different. He looked at a really big fellow with one tusk so curved it almost completed a full circle, while the other was not very curved at all, and its curvature was outwards, nearly perpendicular to his head.

Danudin was wondering how he could kill it and get its tusks as trophies when he noticed the mammoths raise their heads and face toward the west. They stood with ears straight out from their heads, trunks raised, sniffing the air. Danudin followed their gaze. The sky in the west looked strange. He had never seen the sky anything but blue from horizon to horizon, but an unusual blackness was rising rapidly. A shadow raced over the countryside. The sun faded from view. Suddenly Danny was frightened. He edged toward the mouth of his cave.

The ground beneath his feet started to shake.

Then he heard a faint noise far to the west. The mammoths were still facing that way, ears outstretched, trunks raised. Far in the distance the sky was falling. It was pouring down like water. But it was not splashing up after it landed. The falling sky was coming closer. It came very quickly—far more quickly than Danudin could have ever imagined possible. The first mammoths to be struck, more than a mile away, disappeared under a mass of black sky which solidified on impact.

Danny ran for the rock face and dashed in. A deafening thump echoed throughout the cave.

The ground shook.

He was in total darkness.

A thunderous pounding faded into the distance. Then all was quiet. Deathly quiet. Danny trembled.

He groped toward the mouth of the cave. As he neared it he felt strangely chilly. When he reached the entrance he bumped into something hard as rock and very cold.

There was no way out; the entrance was completely blocked. He began to shiver. He moved away from the entrance to find a warmer place but, within a few minutes, the cold had seeped into every corner of the cave. Shivering. Very frightened. He began to cry.

He was still sobbing through his chattering teeth when the earthquake struck.

The deafening crack of rocks tearing apart brought his hands to his ears just in time to save his right hand from being crushed by the corner of a block that fell from the roof. It grazed his shoulder and he felt a trickle of blood wending its warm way down his cold skin. Other rocks fell around him, but only two rather small ones rolled onto him, one pinning his left ankle to the floor, the other holding his right thigh. Light seeped into the cave, and Danudin could make out the chaos around him. It took a few minutes and a lot of effort to free his legs, then he crawled over shattered boulders toward the light.

A narrow crack had split the south wall of the cave. Danny squeezed himself past jagged, broken rock, desperate to get out. Twice he got stuck so tight that he had to tear his flesh to get free. He paid no attention to the pain. He was thinking only of getting out of that terrifying cave.

Suddenly he found himself at the end of the split in the rock and at the start of a crevasse with walls of dirty brown ice on either side and an ugly grey sky overhead. In spite of his exertions he was shivering. His thin clothing was reduced to tattered, blood-stained rags. He squeezed between the ice walls, moving as quickly as he could, wanting to leave the cave far behind. He suddenly stopped. To his right was one of his father's cattle. Its eyes were open. Its mouth was open. Its nose was only a few inches away from his hand. Its body disappeared into dirty ice. Danny reached to touch it, but his hand came up against the wall of ice. The realization that the cow was dead hit him like a hammer blow. It was frozen solid. He hurried past it, lost and dazed.

On his left, a crack rose to the top of the ice wall. Danny stood for a few seconds looking at the crack. He decided he could climb it. In a few minutes, his hands were numb. His feet hurt from the cold and the pressure of ice squeezing them at every step. He was close to exhaustion when he reached the top and struggled out onto the slippery surface of ice. A freezing wind lashed him so powerfully he could not stand up. He clawed his way to the top of a mound and lay there clutching at the ice with his broken fingernails.

He looked around dumbstruck. He could see nothing but an undulating sea of dirty ice. The scenery he knew so well had disappeared. Not a plant or an animal. Just ice. There was no sun, no blue sky, only a grey mass of cloud. He was completely alone in this frozen desolation.

Then everything started to tremble. He looked around in bewilderment. In the distance, he made out a purple-green mass speeding toward him. The dull rumble of it rose to a roar as it approached at astonishing speed. Its top was hidden by the clouds; its bottom was ripping up huge chunks of the frozen landscape. The whole monstrous wall of water, from horizon to horizon, was roiling and foaming, hissing and roaring.

37 Tob

When Tob thrust his flaming torch into the pile of brushwood, he felt a thrill of triumph as the crowd cheered and applauded. He turned toward them, a broad smile on his face, the late-afternoon sun reflecting off his smooth, freshly shaved and oiled head. He held up his hands for silence and yelled, "So much for us all being washed away into the flames of hell and old preacher-boy being saved!"

The crowd roared with laughter and began clapping and cheering again.

Tob's back began to feel uncomfortably hot. He turned to see flames already ten feet high crackling and leaping among the brushwood. He moved away toward the crowd. He began to feel a bit uneasy. It was a big crowd. The heat of the fire was becoming unbearable. He pressed into the mass of people hoping those further back in the mob would give way.

A hush fell on the crowd. The flames were getting very close to the boat. The fire was roaring. The heat began to scorch Tob's face. He began to think of how it would feel for the preacher and his family in a few minutes when the whole thing became an inferno. They couldn't escape now if they'd wanted to. There was only one doorway, and the wood had been piled up against it. If anyone wanted to escape, they would have to somehow push tons of brushwood away. And it was already burning so fiercely they would be roasted the moment the door opened anyway.

His thoughts were blasted out of his mind by a deafening, hissing *thwack.* His hands shot to his ears and he turned toward the din.

Rooted to the spot, he gaped at the astonishing sight of gigantic fountains springing up one after another. In moments, Salem was hidden by jets rapidly spreading toward each other to form a continuous curtain. They soon widened into a solid wall of water jetting upward with incredible force and a deafening roar.

Tob had forgotten the fire. Not only was he riveted by the amazing sight, he was struggling to keep his balance as the earth shook. He jumped when flaming twigs thrown up by an explosion in the conflagration behind him showered down, burning his shaved pate and bare neck.

Suddenly the fire didn't seem like such a good idea.

Suddenly many things didn't seem like such a good idea anymore.

He looked toward the fire. Huge flames were licking the side of the ship when the first drops of water struck him. He turned his face upward to see water cascading down from the sky. It poured into his open mouth bubbling and fizzing like soda water. He screwed up his face in reaction to the saltiness—so strong it made him feel sick. He spat it out, but the taste lingered. His mouth was lined with grit and it grated between his teeth.

The fire threw up more showers of burning twigs as water

turned explosively to steam on impact. People all around him screamed as hair and clothing burned for a few seconds before falling water put out the sparks.

The deluge rapidly strengthened. There were no longer just individual drops of water pouring from the sky, but great sheets which battered down almost making him lose his balance. A hissing cloud of steam bellowed from the blackened mass of branches from which the last flames had already disappeared.

Tob staggered round the steaming pile toward the vessel looking for shelter. Many of his mob were already there, beating on the side and shouting entreaties which could not be heard above the thunderous pounding of the water. Tob was soon also hammering and pleading to be let in. Water was pouring down the sides of the ship. The ground under foot was turning to a quagmire—Tob's ankles were soon covered. The side of the boat became a waterfall, useless for shelter. He joined the mob heading for the trees. The muddy, salty water was now knee deep and he climbed into a tree to get out of it. He had to hold tight to prevent himself being knocked off by the force of the water pouring down through the branches.

He had a ghastly feeling in his gut. A hard knot of fear. Certain he was going to die, he was suddenly full of regrets. If only he'd done things differently. With a pang of foreboding, he thought of that fellow he'd worked over right in the middle of town—in broad daylight. Funny he should think of that one, in particular. After all, he'd killed plenty of others. He remembered the way he'd turned his poster toward the women going into the clinic.

It had been so easy.

He'd been on the sidewalk outside the newly opened abortion clinic. He'd been alone. He was holding that poster. After he and Fareno had sunk their knives into the guy, the whole group had simply moved off down the street leaving the body oozing blood onto his crumpled poster.

Tob was almost in tears, cursing himself for a fool. After all, hadn't everyone known a week ago they were in big trouble? Everybody had realised when the animals started to arrive, though they all made a joke of it. Lots of the kids who had been spying on the preacher instead of going to school had come into town telling about the animals, and most of the townspeople had sneaked off to look, just as he had. It was really weird to see all those animals coming out of the forest like a well-trained circus act. To see tricos—admittedly not the thousand-year-old giants, maybe only twenty years old, but big enough, with horns that could gore a man to pulp—just calmly walking in through the door in the side of that huge boat. It was awesome. And tyranos—sure, only ten-year-old light-weights, but with jaws that could snap off your head in a twinkling. What would he have done if a pair of those had calmly walked into his place? And Lambos! Just think of it, two pairs of them in that wooden vessel, and the preacher's family had been taking great loads of hay in there for weeks. They could set the whole thing alight with one snort. They had just calmly followed the mammoths up the gangway. And what about those lions and cheetahs going in with horses, sheep, and gazelles? Unreal! Not a hint of aggression, not a trace of fear. He'd been scared, just like everybody else watching, but he'd put on a mask of scornful bravado. Now he was thinking what a great fool he'd been not to have gone to ask if he could get onboard, too.

He was roused from his self-pity by the rising water tugging at his legs. He must get to a higher branch. He let go his grip with one hand to reach up just as the whole forest began to shake. The earthquake loosened the roots of the trees. A wave rushed through the forest toppling trees, including his own, into the raging water. He lost his grip and slid screaming into the swirling current. The neck of his robe snagged on a broken branch before he could surface. He struggled vainly trying to free himself, his lungs filling with muddy, salty water. A few minutes later, the current tore his body free. It rose to the surface and joined those of several of his former gang members drifting above the old mag-sledway.

38 Thugs' End

As the stream of people approached the boat carrying their dry branches, Fareno watched Tob directing them toward the dumping site. You had to hand it to Tob. Only a few hundred leaflets, and look at the response. Who would have thought it these days? Just about the only notices that seemed to get any reaction were for the stadium. Still, his leaflet had made it sound as if the fire would be almost as much of a spectacle as a capital punishment fight. And what a success they were! Since the stadium owners had persuaded the judges to sentence undesirables to gang battles, they had become one of the most popular events of all.

Fareno had broken up with Tob, left the Diamonds, and gone into a little business of his own. But they were on speaking terms again and he had offered to help as soon as he heard about the bonfire plan. Each time the pile was big enough, he went into action with his mobile derrick. The grab crunched into the pile, lifted it up, and swung it over to the heap rapidly growing against the boat's main side-hatch. At this rate, it would be up to the deck in about two hours. Little of the hatch could still be seen.

The stream of people stretched off toward the city.

Those who had already left their contribution were forming a huge crowd. The preacher must have made just about everyone in Salem as angry as he was. "Repent!" the preacher said. The self-righteous bigot! Who does he think he is? Telling other people how to live. Fareno was furious. I don't answer to anyone. It's my life. I've got my rights. I can do with it what I want. Who does that old crank think he is? Am I a powdered baby? Rage rose within him as he set the grab into motion again and added another ton of branches to the pile.

❖ ❖ ❖

The sun began to slope down the sky to the west. The last of the wood had been put into place twenty minutes ago. The pile was spilling onto the deck. They had removed the derrick safely out of harm's way, two hundred yards from the pitch-covered boat.

Fareno watched Tob with growing admiration. He really was good at rabble-rousing. Maybe he should get back in with him. Tob looked good wielding that flaming torch—it somehow went so well with that shaved head and bushy beard. Such style as he stuck the torch into the pile. So macho. So casual. Stepping away from the flames with a joke that made those close enough to hear burst out laughing again.

From his vantage point on the little hill close to the boat he noticed a sled approaching. Strange! You don't see lone sleds these days. Word must have spread to other towns. Maybe this is a bunch who heard about the shindig and just couldn't bear to miss it in spite of the danger of bandits. Or maybe it was bandits. Wouldn't be surprising. The preacher's message had spread far and wide. Must be people all over the world who hate his guts.

Tob should have thought about sending leaflets to other towns. But the crowd was already big enough to be scary. You never knew what a mob this size might do. At least they're not going to be disappointed. Just look how those flames are spreading! When those lions and brontos and the rest smell the smoke, they'll go wild. Yeah, they'll be creating pandemonium in there. In minutes, old preacher boy and his wretched sons will be crushed to pulp. Soon, their bodies and his whole menagerie will be well-done barbecue.

The mob around him pressed forward to get a better view. Fareno jabbed his elbow into someone crowding too close behind him.

"Watch it you worthless scum!" came a vicious voice behind him. "Keep your elbows to yourself."

Fareno turned to see two smouldering eyes, one dark brown, one light, both equally full of hatred, glaring at him.

"And who d'you think you're calling scum?" Fareno reached for his knife.

Rendo was too quick for him. Before Fareno's blade came clear of its sheath, Rendo's dagger struck upward from below his ribs into his heart.

❖ ❖ ❖

Rendo barely had time to feel the thrill of triumph before his thoughts were wiped out by a deafening *thwack*. He spun around to look in the direction of the noise. At the same moment, a hulking brute of a man backed into him and trod on his foot. As he staggered back, Rendo tripped over Fareno's body and fell to the ground, cursing. A moment later, the frantic crowd trampled him in their stampede toward the boat.

Rendo regained consciousness with water pouring down onto his face. He struggled to a sitting position on the wet grass. He hurt all over. Looking around in bewilderment, he found himself almost alone on a little hill. Three children were not far away.

One was not moving—probably dead—the other two, covered in blood, moaned weakly. He could just see the preacher's boat through the pouring rain. Oh yes, the bonfire...the thought gradually seeped back into his throbbing head. He drew in a deep breath and sucked gritty, salty, fizzy water into his mouth. He spat it out. Yuck! Must get out of this rain. Rain! A feeling of dread ripped through him. Rain! The preacher had talked about rain. Nobody had believed him. Water coming from the sky! Nonsense. But it's happening! He'd said everybody not on the boat would drown. What if he was right? And where were all the people?

He staggered toward the boat, struggling to keep his balance on the slippery downhill slope with sheets of water battering down on him and the ground trembling. As he drew nearer, he could make out crowds of people around the boat—banging with their fists and shouting things that could not be heard above the driving wind and rain. He stopped next to the pile of brushwood, much of it black as charcoal, cold and sodden.

Preacher had said that everyone not on the boat would drown. Better believe him this time. Must get onboard. Only one way. Got to climb up the wood pile.

It proved difficult. He cut himself on sharp, broken branches. Charred limbs broke without warning. His face and arms were soon ripped and scratched and bleeding. After a gruelling struggle, he reached the top of the pile, which no longer reached the deck.

He looked down at the crowd. They were leaving the boat and heading for the trees, sloshing through water up to their knees, slipping and sliding in the strengthening current. The water was rising. At this rate they'll all drown for sure. Got to get onto the deck before this pile of wood gets washed away! He began pulling out branches and heaping them against the side.

When the heap was big enough, he clambered over the edge and lay on the deck panting, digging his nails into the pitch to keep from being washed off.

A raised section in the middle of the deck had an overhang, shielding ventilation slits from the rain. He clawed his way toward it through a sheet of water. The slats were set close together, but the gaps were big enough to let his fingers curl around and get a grip. He screamed into the vent, begging to be let in. He knew he was wasting his time. He could scarcely hear his own voice above the pounding of the rain. He wrenched at the slats trying to break his way in, but they were too strong, and he only hurt his fingers on the hard edges of the wood.

He looked toward the trees. Hard to see much through the torrents of rain, now being driven almost horizontal by a rapidly strengthening wind. He could just make out people hanging onto branches, climbing higher as the water rose. Then the boat started to shudder violently. He tightened his grip on the vent. A twenty-foot-high wave raced across his view, ripping out the trees and sweeping away the struggling people clinging to them. The boat rocked to one side, rose a few inches from the ground and settled down again as the wave passed.

The scene before him had changed drastically. Only a few trees remained sticking up from a muddy, featureless plain—a plain he had always known as a forest. A few minutes later, debris-laden water surged back again and the forest he had known for so many years became a seething, muddy lake. The howling wind drove water under his sheltered overhang. He wanted to relieve his aching fingers by slackening his grip, but the wind threatened to tear him away. He closed his eyes, clenched his teeth and hung on. The light faded.

When daylight returned, there was no sign of the sun, just

dull greyness all around. Water still pounded down from the sky. Rendo's head throbbed from its constant drumming. He was tired. His hands felt like wood, frozen rigid by their constant grip on the vent. He was shivering. To his left was the roaring sheet of water spurting up to the sky. It was hard to see clearly through the rain, just an eerily changing pattern of light and shadow.

The day dragged on. His fingers were agony. He was hungry. And thirsty. He tried swallowing some of the rain. It almost made him sick. Why was he trying to stay alive? There was no chance of getting inside this boat. No chance of being able to hang on like this for even one more day. No fun to die of exposure or starvation. Why not just let go and drown? But he was afraid of drowning. Must be terrible to find your lungs full of water, must be a horrible way to go. Wouldn't it be better to cut his own throat and get it over with quickly? He always carried his knife. He'd killed plenty of people with it. They'd died quickly—quicker than drowning, surely. But then, he was afraid of dying—quickly or slowly. Better just hang on for as long as possible. Hey, but why hadn't he thought of that before? He had his knife. He could hack his way through the vents and make a hole big enough to get in.

The light was fading. He loosened the hold of his right hand. It was terribly painful to straighten his fingers. The wind snatched at him, but he managed to keep his grip with the left hand. His fingers were numb and he had to beat them on the deck before he could regain enough feeling to grip his knife and draw it from its sheath. He started hacking at the vent, but he had little strength in his benumbed grip and the knife almost slipped out of his hand.

The boat shuddered. It lifted a little and settled back onto the ground. He looked up. Blackness was rising from the horizon.

He glanced all around him. The blackness was coming from all directions. The light was becoming a rapidly diminishing circle directly overhead. The boat began to rise. A thunderous roaring drowned out the sound of the pounding rain and the booming fountain. From all sides, enormous waves raced toward the boat. He let go of his knife and grabbed the vent with both hands. He was thrown about as the vessel accelerated upward, pitching and rolling wildly. His stomach was being left behind. He felt sick but had nothing in his belly to vomit. He struggled to hang on with tired, numb hands. The boat rolled viciously. A wave washed over the deck, hissing and roaring. It smashed into him so hard it knocked the breath out of his lungs and his fingers gave way. He felt the skin rubbed off his knees and elbows as he was swept across the deck. His eyes were two different shades of terror. Then he spiralled dizzily downward in a whirling vortex of dirty, salty water.

39 Tsunami

Jethro was stunned.

After being pressed into his wildly swinging hammock as it rocketed toward the sky, he was nearly too seasick to hold on as his world hurtled downward again.

Now, after the jarring thud which ended the fall, the motionlessness seemed unearthly. The floating forest was no longer rocketing up or down. Neither was it rocking gently and almost imperceptibly as it usually did. It was dead still.

Jethro glanced around and was relieved to see that all his family were still there. They looked sick and frightened, but alive.

He looked toward the pool and was astounded to see the sea

bed. Fish flopped about on the mud between shallow pools. A huge tentacle twitched in the death throes of its invisible owner, crushed beneath the beached forest.

It took several seconds for the fact that the floating forest was no longer floating to penetrate.

Jethro climbed out of his hammock, stood unsteadily for a moment or two, felt a little better and headed for a tree. "I'm going to climb up and see if I can see anything."

"Do be careful. You're not looking too good."

"I'll be all right." He swung up into the branches and began to feel a bit more like his old self again.

"Nina, the island's broken! It must be a mile or two from here. There's a great break where I can see the sea bed. And there's something very strange about three or four miles further away. There's smoke and there's red stuff coming out of the ground. It must be very hot. It's glowing like hot iron and turning pools of water to steam. I think it's flowing this way. I can't see much in the opposite direction—the slope's the wrong way and every-thing's hidden by the trees."

"How quickly is the red-hot stuff moving our way?"

"Hard to tell, but I think we'd better get out of here as fast as we can. We'll head for Lano's. That's just about directly away from it."

He climbed down quickly and joined Nina in making up as many of their meagre possessions as possible into back-packs. In a few minutes, the little family was making its way cautiously eastwards, ever alert for dangerous animals. Jethro carried Leanie on his shoulders, Nina was holding Jed's hand. Bedelia was put-ting on a show of carrying her own back pack. For years Jethro had navigated by the pools of the forest. Now the pools looked strange and confusingly different, with dead fish, unusual creatures, shallow puddles, and rapidly drying mud. The pools were dangerous. Many animals were there to drink, and there was little water to satisfy their thirst. The puddles closest to the edge had already been drunk just about dry, and many animals seemed wary of stepping down onto the exposed sea-bed to reach those further away. Jethro and his family were very thirsty by the time he found a pool which he considered safe to approach. They drank greedily and Jethro caught fish for their supper in the same puddle.

A few miles further on, they came to a break in their island. They could see the remainder across a mile and a half of exposed sea bed. The sea bed was littered with fish and sea creatures they had never seen before. Giant squids and octopuses. Huge, sleek-bodied creatures with powerful flippers, long necks, and enormous heads full of long teeth. Some of the creatures, like massive turtles and whales, were still alive, but obviously dying. Pools dotted the exposed sea bed.

"It's too dangerous to try to cross to Lano's side. Just look at those crocs. We'll have to find a place to sleep. Its nearly sundown anyway. Nina, while you make a fire and cook the fish, we'll string the hammocks."

They walked back a little way into the forest and found a good place to spend the night. After their exertions, the family was so tired that soon after eating they turned in. The dense foliage of the trees hid the sky completely. The red glow from the direction they had come was barely visible. They fell asleep almost at once.

Before dawn, the sound of animals on the move wakened them. A faint red light filtered down through the leaves above them. It was too dark to risk moving. They recognised the sounds of brontos, parasos, tyranos, and many other creatures not very far away from them. They could sometimes make out their shapes gliding between the nearby trees in the dim red glow. All were moving eastward. They would soon reach the broken edge of the island. What would they do then? Move along the shore, or risk crossing to the other side?

As soon as there was enough light to see by, Jethro whispered to Nina that he was going to climb up to see what he could see. He moved slowly and carefully, not wanting to attract the attention of any of the animals. In a few minutes, he was at the top of the tallest tree he could find.

"Nina! That ridge of red-hot stuff! It's huge! It stretches as far as I can see and it's flowing this way. It's setting the forest on fire. Our home is gone. I think it will reach here in a couple of hours. We're going to have to cross to the other side!"

"But how can we move with all these animals around?" asked Nina.

"We just have to hope they're more interested in fleeing the fire than bothering about us. Come on, let's get ready. We have to go."

As they approached the shore, they saw many large creatures picking their way across the sea bed. Most of the smaller animals hung back, afraid to take the first step into the unknown.

"We can try walking in the tracks of one of the brontos," said Jethro. "Where a bronto can walk it's solid enough for us, and I don't think there will be any crocs, or anything else, where a bronto's just put his foot down."

"But how do we get to the bronto's tracks?" said Nina. "Look at those lions on the shore. They might eat us before we get to the sea bed."

"We've got to risk it," said Jethro, moving forward gingerly.

And then they felt the first blast of a hot wind in their faces.

"What's happening?" gasped Jethro. "That's from the opposite direction to the fire. There must be fire ahead as well."

The next blast was hotter and stronger.

"We've got to get out of this wind," shouted Nina. "We'll die if we don't. Come children, let's shelter in the trees."

They blundered back, gasping.

They reached a pool and staggered to a large puddle of muddy water. The wind was so hot that they had to submerge completely, and bring their heads up for air now and then. Jethro had just brought his head up for another gasp of air when he heard the deafening roar of the next wave. He turned to see a thundering wall of water towering three miles into the sky racing toward them.

40 Dream World

How long have we been here in the dark, my love? So many turbulent days and nights. But we're no longer tossing and rolling—let's take advantage of the stillness. Come with me to the light. Come!

The walls are thick, but when we touch them gently, see how soft they feel. Soft like a morning mist. Come glide through them with me to the light.

But how dim the light is, how grey and cold, how bleak this expanse of mud littered with pools—as far as the eye can see.

Our wooden home looks forlorn and forgotten, dumped on top of all these miles of sediment. It seems small and fragile as we soar toward the dark clouds. Who could blame them for weeping so bitterly at the sight of so much desolation?

But look over there, in the far distance. That green smudge against the brown. Let's take wing toward it and see what it can be.

Ah, now I understand. It's a floating forest.

But it's not floating. It's lying on the mud. How pitiful. The leaves are withered and wilted. From up here we can see many animals. They appear to be weak and sick. And over there I can see people. They also seem to be unwell. Do you think we could go and help them, my love?

What was that, my dearest?

Over there?

What can it be?

A wall of water!

Another huge wave. It's coming so quickly, we'd better go back. Come speed with me toward our home.

The wave is picking up the forest and flinging it toward the clouds.

Hurry, my love!

Hurry!

41 Beached

"I never felt so bad in all my life," a shadow of Lano's voice groaned.

Telina offered him a drink of rainwater. "Let's try and…" The roar of the next wave cut her off.

The next one struck within minutes of their being dumped on the latest few hundred feet of mud. The wave after that arrived before they touched bottom again. Life was a nightmare of tossing and rolling, hurtling in every direction.

They lost track of time. They felt so sick that they gave up even wanting to live. They had no idea how many days had passed before they found themselves lying outside their shelter in pouring rain under a leaden sky.

"I'm cold—and very hungry."

"So am I."

Their pool was barely recognizable. The island was on a slope; the muddy surface drained to the downhill side where rainwater dammed up against the roots, forming a small pond. Lano could find no fish in it.

"We'll have to eat leaves. It's not the tastiest meal in the world, but it won't be the first time."

He climbed a tree to get some of the tender young leaves from the top. A few seconds later, he was at her side.

"They don't look so good, but they were the best I could find. Most of the leaves seem to be shrivelling up."

"Oh, yuck, they taste awful. I can't eat them."

"Ugh!" Lano screwed up his face.

They threw the leaves away.

Not far away they found an antelope with one foot caught between two roots. It had obviously been stuck like this for some time and was now weak and exhausted. Lano cut its throat.

"No chance of any dry firewood, so we can't cook it. We'll just have to eat it raw."

They finished off the liver and started on the other organs. They were still eating when they noticed the sound of animals moving through the forest.

"A lot of animals are moving, and they're all going in the same direction," said Lano after a few seconds. "Maybe there's a fire or something they're all running away from."

"Couldn't be a fire with everything soaked and water coming down like this."

"Whatever it is, it's likely to be just as dangerous for us as for them."

Lano suddenly turned to face downhill, tense and alert, eyes darting over the undergrowth, between the trees, and into the leaves. He grabbed Telina's arm and hustled her behind a tree just before two brontos with a baby emerged a few yards away. The female and the baby ignored them and carried on lumbering uphill looking tired and dazed. The male snorted and glared at them, but hardly hesitated in his stride. They disappeared into the trees as quickly as they had appeared.

Lano turned to his left. He signalled Telina to be quiet and edged round the tree to peer into the forest. The undergrowth ahead burst open and a tyrano charged at them roaring.

Lano leapt toward the dead deer shouting, "Run after the brontos!"

He turned to face the tyrano, scuttling backward to get the carcass behind his feet. The tyrano ignored Telina and thundered toward Lano, jaws wide open. Lano spun round, jumped over the deer and raced for the cover of a tree. The tyrano smelled the blood, hesitated, spotted the deer, and stopped.

Lano caught Telina up and gripped her arm, urging her to keep going. "We'd better stick behind the brontos; they don't like tyranos and the tyrano won't come too close to them."

The sound of crunching bones faded behind them as they hurried after the bronto family.

It stopped raining after an hour. Two hours later, they came to the end of their island and nearly ran into the brontos. They had reached the edge of the forest and were surveying a desolate mountain of mud rising gently into a mist which hid the distance. Small groups of animals straggled up the mountain, which disappeared into the mist a few miles ahead.

"Telina, maybe there isn't a fire behind us. Maybe the animals are just trying to get to some food—the forest leaves aren't edible anymore. Maybe they think there's food up ahead."

"Or perhaps they can't face another wave and think the mountain's high enough to be safe," said Telina.

"So what do we do now?"

"If another wave comes, we'll stand a better chance on the island."

"If there's no food, we'll starve if we stay here."

On either side they could see animals reaching the end of the forest. One by one the animals peered into the distance, stepped carefully down onto the muddy surface, and plodded wearily on.

"Let's go." He helped her down onto the mud and they trudged after the brontos.

Every few minutes, they turned around to look back at the scene behind them. More and more of the island gradually came into view and, after half an hour, they could make out the sea beyond it. They stood for a few minutes taking in the scene. The slope of damp sand rose from the end of the forest and disappeared into the continuous grey mass of cloud less than a mile ahead. Looking back the way they had come, the expanse of forest, beached on the foot of the mountain, stretched away to its farthest edge still floating in the grey-green sea.

They resumed their journey up the slope and were suddenly stunned by the blast of a meteorite strike which hit somewhere out of sight to their left. The blast cleared a hole in the clouds and they stared up at the first blue sky they had seen for a long time. How they had taken it for granted all their lives. Now it seemed so beautiful they wanted to feast their eyes on it for a while before plodding on again.

"Oh! Look! What's that?" said Telina pointing to the sky above the sea beyond their island.

"What?" said Lano. "Oh, that flash of light you mean?"

"There it is again."

They watched for a few seconds and the flashes became brighter. After a few moments, they could see that the light was actually continuous but it changed in brightness from barely visible to bright and back to barely visible again. In a few more seconds, the light showed a distinct ripple through its bright phase. Then, as it grew, emerging from the blue haze of the sky, they could make out the distorted, deformed shape of a huge body with sunlight shimmering down a tortuous path along its pitted metal surface. It twisted and tumbled as it hurtled toward the ocean far beyond their beached island. In almost no time, it filled half their field of vision; the blaze of sunlight streaking down its uneven surface was dazzlingly bright.

Telina began screaming hysterically.

Lano stared, unable to move, rigid with terror.

A moment after the enormous body disappeared beyond the horizon, the sea behind their island shot skyward. Above the immense wave, vast clouds of steam and spray rocketed upward, blindingly bright with reflected light. Moments before the giant wall of water reached them, an immense shock wave smashed their ear drums and hurled them a thousand yards up the slope of quaking sand.

42 Awakening

Shem had started to wake up half an hour earlier, but he still felt too drowsy to get up. He could hear slight movement from the bunk below. Sarai must be awake. He wanted to see her. It felt like a long time since she had been in his arms. He made an effort to sit up, but winced as the straps dug into chafed flesh. He had forgotten the straps. He ran his fingers gingerly over his bruises. It must have been a rough ride. He was sure something was very wrong, but could not quite put his finger on it. He seemed a little short of breath.

"Honey, are you awake?"

"Darling, I'm so sore."

Shem unfastened his straps, sat up stiffly, massaged his aches a little, climbed down, and freed Sarai.

"It seems somehow difficult to breathe," she murmured. "Oh, Shem, darling, I'm so glad to see you."

Shem folded her into his arms, caressing her gently as they sank back onto the bunk. They lay in each other's arms for a long time, then he suggested they go and see if the others were awake. In the living quarters, they found everyone else seated quietly around the table. Shem suddenly felt very hungry.

"Mom, that smells delicious! I'm famished. It feels like I haven't eaten for a week."

"Oh, it's much longer than that, Shem! Ready in a few minutes. Sit down. It's good to see you."

After the meal, the men decided to check the animals. Most were still sleeping, but the carnivores were beginning to stir. The lion growled and his mate answered.

"What are we going to do about those two?" asked Japh. "They'll be hungry, and those sheep and gazelles over there will probably smell pretty good to them once they really wake up."

"We'd better open the door. I think they'll go outside without any fuss," said his father.

None of them was prepared for the view which met them when the door was opened.

A dull leaden sky stretched over a drab, brown world. They were on a mountain of mud and sand. Pools of water filled the hollows. A plain far below them was half covered with lakes and ponds. It was dismally cold and damp.

Oh my, what have we landed ourselves in, thought Shem. He shivered and looked at the faces of the others. Their expressions matched his feelings. Nobody said anything. All heard the movement behind them at about the same time. The lions were heading for the door and the other carnivores were not far behind.

"We'd better get out of the way…" Ham spoke the first words since the door had been opened. They moved to the side and the animals trooped slowly to the doorway, stopped, looked around, sniffed the air, and went out.

The lions made straight for the nearest pool, dabbed their paws in, and each flicked out a fish. The tyranos lumbered toward a block of melting ice half a mile down the slope to the south. They tore at the body of a giraffe, its head and some of its neck still hidden in the ice. After eating half of the carcass, they continued down the slope, leaving the rest for the wolves and hyenas.

"Looks pretty dead out there," said Shem. "Let's go and have a closer look."

They found plants a few inches tall growing here and there, and little seedlings poking up through the mud all over the place. Down below, on the plain, they could see patches where the brown had a green tinge.

"I'm cold," said Ham. "Let's go inside and get something warm to put on."

As they climbed the stairway to the living quarters, Shem again had the uneasy feeling that something was not right. "There must be something wrong with me," he said. "I'm out of breath just climbing this staircase."

"Me too," said Ham and Japh in unison.

"Would you mind giving me a hand with the mag-sled?" said Japh.

Just like him, thought Shem with a wry smile. Always eager to fiddle with something technical. But I suppose we'll need that sled pretty soon to take all our gear to wherever we'll go when we leave this barge. "Sure, what do you want to do with it?"

"Well, I looked at the sled just after I woke up, and it was very odd; the meter said there was almost no field. There's obviously something wrong. I need a hand to check everything out."

They reached the main storeroom. Japh slipped easily behind the controls and stopped dead. "Hey, this is weird. Now the gauge says the field is negative!"

"What does that mean?" asked Ham, who had never really been interested in technical matters.

"Well, it means a compass should point South instead of North," said Japh.

"So let's just check the compass and see which way it points," said Ham.

"That would only help if we knew which direction was North," said Japh.

"Easy," said Shem, "just look at the sun."

"Well, maybe you didn't notice, but there wasn't any sun when we went outside just now and even if there was, how do we know which side of the equator we're on?"

"Why not just switch on and see if it goes forward or backward," said Shem.

"If the gauge is right, it won't go anywhere. The field is too weak even to lift it off the floor. But maybe the gauge is wrong, so I'm going to give it a try, and I need you two big strong lads to make sure I don't bump into anything fragile."

Nothing happened. Even at full power, the sled made no indication of lifting.

"Well, chaps, we'd better make sure the donkeys don't leave

until we've decided whether we need them to carry our stuff."

"So it's back to the days of the horse and cart, by the sound of it," said Ham.

"I've always fancied the simple life," said Shem. "But Japh, what will you do with no gadgets like mag-sleds to play with?"

"I guess we'll all have to earn our daily bread with honest, physical labour. And we'd better go and tell Dad we'll need the horses and donkeys. It'll be a lot harder to catch them after we've let them walk out the door."

43 New World

Japh turned his gaze from the plain far below to Malala, standing a few feet away. The sun came out from behind a cloud and danced on her long hair. It reminded him of a dream—was it years ago or just yesterday? He moved toward her and placed his arm gently on her shoulder.

"Lal, my precious, you look even more lovely in the sunshine."

"Pity there's so little of it these days." She smiled at him, then looked away to the plain. "It gets a bit greener over there every day. When are we going down to find a place to make a home?"

Japh did not answer. He had no answer to give.

"Sarai thinks she's pregnant," continued Malala. "I don't think she'll be happy trying to raise a family here."

Lal looked up sideways at Japh and, after a slight hesitation, went on, "I don't want to raise your hopes too much…but I'm beginning to think I might be pregnant, too."

A radiant smile spread over Japh's face as he enfolded her in his arms and covered her face with kisses.

A tremor shook the ground and they looked around to find

several new cracks in the surface not far away.

"Japh darling, I don't like it much on the mountain. It's always groaning and trembling and moving."

"And I'm sure it's getting higher—the plain looks a bit farther away every day. Still, we could be leaving soon. Since the animals awoke, they've been gobbling up the fodder as if they hadn't eaten for a month."

"It's much longer than that, Japh," she said, in a perfect impersonation of her mother-in-law.

Japh grinned. "Well, however long it was, there'll soon be nothing left and they'll have to go down to find grazing."

"I hope the grazing down there is a lot better than up here. The plants up here are so spindly and scrawny, they're quite pathetic. Oh, look, I can see the rabbits coming down the gangway. And here come the emus and ostriches. And many other birds are coming, too."

"You know, Lal, those birds look a bit bewildered. I would've thought they'd just spread their wings and glide off down the mountain in no time."

"Well, some of the little birds are flying away, but I don't remember seeing a bird having to put so much effort into flying before."

"And it looks as if the emus have given up; they're walking down the gangway. The pteros, too."

Two of the pteros waddled toward the cliff on Japh and Lal's right. They stood on the edge with their long leathery wings outstretched. The male gave a raucous call and jumped, the female followed a second later.

"Oh Japh, they're in trouble; just look how quickly they're going down!"

"They're heading straight for the other side of the gorge.

What a racket they're making."

The pteros banked steeply and turned just in time to miss the wall of the gorge. At breakneck speed they curved round and disappeared behind the slope of the mountain, losing height rapidly in the unaccustomed thin air.

"Japh, it looked as if they were learning to fly all over again."

"Well, my precious, we're all going to have to learn to do everything all over again. Nothing's the way it used to be."

The sun disappeared behind a thick cloud. Snow began to fall.

"Oh! Did you ever see anything like it? It's so beautiful!"

"And cold! Come on, both of you, let's get inside."

They climbed the gangway and reached shelter. Lal turned around to look at the snow falling steadily outside.

"Japh, you are right. Nothing's the same. We're in another world."

The End

ⲦPPENDIX

Postscript

THIS story could be considered "Biblical science fiction." The aspects of the story, such as that man lived alongside the huge creatures of Job 40 and 41 ("behemoths"), that the Flood of Noah's time in Genesis 6, 7, and 8* was worldwide, etc., are certain because God's Word is true. The ideas in the story taken from those recognised as "scientists" are less certain. Scientists are fallible, like everyone else, are liable to make mistakes, and are still learning.

Possibly the first scientist to propose that the earth had been struck by a large meteorite was Dr. George Dodwell, a renowned Australian astronomer. Dodwell was born in 1879, became an assistant astronomer at Adelaide Observatory in 1899, became a Government Astronomer in 1909, and represented Australia at international astronomy gatherings. He retired at the age of 73. He derived a size of approximately 200 km (124 miles) diameter for the impacting body. He noted that our moon, unlike the planets, does not orbit over the equator and suggested that this could be because of disturbance due to this impact. His work showed that if an impacting body were responsible for the huge

---

* Unless otherwise noted, Scripture quotations are from the King James Version.

difference between the observed changes in the tilt of the axis and those predicted by normal calculations, then it probably struck the earth about four and a half thousand years ago, which coincides with the Biblical Flood.

Dodwell's idea gained no popularity with scientists during his lifetime since it does not readily fit into the millions of years of earth history which were then universally accepted. Since then, considerable numbers of scientists have come to question this timescale and Dodwell's theory is now being considered seriously.

Unfortunately, the present American copyright holders have not published Dodwell's book on this subject, perhaps purposely to suppress it, and copies made available by the previous Australian copyright holder are scarce and hard to come by. Fortunately, the important first chapter, "Astronomical Investigations of the Obliquity of the Ecliptic," had become fairly well known before the book became obscure.

The idea of meteorite impacts became popular when Walter Alvarez and Luis W. Alvarez published a famous paper describing a worldwide iridium anomaly that they could account for by the impact of a meteorite of about 10 km (6.2 miles) diameter. Their observations were, as I would have predicted, interpreted in a way that squeezed them into the popular geological timescale. Some scientists do recognise that such an event could destroy the fundamental assumptions on which Charles Lyell and his disciples had built that timescale! Evidence has led many scientists to theorize that at least one major meteorite has struck the earth with devastating consequences.

Calculations on the effects of meteorite impacts have been done by many scientists, perhaps the best known being Thomas J. Ahrens and John D. O'Keefe of the California Institute of Technology. In 1982, they showed that a body of 10 km (6.2 miles) diameter would produce tsunamis (formerly called tidal waves) 5 km (3 miles) high that would overwhelm the entire globe in 27 hours. It would also have led to earthquakes millions of times more powerful than those we observe today, thousands of millions of tons of water being thrown up into the atmosphere, etc. They asked how it would be possible for any land-dwelling creature to escape drowning. The scientific community on the whole preferred to ignore this theory, and to speculate instead on dust being thrown up, cutting off sunlight, leading to reduced vegetation, starvation of dinosaurs, etc., and no change to the popular mythology about an earth many millions of years old.

The pre-flood world had no rain (Genesis 2:5). This may be due to the lack of a strong wind system (as would be expected if the axis were not tilted), together with lack of dust in the uniformly fertile and well-watered ("very good") Earth. Without particles to act as condensation nuclei, water vapour does not form drops of water, which, therefore, cannot then form clouds. There was probably a great deal of water vapour in the atmosphere. There is evidence that suggests that the atmospheric pressure before the Flood was about double that of today. Much of the atmosphere could have been blown away into space during an impact event. Most of the water vapour that remained would have condensed on dust particles thrown up by the impact (and by volcanoes) and come down as rain. The present "water cycle" of evaporation, condensation, and precipitation probably began during the Flood.

Findings of unfossilized dinosaur bones containing DNA and red blood cells have discredited the idea that dinosaurs became extinct millions of years ago. Such bones are the remains of post-flood creatures, certainly no older than three or four thousand years. The existence of historical documents, like those of

Geoffrey of Monmouth, Alexander the Great, the old English saga *Beowulf*, etc., describing easily recognizable dinosaurs, points to their existence within the last few thousand years. This agrees with the account in the book of Job (40:15) where God, speaking out of the whirlwind, tells Job to "behold now Behemoth, which I made with thee…." The description appears to fit that of a *sauropod* dinosaur. Dr. David Rosevear, has pointed out that certain dinosaurs (*Lambeosaurus*, *Corythosaurus*, etc.) had structures in their skulls similar to those in the rear end of bombardier beetles. These little creatures fire boiling acid from their twin cannons by exploding hydroquinones and peroxides in an explosion chamber. This offers theoretical support for the existence of such creatures as the one described in Job 41 with the ability to fire smoke, sparks, and hot gases from their nostrils.

All dinosaurs are given abbreviated names in *Another World*: tyrano instead of *tyrannosaurs*, trico instead of *triceratops*, etc. The appendix gives brief descriptions of most of those mentioned in the story.

Dr. Walter Brown's hydroplate theory is detailed in his book *In the Beginning*. It is based on the fact that observed geological features are consistent with vast quantities of water having burst forth from underground reservoirs when overlying basalt was pierced. A crack would spread at the speed of sound in rock until it completely encircled the globe. Dr. Brown does not attempt to determine what led to the cracking open of the basalt over the reservoirs. A meteorite impact is one possibility.

It is quite likely that the force of the water jets could have thrown water into the stratosphere where it would have rapidly cooled to far below freezing temperature. Its violent motion could have prevented it from freezing until it came to an abrupt halt upon hitting the earth. This is similar to what happens in arctic waters when windblown sea spray at sub-freezing temperature hits a ship and turns to black ice on impact. There are many cases of mammoths being found apparently "super-quick frozen" and in a very good state of preservation. The Berezovka mammoth is a particularly famous example. One Royal Society dinner in London featured extremely well-preserved mammoth steaks. Some of the mammoths found had grasses and flowers (notably bluebells) in their mouths and undigested flowers and grasses in their stomachs. This suggests extremely rapid freezing at a very low temperature. The ice in which they are found is often described as very dirty. Others are in "muck" which is no longer fully frozen. This would be consistent with the "fountains of the great deep" eroding material from the sides of the crack leading from the underground chambers to the surface. Dissolved salts and carbon dioxide could explain many otherwise puzzling geological features like "evaporates" and surprisingly pure, widely distributed and impressively huge calcium carbonate deposits.

The earth's rapidly decaying magnetic field was first analysed in 1883 by the famous mathematician Sir Horace Lamb, who pointed out that using well-established laws of physics and any reasonable assumptions about conditions within the earth, the magnetic field must have decreased from an extremely high value only a few thousand years ago. Many observations confirmed his analysis, which was refined by Professor Thomas Barnes in 1973, and subsequently later significantly modified by Dr. Russell Humphreys in the light of more recent observations. His analysis showed how a major disturbance at the time of the Flood could lead to rapid fluctuation in the magnetic field, with possible field reversals. The field would then have risen to a strength less than before the Flood, but several times stronger than today, before resuming decay with the currently observed "half-life" of about fourteen hundred years, which means that at the end of every period of fourteen hundred years, its strength has fallen to half of its value at the beginning of that period.

The idea of the earth's formerly powerful magnetic field being used for transport comes from Professor Emeritus James N. Hanson, of Cleveland State University, who proposed it as a possible means of transporting the enormous blocks of stone used in some huge ancient structures.

The floating forests come from German paleontologist Dr. Joachim Scheven, whose work indicates that many of the world's gigantic coal deposits were formed from vast floating forests of lycopod trees.

These scientists could, of course, be totally wrong. Scientists are fallible but, as far as I can tell, there is good observational support and no conflict between their work and statements of Scripture.

We are generally indoctrinated with the evolutionary idea that man was formerly a primitive descendent of an ape-like creature, a brute with little intelligence and no technological development. We can see that this is untrue when we consider that ancient maritime civilisations are known to have had global navigation systems the likes of which modern man has only achieved quite recently. Some of the blocks used to build the ancient city of Tiahuanaco weigh hundreds of tons. The technology to lift such blocks into place has been with modern man for less than a century. The blocks used to make the great pyramids have edges straight to the accuracy of a modern optical straightedge. The structure is so accurate in its construction and orientation that it required a technologically-advanced civilization to build it. Artefacts that appear to be pre-flood in origin show that a method of rust-proofing iron by a sulphur treatment was known. Such treatment has not yet been redis-covered. It is also noteworthy that ancient civilisations (e.g., the ancient Greeks) looked back to a Golden Age of enormous learning and technological development, which had been lost. It is also noteworthy that the more ancient the language one studies, the more complexity and subtlety one tends to find.

Decay of the magnetic field and the loss of much of the atmo-sphere may have deprived us of most of our original protection from harmful radiation and be leading to ever increasing genetic damage. It is highly probable that the erupting fountains of the great deep brought buried radioactive materials to the surface, leading to further genetic damage. Before the Flood, man lived for about nine hundred years, genetically in far better shape than modern man who lives with the accumulation of more than four thousand years of genetic decay. We would expect the pre-flood population to make rapid strides in knowledge. We could expect a productive career many times that of a modern researcher. We see in Genesis Chapter 4 that quite soon after creation, Tubal-Cain was proficient in metalworking and Jubal was skilled in stringed and wind musical instruments.

Most speculation about the Flood concentrates on the rain that fell for forty days and forty nights (Genesis 7:12). But the Bible notes before mentioning this rain that "in that same day were all the fountains of the great deep broken up" (Genesis 7:11). We are also told that God "calleth for the waters of the sea, and poureth them out upon the face of the earth." (Amos 5:8 and Amos 9:6)

Another detail about the Flood which is often overlooked, is that the "unclean" animals and birds (those not suitable for human consumption—the vast majority) came to the ark in pairs, whereas seven pairs each of the "clean" beasts and birds (those few kinds which are good for human consumption) were taken onboard. "Of every clean beast thou shalt take to thee by sevens, the male and his female: and the beasts that are not clean by two, the male and his female" (Genesis 7:2); note: "by sevens" not seven, and "by two" not twos.

Another World attempts to portray what God states in the Bible, that "all flesh had corrupted his way upon the earth" (Genesis 6:12) and "every imagination of the thoughts of his [mankind's] heart was only evil continually" (Genesis 6:5). If some aspects of this could be considered unsuitable for younger readers, I may have failed to strike the right balance, for which I ask the reader's pardon.

There are many parallels between the pre-flood earth and the circumstances today. There is a worldwide turning away from righteousness and morality. The killing of unborn babies by abortion has been legalised in many formerly civilised societies; promiscuity and homosexuality are being encouraged as acceptable "alternative lifestyles," pornography has become accepted as "freedom of expression," and capital punishment has been abolished as infringing upon "human rights" in most of the countries once considered at the forefront of civilisation. The disastrous consequences—dramatic increases of rape, murder, the breakdown of the family, and general moral decay—seem to be quite acceptable to our "enlightened" post-modern society.

The Bible warns that there will be another judgement, this time not by water, but by fire. It is very likely that the majority of people will be as unprepared as people were in the days of Noah.

Some of the creatures in the story in order of appearance:

Drawings by Henning ven der Westhuizen

Stegosaurus

Stegosaurus were large, armoured dinosaurs that had two rows of large, distinctive plates running down their backs. It was thought that these plates could be held horizontally, sticking out from the top of the animal making a kind of roof over its sides. Hence the name *Stegosaurus* which means "roof lizard." *Stegosaurs* were about as big as a bus. They had short front legs which kept their heads close to the ground. They had very humped bodies, high in the middle, low at the front and rear, and a heavy tail which was probably held high in the air. They had two pairs of long spikes on their tails, which are thought to have been defensive weapons, and strong, hard plates and scales which are thought to have been defensive armour. They grew to about 30 feet (9 m) long and 14 feet (4 m) high and weighed about 4.5 tons. Their heads were small, their brains were about the size of a dog's brain, and they probably ate only tender plants.

Pterosaur

Pterosaurs (the name means "winged lizard") were flying reptiles whose wings were made of skin, muscle, and other tissue, but had no feathers. Some had long tails and many teeth; others had short tails and few teeth. Some kinds of *pterosaur* are called *pterodactyls*. *Pterosaurs* could be very large, with a wingspan of 33 feet (10 m), though others were far smaller. A *pterosaur* was reportedly killed by blasting operations for a railway tunnel in France a little over one hundred years ago. There have been reports of existing *pterosaurs* in remote areas of Africa in the last century. North American Indian folklore tells of a flying creature, the "thunderbird," whose description fits that of a *pterosaur*.

Plesiosaur

Plesiosaurs were large carnivorous reptiles that lived in water. The name means "near lizard" and they are often thought of as being dinosaurs, but are not so classified by biologists. They had long necks and massive, turtle-shaped bodies with four flippers and short tails. It is thought that they swam fairly slowly, but were very manoeuvrable and could turn into position to snap up their prey very quickly. There are many cases of sightings of strange creatures fitting the description of *plesiosaurs*. Perhaps the most famous is the Loch Ness Monster. *Plesiosaur* bones have been found around Loch Ness, though some believe they may have been planted by hoaxers. So many credible reports have been received that serious research into the Loch Ness Monster is being done by professional scientists. There have been many reports of creatures fitting the description of *plesiosaurs* off the coasts of Canada.

Brontosaurus

Brontosaurus (whose name means "thunder lizard") is a controversial dinosaur. Some deny its name and say we should call it *Apatosaurus*. O. C. March, the discoverer of the first *Brontosaurus*, reconstructed it with the head of another creature. Some say this annuls the classification, some say that with the correct head the mistake is fully rectified. Some say it is really the same as *Apatosaurus*, so the name should be dropped. Others say there are significant differences and we should keep the name. Stephen Jay Gould was one of the most famous scientists who championed *Brontosaurus*. Whatever the controversy, *Brontosaurus* is well known and much loved. It was one of the largest land-dwelling creatures that ever lived. It could grow to 80 feet (25 m) long and could weigh up to 35 tons. Its neck was long, its head small, its body was massive, its legs were relatively short and stout, its tail was roughly as long as its neck. It was vegetarian and is thought to have eaten grass and leaves almost continually to feed its huge body by means of such a small mouth. At one time, it was thought to have dragged its enormous tail along the ground, but is now believed to have held it in the air. It is quite likely that the Behemoth of Job 40 was a *sauropod* dinosaur like *Brontosaurus*.

Tyranosaurus

A well known type of *Tyranosaurus* is popularly known as "T-Rex." The *Tyrannosaurus* is one of the best loved dinosaurs. Its name means "tyrant lizard." It was a fearsome creature, growing up to 40 feet (12 m) long and weighing up to 7 tons. There has been controversy over whether *Tyranosaurus* was primarily a hunter or a scavenger. It seems likely that, like present-day hyenas, it both scavenged carrion and killed prey. Which was predominant may have varied from place to place. The *Tyranosaurus* had strong powerful back legs, but surprisingly small, puny, front legs only about 3 feet (1 m) long. Its huge jaws held an array of enormous teeth. Several *Tyranosaurus* skeletons have been found containing DNA, blood vessels, and even blood. The obvious conclusion is that the bones are not millions of years old. Those who wish to cling to the modern myth of vast time spans will, no doubt, attempt another explanation. But there should actually be no surprise in the obviously young age since there are descriptions in ancient literature. One of the most famous is the ancient British saga *Beowulf*. This poem from the early Christian era describes a creature—a "troll" named "Grendel"—that is clearly recognisable as a *Tyranosaurus*. Grendel was a nuisance, killing livestock and even people. Beowulf was able to slay it by tearing off its puny front limbs, after which it was weakened by blood loss. The saga seems to have authentic historical content and to describe the creature so accurately, many years before palaeontologists had reconstructed *Tyranosaurus*, the description must come from a personal sighting. It could be that people exterminated these creatures by means of tearing off the front limbs, though perhaps not in a single-handed encounter like that of Beowulf, but possibly as a joint effort using some kind of trap or ropes.

Lambeosaurus

Lambeosaurus was very similar to *Corithosaurus* and *Parasaurolophus*. The striking feature of these dinosaurs is the unusual crests on the tops of their heads. It is mainly the shape of these crests which palaeontologists use to distinguish between them. They had large bodies, strong back legs, much smaller front legs, and a large, heavy tail. It seems that they could walk on all fours or on their two back legs with their heavy tail acting as a counterbalance. There is evidence to suggest that they could move quickly, and that they lived near water. The biggest could grow to 50 feet (15 m) long and weigh more than 20 tons.

Their crests contained hollow chambers with passages leading to their nostrils. Some scientists have pointed out that these chambers and passages are like those of the bombardier beetle. The bombardier beetle contains a "chemical warfare factory" which produces very reactive chemicals—hydroquinones and peroxides—which are stored in a collection chamber. When the beetle wants to fire its "cannons," it transfers some of the mixture to an explosion chamber, which is surrounded by enzyme glands. The glands squirt destabilizing enzymes into the mixture, which explodes and fires the cannons. Many scientists resist such a possibility for *Lambeosaurus* and its near relatives, apparently not liking the similarity to "fire-breathing dragons," and speculate instead that the crests and their chambers could have been used for making some kind of sound. There are two reasons for suspecting that the first explanation may be more likely. The first is that we have living creatures which use such chambers for a known purpose—storing and exploding reactive chemicals. The second is that the unique construction of the bony snout, or bill, of these dinosaurs would be just what would be required if they did fire hot explosion products from their nostrils.

Kronosaurus

The *kronosaur* is considered to be a *plesiosaur* with a very short neck and a huge mouth. It had a *plesiosaur's* massive, turtle-like body with four flippers. It was one of the largest marine reptiles that ever lived. It grew to a length of about 26 feet (8m) of which nearly 10 feet (2.4 m) were jaws. Its mouth was filled with teeth about 10 inches (250 mm) long.

Velociraptor

Velociraptor, whose name means "swift robber," was a small carnivorous dinosaur, probably capable of running quickly. It was quite small, only about 1.5 feet (0.5 m) high at the hip, with a long tail (probably important for balance) which could apparently flex horizontally but not vertically. It weighed about 33 pounds (15 kg) and had a length, from snout to tip of tail, of about 6.5 feet (2 m). It had an unusual, large, sickle-shaped claw that is thought to have been a weapon for killing its prey.

Triceratops

Triceratops, whose name means "three horns on the face," was one of the largest land-dwelling creatures, reaching about 33 feet (10 m) in length, 10 feet (3 m) in height and 12 tons in weight. Its huge skull could be up to 10 feet (2.4 m) long—about the same as a *Kronosuarus*, but *triceratops* ate only plants. Its teeth suggest that it ate vast amounts of tough plants—perhaps palms, cycads, and bushy material. It had rows of teeth that

grew and were replaced throughout its life. It may have had as many as 800 teeth altogether. Its most distinctive features were the horns on its face and the bony "frill" at the back of its skull. It had one horn on its nose and one above each eye. The two horns above the eyes could be over 3 feet (1 m) long. *Triceratops* seems to have been a very common dinosaur—many remains have been found. Although it is supposed to have died out about 65 million years ago, according to popular mythology, ancient pottery has been found in South America decorated with images of *triceratops*—some apparently domesticated. Illustrations of men riding on a *triceratops* are remarkably similar to present day use of howdahs on the backs of elephants in India.

Dinosaurs in general

The names of all dinosaurs are recent, and none of them would have had a name anything like *"Brontosaurus"* or *"Tyranosaurus"* when they were alive. We have some clues as to what some civilizations may have called some of them (e.g., "Behemoth" was probably the name of a *sauropod*, like the *Brontosaurus*, at the time of Job. "Troll" may have been the name of a *Tyranosaurus* in certain locations in Western Europe in the early Christian era). Descriptions of dinosaurs in historical records (such as Geoffrey of Monmouth's book of history) are usually dismissed as "mythical" additions to an otherwise authoritative history. This is because of the indoctrination of modern historians in the popular myths of "geological time," which would require all such creatures be extinct millions of geological years before Geoffrey of Monmouth, or the authors he cited, were around to describe them.

Dinosaurs, the name means "terrible lizard," were almost certainly reptiles, which, unlike most vertebrates, do not stop growing throughout their life. Before the Flood, man lived to be almost a thousand years old. Reptiles would probably also live about the same length of time and would reach an enormous size. After the Flood, with the earth's magnetic field drastically reduced by disturbance to the iron core, together with a much thinner atmosphere, far more harmful cosmic radiation would reach the earth's surface. This, possibly together with radioactive materials brought to the surface when the fountains of the great deep were broken up, is possibly a major reason for much shorter life spans today. Although dinosaurs thrived before the Flood, conditions after the Flood do not appear to have been favourable for them. They probably never reproduced in great numbers, never grew to their enormous pre-flood size, and were, in all likelihood, exterminated by man.

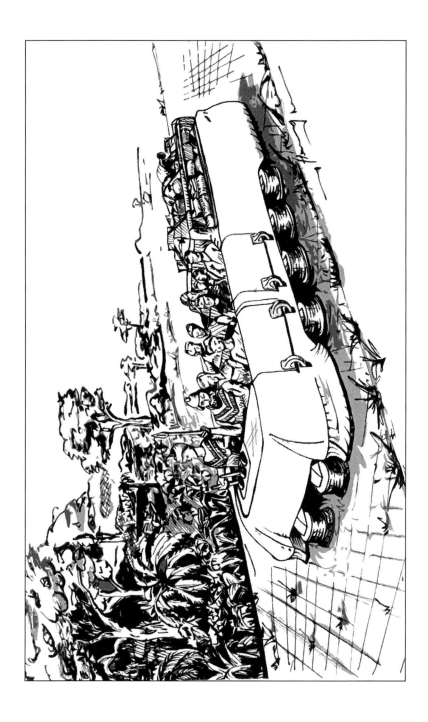

Mag-Sleds

Drawing by Henning ven der Westhuizen

Some exciting research points to possibilities of how mag-sleds might work.

Townsend Brown, an American scientist, spent about fifty years doing experiments with gyroscopes in electric and magnetic fields, a subject he called "electrogravitation." His discoveries enabled him to make objects lift from the ground. His "electro-gravitic discs" look remarkably like flying saucers.

Brown's work has not received much publicity, but that of Eric Laithwaite, an English scientist under whom I had the privilege of studying for a year, certainly has. His revolutionary ideas raised outrage from the scientific establishment and scathing headlines from the British press.

Laithwaite's work led to the invention of the "maglev" system, which has been used to produce magnetic levitation trains in Germany and Japan. These trains use magnetic and electric fields to raise themselves above the tracks and propel themselves without any contact with the rails.

Laithwaite later became interested in the gravitational effects of rapidly spinning gyroscopes and his research led to demonstrations of "mass transfer effects" (popularly know as "anti-gravity") and the invention of the "reactionless drive." The combined power of his linear induction motors, reactionless drive, and mass transfer effects opened up exciting possibilities. In 2000, Laithwaite was commissioned by NASA to develop the technology to launch space projects using his revolutionary ideas instead of rockets. He died when the project was still at an early stage. His work is being continued by William Dawson.

℞bout the ℞uthor

Philip **Stott** was born in England in 1943. He studied at Manchester University, where he obtained B.S. (with honours) and M.S. degrees in Civil Engineering. He lectured at universities in Nigeria and South Africa and carried out research in the analysis of geometrically nonlinear structures. He shared the Henry Adams Award for outstanding research in 1969. While lecturing at the University of Witwatersrand in Johannesburg, South Africa, he studied biology. After leaving Wits he joined an engineering consulting firm. His ongoing interest in all aspects of science led to studies in mathematics and astronomy with the University of South Africa and, later, to four years of part-time research with the Applied Mathematics Department of the University of the Orange Free State in Bloemfontein, South Africa.

After many years as a firm atheist, he was converted to Christianity in 1976. Following several years of studying the conflicting claims of secular science and Scripture, he actively entered the Creation/Evolution debate in 1989.

In 1992, he was invited to address a conference in Russia and since then has lectured, addressed conferences, and taken part in debates in eastern and western Europe, America, Canada, and southern Africa. Venues have included the European Centre for Nuclear Research (CERN), a UNESCO International Conference on the Teaching of Physics, and the Russian Academy of Sciences.

Philip Stott is married to Margaret (born Lloyd). They have two children, Robert and Angela; and two grandchildren, Sean and Julie. They live in Bloemfontein, South Africa.

It has been my privilege to benefit from Philip Stott's superb ministry for more than twenty years. He is a brilliant Creation Science lecturer and I have frequently sat spellbound at his dynamic presentations.

It has been an education to watch Philip Stott at work at secular universities. Even in the face of the most hostile audiences, Philip Stott remains calm and confidently presents the irrefutable scientific facts in support of the Biblical creation position. His *Vital Questions* book is one of the very best scientific books I have ever read.

It is a privilege to recommend the writing and speaking ministry of Philip Stott. He is our favorite Creation Science lecturer at the Biblical Worldview Summits.

——Dr. Peter Hammond
Director, Frontline Fellowship,
Cape Town, South Africa

Publisher's Word

When the Lord saw that the wickedness of man
was great in the earth, and all the imaginations of the
thoughts of his heart were only evil continually,
Then it repented the Lord that He had made man in the
earth, and He was sorry in His heart.
(Genesis 6:5-6)*

Casting down the imaginations, and every high thing
that is exalted against the knowledge of God,
and bringing into captivity every thought
to the obedience of Christ.
(2 Corinthians 10:5)

AFTER the Creation, the Fall, and the First Coming of Christ, history's fourth most important event is surely the Great Flood of Genesis. While the Fall of Adam is certainly the greatest tragedy among mankind, the Great Flood must rank second. The Great Flood is simply the greatest material destruction the earth has ever known. Modern man can barely fathom the Flood's impact on the quality of life on earth. It displays God's perfect and righteous justice for man's sin and rebellion against man's Creator.

Additionally, that the late antediluvian world knew almost nothing but vicious wickedness and its accompanying evil is equally unimaginable. In this day of Christ's reign, we may now see pockets, some large, of utter sinfulness and its consequences. These are so repugnant we will scarcely consider them. With such inhumanity as the world witnessed in World War I, World War II under Hitler, and then Stalin's and Mao's regimes, the

---

* Scriptures in the "Publisher's Word" are quoted from the 1599 Geneva Bible. Republished by Tolle Lege Press, White Hall, West Virginia, 2006. www.genevabible.com. Used by permission.

Killing Fields of Cambodia, and the genocide in Rwanda, the Sudan, and elsewhere, we obtain some inkling of mankind's massive depravity at the time of Noah. As brutally evil as these examples seem, according to the Bible they are a drop in the bucket to the dimensions of evil in the earth before the Flood. The Flood era may equal or surpass all the combined atrocities and evil of history since. That God would justly destroy nearly the entire human population of perhaps billions of people* to protect the last remaining righteous few for the salvation of future generations boggles the mind and wrenches the heart.

It is natural to avoid such unpleasantness. However, the Bible itself uses both a carrot and a stick to engage God's people. The carrot is the great mercy and goodness of abundant life and eternal salvation available to us through Christ's atonement and our salvation. The stick is God's angry but righteous judgment over personal rebellion against Him, such sinful rebellion resulting in supreme human wickedness, injustice, and tyranny.

How does our culture—and the church in particular—today render the story of the Flood? Is it not typically in the form of a cute Sunday school story? Noah's animals span the landscape in a long cue, two by two. They all go for a lengthy boat ride on top of the world. Then comes the rainbow. While these redeeming elements are surely warranted in the church's teaching, it should also be important to emphasize the ugly result of sin from which Christ has redeemed us! We need to know from what (and to Whom) we are saved. Where are the cautionary sermons from Genesis Six through Nine? We can hope we will hear more, with good fruit forthcoming, in the future.

---

* "Even if we use rates appropriate in the present world (x=1 and c=1.5), over 3 billion people could easily have been on the earth at the time of Noah." Henry M. Morris, *The Biblical Basis for Modern Science*, (Green Forest, AR: Master Books, 2002), 392.

In the meantime, this novel, *Another World*, renders a most unique and stimulating treatment of the Great Flood. In it, accomplished scientist, Biblical creationist, teacher, Christian gentlemen, and my friend from South Africa, Professor Philip Stott, illustrates the multifacetedness of the antediluvian era. He draws portraits of the character of the natural earth and of the true human character with forthrightness, imagination, and restraint. Then he dabs the painting with a touch of God's redemption story that a sound representation of the Bible would demand. The story is engaging. It is woefully painful, yet hopeful. It is human in both the worst (sinful) and best (restoration) senses. It suggests the natural wonder—the beauty and the severe dangers—of primeval, fallen earth. That *Another World* is a cautionary tale for our age will not be missed. Altogether, Nordskog Publishing heartily recommends *Another World* to anyone who wishes to understand and appreciate both the significance of the heavenly rebuke and the world's magnificent redemption in the Great Flood of Genesis.

Without God's merciful grace, none of us would be here to read this novel based upon history as told by the ancients in God's Law-Word, and the great story of the destruction of the human race, but also God's redeeming salvation through Noah and his ark.

Another World certainly depicts a world millenniums ago and unknown to modern mankind. Here we find some of the ancient mysteries through a Godly speculation. May it lead you to "another world" in God's future eternal kingdom. Praise be to God from Whom all blessings flow.

—Gerald Christian Nordskog
Publisher
Christmas 2009

(See selected Scriptures following.)

Select Scripture from
Genesis Chapters Six through Nine

When the Lord saw that the wickedness of man was great in the earth, and all the imaginations of the thoughts of his heart were only evil continually, Then it repented the Lord that He had made man in the earth, and He was sorry in His heart. Therefore, the Lord said, I will destroy from the earth the man, whom I have created, from man to beast, to the creeping thing, and to the fowl of the heaven: for I repent that I have made them. But Noah found grace in the eyes of the Lord. (Genesis 6:5-8)

And I, behold, I will bring a flood of waters upon the earth to destroy all flesh, wherein is the breath of life under heaven: all that is in the earth shall perish. But with thee will I establish my covenant, and thou shalt go into the Ark, thou, and thy sons, and thy wife, and thy sons' wives with thee. (Genesis 6:17-18)

Noah therefore did according unto all that God commanded him: even so did he. (Genesis 6:22)

For seven days hence I will cause it to rain upon the earth forty days, and forty nights, and all the substance that I have made, will I destroy from off the earth. (Genesis 7:4)

[T]he same day were all the fountains of the great deep broken up, and the windows of heaven were opened. And the rain was upon the earth forty days and forty nights. (Genesis 7:11b–12)

So He destroyed everything that was upon the earth, from man to beast, to the creeping thing, and to the fowl of the heaven: they were even destroyed from the earth. And Noah only remained, and they that were with him in the Ark. And the waters prevailed upon the earth an hundred and fifty days." (Genesis 7:23-24)

Then God spake to Noah, saying, Go forth of the Ark, thou, and thy wife, and thy sons, and thy sons' wives with thee. Bring forth with every beast that is with thee, of all flesh, both fowl and cattle, and everything that creepeth and moveth upon the earth, that they may breed abundantly in the earth, and bring forth fruit and increase upon the earth. (Genesis 8:15-17)

Hereafter seed time and harvest, and cold and heat, and Summer and Winter, and day and night shall not cease, so long as the earth remaineth. (Genesis 8:22)

And God blessed Noah and his sons, and said to them, "Bring forth fruit, and multiply, and replenish the earth. Also the fear of you and the dread of you shall be upon every beast of the earth, and upon every fowl of the heaven, upon all that moveth on the earth, and upon all the fishes of the sea: into your hand are they delivered. Everything that moveth and liveth shall be meat for you: as the green herb, have I given you all things. But flesh with the life thereof, I mean, with the blood thereof, shall ye not eat. For surely I will require your blood, wherein your lives are: at the hands of every beast will I require it: and at the hand of man, even at the hand of a man's brother will I require the life of man. Who so sheddeth man's blood, by man shall his blood be shed: for in the image of God hath He made man. But bring ye forth fruit and multiply: grow plentifully in the earth, and increase therein."

God spake also to Noah and to his sons with him, saying, "Behold, I, even I establish My covenant with you, and with your seed after you, And with every living creature that is with you, with the fowl, with the cattle, and with every beast of the earth with you, from all that go out of the Ark, unto every beast of the earth. And my covenant will I establish with you, that from henceforth all flesh shall not be rooted out by the waters of the flood, neither shall there be a flood to destroy the earth anymore."

Then God said, "This is the token of the covenant which I make between Me and you, and between every living thing that is with you unto perpetual generations. I have set My bow in the cloud, and it shall be for a sign of the covenant between Me and the earth. And when I shall cover the earth with a cloud, and the bow shall be seen in the cloud, Then will I remember My covenant which is between Me and you, and between every living thing in all flesh, and there shall be no more waters of a flood to destroy all flesh. Therefore the bow shall be in the cloud, that I may see it, and remember the everlasting covenant between God and every living thing, in all flesh that is upon the earth."

God said yet to Noah, "This is the sign of the covenant, which I have established between Me and all flesh that is upon the earth." (Genesis 9:1-17)

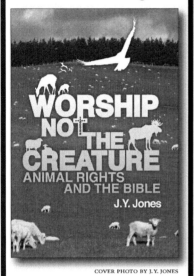

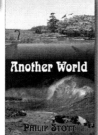

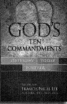

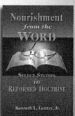

History, Bible, and Current Events
Excellent for Citizen Education and Homeschool

The Book That Made America: How the Bible Formed Our Nation by Jerry Newcombe, D Min

All that is positive in our foundation can be traced back to the Scriptures. Recently, President Obama declared that America is not a Christian nation, while *Newsweek* announced the demise of Christian America. This book is the answer to America's critics with the facts of history.

DEDICATED TO
★ D. JAMES KENNEDY ★

FOREWORD BY
★ JENNIFER KENNEDY CASSIDY ★

PB 6"x9" 404 PP ISBN 978-0-9824929-0-1 2009 **$18.95**

★ **ANN COULTER** ★
NY Times #1 Bestselling Author
"Say that America is a Christian nation and you'll be brought up on hate crime charges – or at least thought an ignoramus. But what are the facts of history? This book demonstrates that there once was a Book even more integral to this nation than Al Gore's *Earth in the Balance*. I recommend Dr. Newcombe's book highly!"

★ **PETER LILLBACK** ★
President of The Providence Forum
"Jerry Newcombe combines accurate scholarship and careful analysis with very engaging writing. This arsenal of historic wisdom from our Judeo-Christian heritage should be in your library."

★ **PETER J. MARSHALL** ★
Author, *The Light and the Glory*
"...a major weapon for the moral and spiritual civil war being waged for the soul of America."

★ *Also endorsed by* ★
MARSHALL FOSTER
Author, *The American Covenant*

CHARLES HULL WOLFE
& PAUL JEHLE
Plymouth Rock Foundation

KERBY ANDERSON
Probe Ministries International

STEPHEN McDOWELL
Providence Foundation

WILLIAM J. FEDERER
Amerisearch, Inc.

★ *& Homeschool Leaders* ★
MARY-ELAINE SWANSON
JAMES B. ROSE

The Battle of Lexington: A Sermon and Eyewitness Narrative
by Lexington Pastor, Jonas Clark, 1776

With powerful voice Jonas Clark tells of the principles of personal, civil, and religious liberty, and the right of resistance. Today our country lacks enough preachers like Clark who gave his congregation courage to stand and make a difference.
—*Introduction* by Rev. Christopher Hoops

Includes biographical information on Pastor Clark, facsimile title page from the original 1776 publication, four classic poems commemorating Paul Revere's Ride and the "shot heard 'round the world," and illustration.

PB 5"x8" 96 PP ISBN 978-0-9796736-3-4 2008 **$9.95** • E-BOOK ISBN 978-0-9824929-7-0 2009 **$8.95**

Brave Boys of Derry: No Surrender!
by W. Stanley Martin

The true historical narrative of how heroic young apprentices helped save their besieged Protestant town of Londonderry in Northern Ireland in 1688–89.

Republication coming soon!

Worship Not the Creature: Animal Rights and the Bible by J. Y. Jones, MD

Radical animal rights activists are well described in Romans 1:25 (NASB):
"They exchanged the truth of God for a lie, and worshiped and served the creature rather than the Creator."

J. Y. Jones delivers the most forthright and engaging presentation of the Biblical view of animals in print.

Dr. Jones, long an accomplished physician, scholar, writer, outdoorsman, hunter, and man of God, powerfully exposes the radical political agenda of animal rights activists. Applying Biblical and scientific knowledge, he reveals the underlying goals of the animal rights movement as a potentially significant menace to liberty and even to Christianity itself.

HB DUST JACKET 6"x9" 192 PP
ISBN 978-0-9824929-1-8 2009
$19.95

"This is the first book I have read that endeavors to present a true Biblical response to the animal rights agenda. I recommend this book to anyone who wants to better understand this insidious movement and the Biblical viewpoint a Christian should have toward it."

Dr. William Franklin Graham IV
Billy Graham Evangelistic Association, Charlotte, NC

The Death Penalty on Trial: Taking a Life for a Life Taken
by Dr. Ron Gleason

Dr. Gleason challenges both sides of the death penalty debate with clarity and cogency, citing history, Scripture, the confessionals of the historic reformed church, and the leading voices of today. He examines the objections from both secularists and liberal Christians, down to the underlying premises. As readers are led to the heart of the matter, they may find themselves drawn persuasively to Gleason's conclusion.

PB 6"x9" 152 PP
ISBN 978-0-9796736-7-2 2009
$14.95

ORDER FROM

4562 Westinghouse Street, Suite E, Ventura, CA 93003
805-642-2070 • www.NordskogPublishing.com

Also distributed by
STL & Anchor

MEMBER
Christian Small Publishers Assn.

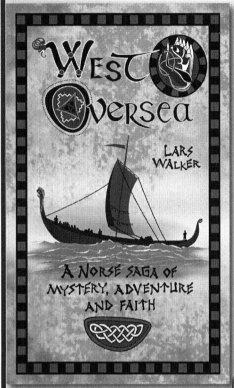